Fire & Ice

Books by Mary Connealy

From Bethany House Publishers

THE KINCAID BRIDES

Out of Control
In Too Deep
Over the Edge

TROUBLE IN TEXAS

Swept Away
Fired Up
Stuck Together

WILD AT HEART

Tried and True
Now and Forever
Fire and Ice

A Match Made in Texas: A Novella Collection

—— *Wild at Heart* ——
BOOK THREE

Fire & Ice

MARY CONNEALY

BETHANYHOUSE
a division of Baker Publishing Group
Minneapolis, Minnesota

Published by Bethany House Publishers
11400 Hampshire Avenue South
Bloomington, Minnesota 55438
www.bethanyhouse.com

Bethany House Publishers is a division of
Baker Publishing Group, Grand Rapids, Michigan

Printed in the United States of America

                    Library of Congress Cataloging-in-Publication Data
Connealy, Mary.
    Fire and ice / Mary Connealy.
        pages ; cm. — (Wild at heart ; book 3)
    Summary: "In the late 1860s West, two independent ranch homesteaders
    go head-to-head over prized land, until Gage Coulter proposes an
    unexpected plan to Bailey Wilde and, in a moment of weakness, she
    agrees"— Provided by publisher.
        ISBN 978-0-7642-1180-5 (softcover)
        1. Ranchers—Fiction. 2. Frontier and pioneer life—Fiction. 3. Man-
    woman relationships—Fiction. I. Title.
    PS3603.O544F56 2015
    813'.6—dc23   2015014731

Scripture quotations are from the King James Version of the Bible.

Cover design by Paul Higdon
Cover photography by Mike Habermann Photography, LLC

Author is represented by Natasha Kern Literary Agency

15   16   17   18   19   20   21   7   6   5   4   3   2   1

Max Weber is a new addition to our family. I dedicated the first two books in this series to my other sons-in-law, so it's only fair that Max gets a turn.

He's a smart, hardworking, wise young man. Welcome to the Connealy clan, Max. And thank you for putting that glow of happiness in my daughter Katy's eyes.

The bullet spit dirt up in Gage Coulter's eyes, and he didn't even flinch.

Wilde always missed him. Granted, he missed by inches.

"Don't you ever sleep, Wilde?" Gage had come early, he'd come late. He'd come in peace, and now this was it—he was coming in war.

"The only reason you'd ask that was if you wanted to sneak in here. Now get off my land." Another bullet, this one even closer to his toes.

Gage ignored it. The shots were to keep him back. Trouble was, if he came closer, Wilde might stop trying to scare him and get serious.

"You aren't gonna shoot me and you know it."

At least Wilde never had. That confounded nester had stolen his best land by claiming a homestead that stretched right across the opening to the most fertile canyon on the

7

entire C Bar range. It was a long ways north and a lot higher up than Gage's ranch house. But he'd done a lot of scouting in his years out here and he'd found this canyon and bought it and used it mainly for winter pasture.

He owned it, but Bailey Wilde wouldn't let him cross on this measly little homestead to get his cattle to the grass.

"Trespassing is against the law, Coulter!" Another shot cut through the thin mountain air and landed a few feet in front of Gage's boots. "I've got a right to defend my land. Don't bet your life I won't shoot. I survived the Civil War and sent more than one man home in a box. I ain't afraid of killing, and I sure as certain ain't afraid of killing you. Just give me a reason."

"This is your last chance, Wilde. Let me come in there and we'll talk. Let's figure out a way my cattle can pass on your land with the least amount of damage." Except there wasn't a way short of ripping Wilde's house down, because the young fool had built it right across the mouth of the canyon, and done it deliberately, too. Oh, there was a narrow stretch of the canyon mouth open, but Wilde had a sturdy fence across it.

"I own that canyon and I need the grass. I'm not going to settle for anything less than getting it." Gage had been checking on nesters all over the range he considered his. This canyon was so far away, and this season had been crazy with some ugly threats against nesters that had been laid at Gage's door.

Gage owned the canyon behind the strip of land homesteaded by Wilde, yet he'd never thought to buy up this rocky piece just outside. Who'd ever want to homestead it?

Someone who realized claiming the land in front of the canyon gave him possession of the canyon too, that's who. And that made Wilde mighty savvy. Add in the deadly accurate skill with a gun and Gage didn't fool himself that he was dealing with a weakling.

By the time he'd found out Wilde had settled here and built this house, the varmint had been dug in deep. Wilde was ready to fight at the drop of a hat too, and he looked eager to drop it himself.

A laugh as wild as his name echoed out of that house. It wasn't the first time Gage had wondered if Bailey Wilde was entirely sane.

What the nester didn't know was that Gage meant it. He'd been trying to just have a simple talk with the stubborn youngster for weeks, ever since Matt Tucker, the mountain man who'd married Wilde's sister Shannon, had come riding out here to find his wife. And Gage had come along and found he'd lost access to the richest pastureland on his range.

Wilde would have nothing to do with him that didn't involve flying lead.

Gage had appealed to Bailey's family. His sister Kylie, who was within days of taking off for the East with her husband, Aaron Masterson, and Shannon, who had plans to move up into the mountaintops, to the cabin owned by her husband, Matt.

Kylie and Aaron, well, he didn't know them that well, but Shannon ought to have helped more. Matt Tucker was a good friend who worked for Gage most summers, and Gage thought that fact should have earned him some loyalty. But nope.

Both Kylie and Shannon refused to cooperate. Their husbands advised Gage to leave Bailey alone.

The harder he pushed, the more they assured him Bailey wouldn't budge. Both sisters had homesteaded on Coulter range, and when they'd married, their husbands hadn't wanted the land. They'd signed away their rights to it, and then Gage had immediately bought it. Shannon had wrung a promise out of Gage to let her and Tucker live on her land when they came down from the mountains, which Gage didn't mind a bit. So long as they didn't bother his cows.

He'd known there was a third member of the family, a brother, Bailey. But he was a while finding out where the third Wilde had set up his holding. And Bailey had no intention of selling out.

Gage had tried being nice. But that wasn't his only choice. He wasn't a man to break the law, but he was going to bend it right around Bailey Wilde's neck if the kid didn't let Gage in that cabin right now.

"This is your last chance, Coulter. I'm tired of fighting with you."

Funny, Gage had been thinking the exact same thing.

"I've told the sheriff you're harassing me, and I told him if I catch you trespassing he can expect to have to fetch your body. He knows about your threats."

"This is your last chance, Wilde. I'm tired of fighting with you." Gage took smug pleasure in echoing Bailey's words right back at him. "You've been warned. Are you going to let me in there so we can talk or not?"

Gage had done more than spend his time yelling. His

cattle needed that grass as the winter closed, and Gage was going to get it.

Another bullet cut through the dirt at Gage's feet.

"That's your answer then?"

"That's the only answer you're going to get." Wilde cocked the gun again, the muzzle emerging from the cabin window. Wilde never showed himself. He'd never had more than a quick look at the kid and then only from a distance. Well, that was about to change.

"You want to do this the hard way, Wilde, we'll do it the hard way." With a tug on his hat brim, Gage turned and strode away.

Bailey watched him walk out of sight. The last few times he'd come, he hadn't ridden in, he'd walked. He said her gunfire upset his horse. She'd told him to stay away and that'd settle his horse right down.

Instead, he must've tied that beautiful brown stallion somewhere nearby, because he'd started showing up on foot.

Which meant he was even quieter. Bailey had learned to stay on edge. He'd come day and night. No rhyme or reason to it.

She listened close and finally heard hoofbeats thunder away. When they faded in the distance, she uncocked her rifle with a hard, metallic click. Exhausted, she turned her back to the wall, leaned against it, and slid to the floor. He was wearing her down. One of these days he'd catch her napping. He'd even admitted as much when he asked, "Don't you ever sleep?"

She'd never seen a man with that kind of relentless confidence.

Well, it wouldn't matter. All his catching her would do was let him figure out she was female. Right now he believed she was Shannon and Kylie's brother. She dreaded the day that changed. A man treated a woman differently.

Something she knew all too well.

But however he treated her, she'd never let him cross on her land. The pleasure she took in denying him was as heady as strong drink—something she knew nothing about except as witness to others indulging.

Shuddering at the memory, she went back to fuming about Coulter.

She had to take this chance to rest.

He'd made a mistake with his visits. He never came back right away. She'd learned to take a nap right after he'd been by. Or if she wasn't too tired, she'd rush with her chores and then sleep awhile before going back to her vigil.

Right now she should ride out and see to her cattle—happily getting fat on the lush autumn grass in Coulter's canyon. But she didn't have the energy.

And that was his fault too, because he hadn't been here for two days and she'd been watching for him the whole time, which meant no sleep. No chores.

Her heavy eyelids were too much. She didn't even get up to climb into bed. She just laid her rifle on the floor, along the length of her leg, within easy grabbing distance.

Then she rested her sleepy head against the log wall and let her miserable, lonely life slip away into peaceful sleep.

2

A hard weight crushed her to the floor.

In the dark, she clawed for the rifle she'd laid beside her on the floor with what limited motion she had and found nothing. Her rifle was gone. She was mixed up. Had she rolled away from it?

"Get off!" Striking at whoever had her, she got one good punch in, then found her arms pinned. She wrestled, shoved, fought, shouted. Nothing gained her any ground.

She felt a tug at her clothes. For a second she froze. Was this a nightmare? She was swept back to the war, to memories that haunted her. A nightmare that she'd barely survived. There was another tug, then another. Shaking her head she tried to force herself to wake up, hoping desperately she was dreaming.

The tugging stopped. She heard a sound, part gasp, part grunt. It was the first she'd heard from this man and it wiped away any hope she had that she was sleeping.

A hand slid down her side, following from under her arm to her waist to her hip down the hourglass curve. With a yelp, not unlike a dog with a pinched tail, the man rolled off her.

"You're a woman!" Gage Coulter's voice cut through the horror that had frozen her. He moved so fast you'd've thought he was lying on a bed of rusty nails.

Bailey scrambled for her gun.

He leapt to his feet. "You can quit looking. I've got it." His arm swooped up, her rifle silhouetted in the dim light, held high over his head.

"*Miss* Bailey Wilde." The disgust in his voice almost shook the cabin walls. "Now, why didn't I know you'd be a woman? I've seen your sister Shannon running around in britches. I've heard your pa go on and on about his son Jimmy—the way a man might talk if he only had one boy."

Bailey suddenly realized she was free. She clawed at her holster.

"I got your six-shooter, too." Gage lifted his other hand. "And don't bother searching for the knife up your sleeve or the ones in your boot or your belt."

He'd scooped up every weapon she had. The tugs she'd felt. Not a man assaulting her, but a man disarming her. Annoying, and yet it was better than what she'd feared.

He tossed the knives on her kitchen table, along with her guns. The clatter shook her into action. She lurched to her feet and ran for the nearest deadly object.

Coulter moved fast for a big man. He put himself between her and the table. She ran right into his broad chest and bounced backward. He caught her by the forearms or she might've fallen right back to the floor where this had all started.

"All I want to do is talk. Will you quit fussing and sit down?" Coulter's gray eyes narrowed as he looked at her. "This is why you've been as good as hiding from me ever since the first time I came across you in your sister's cabin, all the way back before Kylie married Aaron. You didn't want me to know you were a woman."

Bailey jerked at the grip he had on her arm.

He didn't even pretend to let go. "Does Tucker know?"

She was in no mood to be questioned. Instead, though it made her a little sick, she knew how to be a female. Mainly she'd learned it from watching Kylie.

She tugged harder, and knowing how men behaved, she said, "You're hurting me." At least she knew how decent men behaved.

"I'd say you're hurting yourself, Miss Wilde." Coulter apparently wasn't too worried about being decent. Or maybe he wasn't interested in letting her near the guns and knives. A woman could almost respect that.

"Now then, Miss Wilde . . ." Coulter leaned down so close that Bailey could smell him, smell him every time she breathed. And a woman had to breathe, blast it all. "We're gonna sit down and have ourselves a little talk."

A quick glance at the table told her she'd be right near her guns and knives, so she wasn't completely opposed to it.

"Before we start, I think it's only polite to tell you I've found another way into my canyon."

"What? No. There's no other way."

The solid confidence in his expression made Bailey's knees give out. All the fight went out of her, and Gage knew it, the polecat, because he had to hold her upright and drag her to the table, where he plunked her into a chair.

He didn't even bother to move her weapons out of reach. He actually turned his back to her and took a few seconds to turn the wick up on her lantern so she could see the light gray of his eyes.

They weren't as cold as she thought they'd be. The closest she'd ever gotten to him was the time she'd watched him out the window at Kylie's house. She'd been close enough to see those light-colored eyes, and they'd always struck her as pure bitter ice.

Of course, right now he was feeling warmed by victory. Those eyes were so light against his tanned skin and dark brown hair that it was hard to look away, and he sure kept his eyes right on her.

He sat down in a chair around the corner from her, within grabbing distance, so maybe he wasn't completely sure she wouldn't decide to shoot him. That made her feel a little better.

Then the big lug smiled. "I've been working on a trail ever since I found you in here. It's a hair-raiser, and the last stretch is going to take some dynamite, but I'm ready to start setting off charges come morning. Up to now, my work has been done quietly, but I figured you'd notice explosions, so I near to broke my neck climbing in here over the canyon wall to warn you."

"That's a box canyon. I've scouted it. I can't believe you've found a trail. You're just trying to trick me into believing you've found a way in so I'll give up and let you cross on my land. But I'm not letting you. Not even once, Coulter."

"Listen in the morning, Miss Wilde." Coulter shook his head and leaned closer. "I can't believe you've hacked your hair off so short. That is plumb shameful. You're not a proper woman at all."

Bailey glared at him for a second, then said, "Thank you."

That wrung an unexpected laugh out of him. "Start planning on where to move your cattle. I walked through your herd on my way in here and it's sizable. I don't know how many cows you came into the area with, but if you were like your sisters or your pa, it wasn't many. You've done a good job expanding. I doubt you can feed them on one hundred and sixty acres. I reckon you'll have to sell about half. It's mighty ambitious of you to increase the herd when you own so little land."

Coulter slapped the table lightly. "Oh, that's right, you thought you could steal five thousand acres from me. That's how you intended to feed them."

He arched his brows, and the lantern light caught the rich brown of them and seemed to cast reddish streaks in his dark hair. "You've got about a week to get your cattle out of there. The day I drive my herd onto that grass, you're going to have to start paying me rent."

Bailey opened her mouth to speak, but no words came out.

"If I was a little less friendly sort of a neighbor"—she snorted at that—"I'd demand you pay for every day since you moved in."

"I built this cabin last summer. I ran cattle in that canyon all winter. You've never tried to get in here before. Where were you then?"

"Last year I used the canyon early. I put my spring herd in there and had them moved off before you homesteaded. And don't tell me you didn't know someone was using the canyon."

She had known all right. She'd tried to homestead inside the canyon when she was scouting for a likely spot to claim and had seen that beautiful grass. She'd found out Coulter owned it the first minute she'd asked.

And then she'd asked about the trail into the canyon, and lo and behold, it was unclaimed.

"You may be a bur under my saddle, Miss Wilde, but I can tell a shrewd rancher when I see one. I know how good a shot you are, too. A man don't get shot at nearly every day for two weeks and not learn if the one doing the shooting knows where to put her bullets. Just from walking through your herd this once, I can see it's well tended. Your cabin's solid and true, and Shannon and Kylie told me you helped build theirs."

Bailey was strangely warmed by his compliments. It was an odd feeling to be flattered and want to punch a man at the same time. It was so confusing to hold both feelings at once . . . her skin was getting a little itchy.

"Of all the poor folks struggling to survive in this rugged land as homesteaders, you're one who's suited to living out here, and I can see you've got the know-how to make it as a rancher. That means you're smart enough to know you were moving your cattle in where there'd been a good-sized herd. Hundreds of cattle leave plenty of sign. 'Tweren't no accident you staked your claim on this rocky stretch of wasteland like you did, and built this cabin right over the mouth of the canyon. And I don't rightly believe you had your head in the clouds enough not to hear whose canyon it was, either. The land agent is your brother-in-law; he'd know I owned it."

"I claimed it before Aaron came along."

"Then the land agent before him knew, and don't you bother denying it. You built here deliberately so that I couldn't get back in with my herd."

The land agent had known what she was doing, but he didn't have a right to tell her she couldn't homestead on unclaimed land. "I—"

"Don't protest your innocence." Coulter made a chopping wave with his hand. "It insults us both."

Bailey glared at him. She'd had no intention of protesting her innocence. She'd planned to throw her knowledge right back in his face. Now she waited. Knowing what was coming.

"What I want to know, Miss Wilde, is—"

"Just call me Bailey. I'm not Miss Wilde."

"Sure you are."

"It's Bailey. If you know I'm a woman, then fine, there's nothing to be done about it. But I don't want the whole world to know, so stop calling me *Miss*. You're doing it to torment me now, but I don't want you to get in the habit." Bailey leaned forward. "Not that I plan to spend much time talking to you. But if you can really get your cattle in the canyon, then you and your men will be in there working. I don't want them all knowing I'm a woman."

"For the love of heaven, why not?"

"I just don't."

"Well, that's just stupid."

"And don't call me stupid." Bailey's eyes went to her rifle.

Coulter laughed again.

She didn't want to shoot him . . . well, maybe a little. But one good solid butt stroke across the head, *that* she might enjoy. "Men act different towards a woman."

"As true as summer following spring, that's no great piece of news."

"They pester them. They think women want attention and help."

"If you ever needed any help, my men and I would—"

"Shut up!" Bailey slashed a hand at him. Not a butt stroke, but the best she could do. "You see what I mean? Men think a woman wants them to come a-courting."

"Most women do."

"Well, I *don't*. I want none of that. No matter what I say, no man is going to believe I just want to run my ranch, my way, alone. But they'll believe a young man would do such a thing. So don't tell them I'm a woman. And keep them away from me so they don't find out. And I don't care how steep that canyon trail is, you're using it every time you come in and out. Not a one of you is crossing on my land."

Coulter folded his arms on the table and watched her, his expression dark and intent as if he wanted to see inside her head and figure her out.

She sincerely hoped he couldn't. "Well, can you do that? Keep my secret?"

"How many cattle are you going to have to sell if you don't have that canyon?"

"Answer my question."

"Answer mine."

It made Bailey furious to answer his, because she didn't want to sell a single one. She'd done a good job of building her herd, better than she'd dared hope. She had over fifty head in less than a year. She'd bought cattle from folks who were selling out and heading back east. She'd rounded up some longhorns she'd found running wild. She'd bartered and pinched pennies and babied her cows so that every calf survived. And now she didn't have the land to support them.

Coulter didn't wait. "I'd say half are going to have to go. I've had a good look at your land with all my visits over here to try and talk to you. You've got a few good pastures and plenty of heavy forestland, too. I'll buy twenty-five head."

"No!" She shoved herself to her feet. "I'd rather do business with the devil himself."

Another laugh. When there wasn't one thing funny about any of this. The only thing keeping her from grabbing a gun was the plain bald fact that she wasn't a killer, which sometimes was just a shame.

Also, he probably wouldn't let her.

"When you calm down and quit saying stupid things, consider selling me half your herd."

Bailey curled her knuckles on the table and leaned

forward. "The next time you call me stupid, I'm going to shut your mouth with my fist."

Coulter stood. He was about six inches taller than she was and outweighed her by seventy or eighty pounds. He probably wouldn't punch her back, though, now that he knew she was female, so she might get away with one good hit.

"I don't think you're stupid."

"You've called me stupid twice."

"I happen to think you're one of the smartest nesters to come into these mountains. Maybe the best one I've seen. So when I hear you say something stupid, I have to wonder about it. Seems to me a smart woman like you must have a reason for most everything she does. Not wanting me to tell my men you're a woman so they won't pester you, I don't see why you can't just tell them to move along. My men are decent. They don't harass a woman who wants to be left alone. And you'd rather do business with the devil himself than me? I suspect that's not a wise thing to say, but it does tell me you've got a powerful dislike burning for me, and I'm not real sure why. Except of course because you stole my land, but that doesn't strike me as fair. Nope, I don't think it's all about me wanting my canyon back, and I don't think it's about not wanting my men to know you're female. So what is it about, I wonder? There's a lot about you that don't make sense."

Again, Bailey felt her hands curl into fists.

Coulter glanced down and noticed, and his lips twitched into a smile. "I know what you're thinking. And no, I wouldn't hit a woman. But I wouldn't stand here and let you get in a punch, either. And something tells me blocking one of your swinging fists might just end up with us in a wrestling match."

Coulter leaned closer, much closer, and suddenly Bailey knew better than to punch him. A wrestling match was a bad idea.

"I think that ending up in a clinch with me might be about the worst idea either one of us ever had." He towered over her, almost like he was asking her to take a swing at him. Almost like he wanted to wrestle—end up in a clinch. Something strange twisted deep inside her. She had no idea what it was, only that it scared her right down to the pointed toes of her boots.

He leaned a bit closer. "Or maybe it'd be the best."

Another second passed as those light-gray eyes—that should have been cold—burned into hers.

"You've got eyes like your baby sister's, except more colorful like blazing gold, and hot enough to brand a man. Prettiest things I've ever seen." When he said that, she thought for a second he was going to lean closer still. Then he shook his head as if to clear it of whatever nonsense was going on in there, straightened, and headed for the door. He turned his back on her then, as if not caring that she was within grabbing distance of an arsenal.

When he opened the door he spun around, and those too-pale eyes locked on hers. "I'm going to stop calling you stupid. I apologize for that. Instead, Bailey"—he stressed her first name; no "Miss Wilde" this time—"every time you say something that strikes me as stupid, I'm going to ask myself, What is that little fire-eyed woman up to now?"

He stepped out the door, but just before he swung it shut, he seemed to look all the way inside where he could see secrets she'd never told anyone. "I'd advise you to get some sleep. My dynamite will blow you wide awake come morning." Then he slammed the door and was gone—taking her beautiful canyon home with him.

A home where she'd held her safety in her own two hands. A home where she'd obeyed no man, saluted no man, taken no orders. On her own land she'd never again be forced to stand silent before madness.

With a single slammed door, he closed away the dream she'd thought was within her grasp ever since she'd seen this canyon and dreamed of building a vast herd to fill it.

She turned down the lantern, staggered over to her bed, and collapsed onto her back without taking her boots off.

Was there any way to stop him? Where was he coming into the canyon? She should have asked. She knew the canyon well, inside and out, and couldn't imagine anywhere a trail could be cut.

Could she fight him? Trick him? Her mind churned like the muddy waters of the Mississippi in August. She couldn't think of a plan, but she did decide that whatever he had planned, she wasn't just going to sit here wringing her hands and let him have his way.

There was no reason in the world she had to make it easy for him.

With that, she decided he was right. She needed to get some rest, because she was going to have to beat him to the blasting site in the morning. And that was going to take some scouting because she didn't even know where to look.

3

*Y*ou're going to drive your cattle up here?" Bailey stepped out on the trail as Gage rode up.

How early had the little pest gotten up to find where he was working? Gage reminded himself, and not for the first time, never again to underestimate her.

She'd come down on the side of the canyon right where Gage was planning to blast. It wasn't fit to ride on and took a fair amount of mountain-climbing skills to walk down.

Her voice was different. Completely female.

She'd been disguising it when she shot at him, the little sneak. It was still a deep voice for a woman, slightly raspy, yet smooth enough to be worth listening to. "What did you plan to do if my men rode with me? They'd have seen you and known in a second you weren't a man."

"I didn't step out until I saw you were alone. If they were with you, I had plans to get you alone."

When she talked about getting him alone, Gage felt

something reckless and primitive stir to life inside him. He'd never felt it before and it shocked him. At the same time he couldn't believe how much he liked it. Strangest thing he'd ever felt, and he had no idea what it all meant or what to do about it. Probably a sign that Bailey Wilde was driving him completely out of his mind.

He didn't know much about women, but he knew this one was infuriating and fascinating, and when she wasn't trying to kill him, he thought she was about the most interesting female he'd ever met.

Oh, who was he tryin' to fool? She was interesting when she was trying to kill him, too. Which made her a very hard package to handle. Not unlike the dynamite in his saddlebags.

He planned to set the charges, blow them, check for loose rocks, and when things were settled, he'd let his men come in and clean up the rubble. It was risky work, and he wouldn't ask any of his men to do it. Although a couple of them said they knew dynamite—especially Rowdy, his foreman.

"You're out of your mind if you think you can get a herd of cows up this trail." She plunked her fists on her neat hips, and if Gage noticed that and looked too long . . . well, he'd just have to apply himself to getting his eyeballs under control.

"The out-of-my-mind part might be right." In the dim light of approaching dawn, Gage swung down off his stallion and ground-hitched him. He closed the distance between himself and Bailey. She wasn't a big woman, no more than five and a half feet tall, and skinny. When he thought she was a young man, *skinny* might've been right, but now . . . maybe *slender* was a better word. He'd felt those curves for himself last night. Gage looked close to be sure he remembered right.

"So forget the blasting, Coulter."

But he couldn't just enjoy looking, not when the woman wouldn't shut up.

"Give it up and cut your herd," she said. "You've got plenty of land. You don't need this canyon."

She wore no hat; maybe she'd lost it in the climb. Her hair was too short to be tied back, so tight curls less than an inch long danced on her head in the breeze. Those golden eyes glinted in the first rays of morning light. Shaking his head to get his thoughts in order, he knew whatever her size, she sure cast a big shadow, and that had nothing to do with the way the sun hit her.

Was she just here to complain or was she up to something?

"I own this canyon. But this summer I've learned the hard way that I've been mighty foolish about buying up land. I never dreamed homesteaders would want to settle in such a rugged place. They think they're going to be farmers, till up the soil and get corn to grow, but this land won't support crops. It's for trees and grass and precious little else. And the seasons are too short for any crop I know. Now I'm working hard to buy up every piece I use that's still available, and I'm waiting and watching for the nesters to come to their senses and figure out you can't farm the side of a mountain. When they pull up stakes, I'll buy up their claims. But this canyon is one of the prettiest stretches anywhere. Almost no trees. Perfect shelter from the wind. A stream that flows year round. I had the sense to buy it up right away."

"But not the sense to buy the land outside it," Bailey said.

"I need to go back to the land office first chance I get and see what other pieces of my land can be locked away from me this way." Gage couldn't think of any right now, but he'd better get smarter about such things.

"You're too late here, Coulter. You need to quit this madness, admit defeat and go home." Bailey took one more step toward him as she sassed him, her little nose in the air. Those golden eyes catching the sun as if on fire. Not one speck afraid of him. That was probably a mistake on his part. He probably ought to figure out a way to make her afraid, yet he was downright proud of her for that streak of pure courage.

"Admitting defeat isn't my style, Bailey. I *will* get my cattle in here. I'll do it if I have to reduce the entire Rocky Mountains to rubble. You know the Bible says every mountain and hill shall be made low. God may have to come in and finish that up, but I reckon I can go ahead and get started on it."

That tricked a smile out of her. She shook her head and looked around.

A moment of less than rage. He knew it was a waste of breath, but he had plenty, so he went ahead and wasted it. "Why don't you let me pay you a fair price to let my cattle cross on your land? My cows would walk across a few acres, then later walk out. Two crossings a year. I'd do my best to see that they did no damage, and if there was damage, I'd pay you what you thought it was worth."

"There's no space. They'd wreck my yard, knock down my fences."

"They probably would." She was giving him reasons—that wasn't the same as just hollering no in his face. It gave him hope.

"You positioned your yard and built fences to block the canyon for just this exact reason." Her house covered as much of that canyon mouth as it could. The canyon was too wide, though, and Bailey's house wasn't grand. The mouth was probably more than fifty feet across, and she couldn't shove the house right up against it or she wouldn't be able get her own cattle in and out. There was a sturdy log fence stretching from the house to a barn off on the south side. No gate. Bailey had to tear a section of that fence down every time she wanted to get her cattle out.

That wasn't by chance. Nothing this woman did was by chance.

"I'll take your fence down and then I'll put it back up. I'll keep my cattle calm and do my best to send them through in singles or pairs. That way, they won't bother a wide swath of your land."

"You ran your cattle over Kylie's homestead. She had to fix all that damage herself."

"I didn't even know she was there until I rode up behind my cattle. And she fixed it herself before I could offer."

Bailey sniffed at him as if she didn't like his smell. A shame when he was just catching a faint womanly scent coming from her and liking it real fine.

"And you saw how we handled things at Shannon's. I rented use of her pasture and water. The fence I built gave her sheep plenty of room and kept them safe. I can do the same here if you want, except there's one big difference."

"What's that?" Bailey bristled at him like a little porcupine, and her eyes flashed fire so hot he thought she might've singed his cheeks.

"I didn't own your sister's homestead. She had full rights to claim that land and water. I do own this canyon, however."

"And I own the land you want to cross on."

"True enough. But you can't use all the grass in that canyon. Seems to me we could strike a fair bargain." Gage figured they ought to trade straight up. She let him cross; he let her cattle stay and graze. He sure wished she'd get to that on her own because, tough talk aside, getting his cattle up this trail was going to be a killer.

She crossed her arms and looked at him, as stubborn as any mule in the history of the West.

He decided he had to spell it out for her. "In exchange, you can leave your herd in the canyon. I won't crowd so many cows in there that yours won't have their share of grass, and I won't expect a dollar of rent."

He took another step toward her while knowing full well he should stay away. He was too close, and the reckless, primitive nonsense boiling inside him was goading him on. "We can be neighborly and you know it, Bailey. This is only war because you want war."

That shook a gasp out of her, and she backed up so fast she stumbled.

Coulter's hand shot out and caught her or she'd have probably fallen over her own two feet.

"I don't want war. I never, ever want war again."

"Again?" Coulter's tanned brow knit into furrows. He was so dark, his skin, his hair. He wore a black Stetson and even had his back to the rising sun, casting his face in shadows. Those eyes glowed out of his face, gray and unnaturally light and almost hypnotic. "What do you mean by 'again'?"

"I mean I never want to go to war again. I had enough of that fighting in the Civil War. Enough to last a hundred lifetimes."

Coulter's hand relaxed on her arm, but he didn't let go. "You fought in the Civil War?"

That pulled her up short. Coulter had been so intertwined with everything that had happened. He'd been friends with Tucker. He'd bought Kylie's land. He'd helped catch the man who'd been after Shannon. He'd been around so much, he was practically family. Family she disliked and avoided like the plague. Which made him a lot like Pa.

"I thought you knew."

"I . . . I did hear such a thing. I've talked to your pa." Gage got a sour look on his face that told Bailey he had indeed talked to Pa. "He said his sons fought in the war. Once I realized you were a woman, I just figured that didn't apply to you. Except he did say sons. And he only has—had one—Jimmy, the one who died." His hand resting on her upper arm slid up and down from her elbow to near her shoulder, then back to her elbow again. "You mean it? You actually fought in the war?"

Then his eyes softened. Instead of the sour look when he'd spoken of Pa, he looked kind, concerned. That strong hand of his went up and down again. This time it felt like a caress.

"Is that why you're dressed like this? You passed yourself off as a man so you could fight? And now you're still dressing like you did then?"

The touch was too much. The concern. She might even call it pity. Wrenching free, she considered just how close she'd come to buckling under to his slippery offer. He was a man used to getting what he wanted, but not from her.

"Teach your cattle how to mountain-climb, Coulter. Not one hoof touches my property. Not one." She whirled away and stomped up the trail.

"Bailey, come back. We can figure something out."

She didn't look, and he didn't chase her. She was relieved because she didn't want his hands on her again. Ever.

It wasn't long before she was almost on her hands and knees. Doing more climbing than walking. The last twenty feet at the top was sheer rock sticking straight up. No dynamite could make this passable. Coulter might think he was the king of this whole part of the Rockies, but no amount of power, money, and arrogance could make a cow climb a mountain.

She'd gone over the lip of the canyon and was all the way to the floor of it, had found her hat and caught up her horse, and was most of the way home when the first blast shook the ground.

Too bad Coulter was going to have to figure out the hard way that his cows weren't mountain goats.

Bailey waited until the last explosion of the day ended before she led Shannon and Tucker out to where Coulter was blowing up a mountain. The blasting usually lasted about half a day, then silence until the next morning when it started again. She'd done some spying and knew they spent the other half of the day moving rubble.

She also knew Gage always took the toughest job and the most risks.

"He's building a trail up this slope?" Shannon looked over the canyon rim, then turned to Bailey, her eyes wide, her voice laced with doubt. "He'll have to move half the mountain."

There was a small army of men working about halfway down on a dizzying stretch nearly a quarter mile long. Gage was in the middle of it, hoisting rocks and throwing them aside. He straightened. Shannon's voice must have carried. He swiped his forearm across his brow and started toward them. He had his coat off and had tossed his Stetson aside, despite the cold October weather.

He strode along steadily until he got past the part that had been blasted. Then he had to climb, pulling himself along, scaling the mountain in a way no cow could manage.

"You can't get your cattle up this slope, not if you blast from now till kingdom come." Tucker, pure mountain man, dressed in leather and fur, stepped up beside his wife, who was dressed in doeskin, wearing warm leggings. If

Shannon had to give up on wearing britches, she'd chosen well.

Coulter came around a boulder, reached a slightly less treacherous spot and stood upright. "I can and I will, Tucker."

Tucker looked down, shaking his head. "This slope would give a mountain goat the vapors."

Coulter walked the last few dozen yards before he stopped about twenty feet straight down. There was no way to get the rest of the way up without turning mountain climber.

Bailey gritted her teeth. He had made it better. She could see that on the lower parts of the trail. But he had a long way to go. And what would he do about this last stretch?

"I've got longhorns mostly, and they're mighty good in rough country. All I've got to do is get the first one to climb up here and the others will follow. And I've got mountain-bred mustangs that will forge the trail, and the cattle will follow them, too. They'll make this climb with only a couple more days of work. I think I could get your grulla up here now. At least to this spot where I'm standing."

Tucker's gray mare was legendary. His horse, called a grulla, which Tucker pronounced *grew-ya*, a strange word Bailey had never heard before she'd come out here, had a black mane and tail on her gray coat. That horse had fought at Tucker's side more than once. Bailey envied him the staunchly loyal critter.

"If any animal can climb this steep trail, it's Gru." Shannon stared down the mountainside.

Bailey couldn't get over the change in her sister. Her hair was still short for most women, but it was definitely growing longer, and the cap of black curls was pinned back and looked female for sure. Even more so now that Shannon was wearing a dress.

Sunrise, the Shoshone woman who'd raised Tucker, had helped Shannon make it along with the leggings. Her sister was dressed in a purely womanish fashion. The outfit also looked warm and fairly rational. Still, it wasn't as safe and comfortable as britches. Bailey was the only one of the Wilde women who still wore them, and she was sorely disappointed in both her little sisters.

"You're tearing the heart out of this land, Gage." Tucker crossed his arms and added with disgust, "It ain't normal to blow up a whole mountain like this."

"You know why I'm doing it, Tucker, so don't act like this is my fault. I need that canyon grass and"—he gave Bailey an explosive glare—"your sister-in-law won't let me dirty up her pretty ranch yard with my cows. Well, I have to get in here somehow."

"No, you don't." Tucker loved these mountains, and his frustration at this blasting showed plain. "Cull your herd. Get along on less land. You're rich enough to eat for six lifetimes. Leave the mountain alone. Be satisfied with what you have and let Bailey have the canyon. This isn't about grass; this is about refusing to take no for an answer, refusing to stop fighting until you win. I can't figure out why you didn't go to war. You'd've been great at it."

"I own this canyon." The cold in Coulter's gray eyes was haunted, as if a ghost lived inside him. Bailey had never noticed that until Tucker mentioned war. "It's mine, and no one's gonna tell me I can't use what's mine."

Coulter's voice was just as frigid as his eyes. "You need anything else before I get back to work?"

Tucker frowned at the damage being done. "My Gru could make it to where you stand if she wanted to." Tucker paused, then added, "But how are you gonna make 'em want to, Gage? I don't know as you can drive anything up here, but even if you could, what about these last twenty feet? This rim is impassable." Since they were standing twenty feet overhead of Coulter, and they hadn't climbed down and he hadn't climbed up, those words seemed like the simple truth.

"I'll manage it," Coulter replied flatly.

Bailey heard such confidence in his voice, she had no doubt he'd somehow find a way.

"Like I said, once I get a few of my best climbing critters up here, the others are sure to follow. And the inside of the canyon isn't as bad. I don't think I'm going to even need to blast on that side."

Bailey looked behind her. The first twenty feet were the same sheer, vertical rock. After that it was a much gentler slope. The inside of the canyon looked like a huge bowl. The walls were covered with aspens and were very steep, but nothing a cow couldn't handle.

Coulter turned those gray eyes on her. "I've built most of the trails in this area, Bailey. Most of the nice, easy roads you ride between here and Aspen Ridge weren't here five years ago. I wasn't afraid to throw the strength in my back into tearing civilization out of wilderness. And I've still got plenty of strength left. So this is the next road. It won't be my last."

36

She had thought his eyes were cold before. Now they turned to chips of ice. At least the ghosts had gone, replaced by cold confidence. She knew going to war had cost her terribly. Was it possible *not* going to war could cost a man something?

From somewhere he'd grown a spine as hard as this granite he was blasting. There was no back up in the man. She had no idea how to stop him, short of sending an avalanche right down on his head, and she didn't have the ruthless streak in her to do such a thing.

So, if she couldn't keep him out, that left her with only one thing she could do.

"I need to get back. I got chores." She turned, picked her way past the first ugly stretch, then stalked down. Good luck to his cattle.

As she wove between the clumps of slender aspen with their spinning yellow leaves, already falling in the autumn weather, she knew Coulter was right in that once his cattle were up, they wouldn't have trouble coming down into the lush grass of the canyon.

She was about to be invaded.

4

"One more day and we're going to invade that canyon."
Gage looked at the three men who'd ridden over with him. At the start, he'd been doing the blasting himself, but these three had pestered until he let them help. And they were good—better than him if he cared to admit it, and he didn't.

His foreman, Rowdy, and these other two, Manny and Ike, had proven their skill and now helped him to lay the charges.

Most days they faced a new layer of snow, but so far it hadn't been deep. One of these mornings it'd be heavy enough that Gage would face another barrier to getting his cattle up this trail. Winter coming was like a ticking clock counting down the moments until his cattle starved.

It'd taken him longer than he'd expected, but they'd finish today and drive the cattle in tomorrow or his name wasn't Gage Coulter.

Looking up, up, up the twisting, mean, Rocky Mountain rattler of a trail, he knew that if his cows didn't faint dead away on the climb, he was going to get into his canyon without needing the cooperation of that stubborn little filly.

"Let me take over the blasting today, boss," Rowdy said, the oldest of Gage's hired hands. A white-haired old-timer, he was the talker of the bunch. "The last few charges have to be set just right."

Gage felt his jaw tighten. "I don't like it. Blasting that last stretch is mighty dangerous, and I can't ask a man to do a job I won't do myself. The risk is mine."

Rowdy nodded. "It's dangerous for a fact, Gage. That's why you need someone who knows what he's doing, and I've shown you I'm better than you. And these two"—he jerked his head toward Manny and Ike—"are better than you, too. For most of this blasting we've all been good enough, yet this last part is tricky. I've done this enough to make it a lot safer for me than it'd be for you."

"We'll be fine," Manny said. The skinny Mexican who didn't look much older than a kid flashed an easy smile. Manny showed up one day out of the clear blue and talked his way into a job, and since then he'd taught them all a thing or two about roping and riding.

Ike tugged on the brim of his Stetson. "Let us do it, Gage." Ike, thin and wiry, was the best hand with gentling a green-broke mustang Gage had ever seen, and the smartest man of the bunch. Trail-savvy, quick-witted. A man Gage liked having along on any job.

Rowdy went on, "It won't take us long to be ready to

blast, and you need to tell Wilde so he gets his cattle out of there, if he hasn't already. Once we start blasting the rim, rocks might fly in. We don't want to kill one of his cows by accident. Reckon he don't need any more reasons to hate us."

That meant he had to go see Bailey again. He hadn't seen her since the day she'd brought Shannon and Tucker over to try to convince Gage this was impossible. It was all he could do not to climb that canyon wall right now and rush over to her house. There was a tug of war going on inside him when he thought about seeing her. A big pull in one direction was his desire to gloat, to just plain throw it in her face that he'd gotten hold of his own land despite her best efforts to keep him out. Even stronger than that was the need to apologize, to offer again to let her keep her cows in the canyon. Try and wheedle a friendship out of the stubborn woman with the outsized ranching skills. Mixed in with all that was a small but strong urge to pull her into his arms and kiss her.

That shocked him clear to his bones. And since she was likely to loosen his teeth if he tried, it was a pure waste of time thinking of it. His bad intentions would only make her hate him even more. His good intentions, well, he was sorely afraid they wouldn't make her hate him any less.

All and all, he probably ought to just send Manny to talk to her and avoid her for the rest of his life.

But he'd promised to keep his men away.

"I'll go talk to h—" Gage almost said *her*. He did his best never to talk about Bailey for this very reason. No possible way could he think of Bailey as a man. Not anymore. And lying didn't suit him, which made him think of the huge lie he'd just included in a letter to his ma.

"I'll try to widen the trail down here," Gage said, shouldering his pickax. "Once the charges are set and you're ready to blow it, go ahead and holler, and then I'll run into the canyon and move the Wilde cattle to the far end. I don't need to talk to . . . Wilde. I just have to make sure no cows are too close to the blast site."

All three headed for the top. Gage saw where they slipped and struggled to stay upright. He hurried after them to the spot giving them trouble, to make it more passable. Where a man couldn't walk, a cow was going to have trouble.

Hammer blows overhead told him his men had started work. Gage swung his ax.

"Look out!" Ike, in the middle of the three, shoved Manny backward, then dove forward and tackled Rowdy. The two of them rolled to the side. A rumble drew Gage's head up. In horror he watched a rockslide tumble straight for his men.

The rocks pelted Ike and Rowdy as they scrambled along the face of the mountain.

Manny came tumbling head over heels downhill, only yards ahead of the avalanche. Gage dropped the pickax and sprinted straight into the teeth of the rockslide.

Manny got control of his fall, gained his feet, and ran several paces, then staggered and went back to rolling. Gage had one chance to catch Manny and yank him out of the path of the heavy boulders.

Gage ran faster, not easy going uphill on the treacherous slope, judging what was to his left and right, trying to pick a spot, watching the stones bounce, knock more rocks loose, grow and spread and spin straight for him.

"Get ready to jump!" Gage only hoped that Manny saw him, let alone heard him or read his mind about what he planned to do. There was no time to say more. A gap to Gage's right opened just ahead. He reached it, braced himself. Manny slammed into him, but the man must've heard Gage yell, because Gage felt the young Mexican bunch his muscles and heave himself to the side just as Gage did.

The force of Manny's fall knocked them backward. Gage slid on shattered rock, tearing his clothes. Clawing toward the sheltering stones, he kept an iron grip on Manny's shirt. His knees rammed into jagged rocks and tore his skin, even though he wore sturdy clothing. They managed to heave themselves behind a rock shelf just as the avalanche approached. Gage looked behind him to see boulders tumbling and bouncing like man-sized hailstones.

Gage dragged Manny beneath an overhang of rocks as the avalanche went on and began raining past their shelter like a curtain of dirt and stone being pulled shut. Grit and gravel blinded them. The impacts of some massive stone shook the rocks over Gage's head and caved in. What had been protection became a crumbling tomb.

Gage grabbed Manny to pull him from harm's way. Manny was moving on his own. Gage took that as a good sign. Gage threw up his arm to ward off the pelting stones as they scrambled away from the collapsing shelter. They ducked behind another group of boulders to watch more rocks collapse and join the avalanche and sweep their way down the mountainside.

This refuge held.

Gage forced himself to wait as a few more rocks tumbled past. He didn't emerge, afraid more rocks might come raining down and start a new slide. Manny was bleeding but awake and alert.

Finally, Gage's control broke. "I've got to check on Rowdy and Ike. Stay here."

"Gage, you all right? Manny?" A shout from overhead stopped Gage from jumping out to start climbing.

Gage looked at the blood trickling down Manny's face. They were both coated with dust. His teeth crunched on grit, and he spit downhill after that ravaging slide. He was sickened to think he'd sent his men into danger while he stayed behind.

"We made it, Ike," Gage called. "Are you and Rowdy okay?"

"Rowdy's got a nasty gash on his head, but we made it."

"You reckon it's over?"

"Yep," Ike said. "I saw where it started, and the whole slope is swept clean. It's over."

"I thought it was swept clean last night. We spent a lot of time knocking all the loose rocks off that ledge yesterday." Gage wiped his mouth and saw blood on the back of his glove.

"We did, boss." Ike's voice was colder than the October wind.

Gage stood and saw that Ike had the right of it. "Then how'd they come down?"

"Someone set a trap." Ike sounded mad enough to tear the rest of the mountain down with his bare hands.

"What?" Gage wasn't expecting that. "You're saying this wasn't an accident?" Gage rounded the rock, and his men came in sight.

"It was a deadfall trap with a single slab of rock positioned to fall against a bigger pile of rocks. That started the avalanche." Ike was bleeding too. His neck was soaked red, and the front of his shirt had a growing circle of blood. He hadn't mentioned that.

"I'm the one who tripped over a stretch of rawhide hidden in a pile of leaves and triggered it, boss." Rowdy's voice was slurred. "I brought it down on all of us."

He leaned hard on Ike, barely able to stand. He had a lump on his forehead that was swelling fast.

Gage rushed for him and slid an arm around his back.

Manny came out into the open, steadying himself on the rocks. Gage got a good look. Manny was filthy. He and Gage had been farther down and had been swallowed up in the cloud of dust, more than Ike and Rowdy. Gage figured he looked a lot like Manny did.

"You know only one person had a good reason to stop us from blasting, boss." Ike was a thinking man, and he and Rowdy had been saddle partners a long time.

"Bailey Wilde." Gage couldn't believe it. But what other explanation could there be?

"We'll take Rowdy down and see that he's resting. Then Manny and I are going to finish this."

Rowdy waved a hand. "I ain't up to no more blasting, but I can ride a horse. I'll head back to the C Bar and send the men over with the herd. That rockslide cleared the trail enough for the cattle to make it in." Rowdy looked fighting mad. "Ike, you and Manny finish the blasting, and by the time we're back with the cattle, they'll just walk right into Wilde's canyon. If he thinks he can run us off, he's in for a big surprise."

Ike and Manny were as furious as Rowdy.

"No one's going to scare us off." Ike turned to the young Mexican. "That right, Manny?"

Manny gave a hard nod of his head. "Let's get back to blasting."

Come to that, Gage was more upset than all three of them. Hard as it was to believe, he had no idea who could have done this other than Bailey Wilde.

"Bring some of the greenest mustangs with you, Rowdy. They'll handle the climb the best. Once the cows see them go over the wall, they'll follow."

Rowdy nodded and started downhill, looking steadier with every step, his temper driving him forward.

"I'm going to go shove Bailey's cattle away from this side of the canyon, and then go have a talk with my new neighbor." He gave each of his battered men one more furious look. "Blow the side out of the mountain."

Gage spun away and stormed up the slope so angry he was afraid to say another word—except to Bailey.

He knew he'd failed as soon as that old-timer had headed up the hill and left Coulter behind. Fury like he'd never known stormed through him. Coulter was alive and well and maybe he'd be able to read sign.

A couple of the men were moving slow. He hoped they

didn't get to looking around. He'd expected to have plenty of time to cover his tracks after Coulter was dead.

It made him sick to think of killing, but the anger had given him the belly to do what needed doing. For one second, he felt relief. He hadn't committed murder.

But he'd done enough. He didn't want Coulter finding out who'd done him wrong. He stayed, waiting for the chance to slip over and make sure his tracks were covered.

"Don't underestimate Coulter or his men," he muttered, then hunkered down to watch, planning to hang around until the men were done and gone. He'd outlast them even if it took all day.

Coulter didn't need to take over the whole country! He had enough.

"I can't believe Coulter blasted his way up that whole mountain. I ain't never seen the like." He still meant to have it, but it was going to be a little harder, that's all. Somehow he'd find a way.

He thought of the rocky soil his own land was resting on, all the stumps that needed to be pulled and the stones that needed to be hauled away. A body could wear himself out trying to do it.

But a smart man did things a different way. A smart man saved his strength and watched a fool like Coulter break his back on that kind of labor. Then when the work was all done, the smart man stepped in and staked his claim.

He reached the bottom of the slope and walked to where they'd picketed their horses, well away from any rolling rocks.

Coulter went up and over the edge of the mountain into the canyon.

Two others stayed to work, and going by the ringing of hammers on steel, he knew they were setting dynamite to blow.

Watching those men go back to work on that mountainside only deepened his resolve to find a way so that soon it would all be his.

5

The canyon was empty.

Since his horse wasn't up to climbing over the canyon, Gage was on foot. With every step he took across the rich grassland, his temper grew.

It was only their quick thinking and fast reflexes that kept them alive. Had Bailey hoped it would be passed off as an accident? Was she hiding, and her cattle along with her, hoping to lay low until her damage was over and done?

This was coyote behavior, and she seemed like the type to face a man, take him on directly. But he'd cornered her; he knew that. And when a person was cornered, often they fought back. Maybe he should have expected this, but instead he was bitterly disappointed in her. He'd looked Bailey in the eye and seen a worthy opponent, someone he could respect.

He couldn't put up with her moving onto his land, but

he'd thought he was dealing with a strong and honest woman.

Now he knew better.

Setting that trap was the act of a coward. A back-shooting coward.

He'd just reached her cabin when the first blast sounded. He turned to hear five more explosions go off just seconds apart. The peak of the canyon wall collapsed, blowing debris in all directions. When the dust finally settled, it was like a giant bear had taken a bite out of the rim. What once had been a peak a man had to drag himself over was now a low saddleback, easily passable. His cattle were going to walk right into this place.

He was going to find Bailey and drag her back here and make her watch them set foot on this land. He was going to enjoy every minute of crushing her. And then he was going to throw her in jail.

Turning back to his search, he found her cabin deserted, still no sign of cattle. But he could read the land. She'd herded them through here sometime yesterday. That trap had been difficult to set. Propping up rocks and bracing them so they're set to tumble, arranging a trip wire to be triggered by a man passing on foot. She'd spent hours on it, and it most likely was done after they'd quit late last night. Although she'd certainly been plotting it for longer, no doubt ever since she'd brought Tucker and Shannon to see where he was blasting out his trail.

And she'd done it on her own, too. He didn't know her sisters that well, so maybe she could have talked Kylie and Shannon into helping her, but he'd never believe Tucker would have any part of it. And Aaron Masterson, Kylie's husband, had the kind of upright nature that would never let him do something so low-down.

Of course, Gage would have thought Bailey's nature was the same.

Mighty tired of walking and determined to find Bailey and have this out with her, he found the mustangs she'd caught and broken. He saddled and bridled the biggest of them, a buckskin stallion, and set out trailing after her herd.

He was an hour finding the cattle, not because it was hard—trailing fifty cattle took no great skill—but because it was a twisting, rugged ride. Bailey was a long way from home. As he rode down the well-marked trail, finally he saw longhorns with her brand—two Ws, with one on top of the other. He'd heard her call it the Double W Ranch.

He noticed the cattle were inside a fence. He rode around the edges of it. He saw a saddle slung over a split rail, and her horse was grazing, haltered and staked out inside the fence with the cattle.

Riding around the outside of the fence, the woods thinned. Through the trees he saw Bailey about a hundred yards off. She was crouched by a crooked post, wearing her britches, of course. There was a nice stack of split rails, plenty to close the rest of the gap in the fence.

The pounding of a hammer on wood rang out. She was building more split-rail fence along one side of the grassy stretch in the middle of the woods. It could almost be called a clearing. A spring ran out of the woods on the far side and cut through her pasture. So she'd found water and grass enough to keep her herd. Gage would have been proud of her if he hadn't been so furious.

It was a cold day, but she'd tossed her buckskin coat aside and wore only a broad-brimmed hat. As he closed the distance between them, he could tell she'd made both herself. The woman knew how to live off the land.

The trees were sparse enough that there was good grass. It was a steep slope, the ground broken and rocky. Nothing like the lush canyon grass. Grudgingly, Gage admitted the woman had found a place to feed her herd that would last the winter. It was off her claim, and that left some land she owned close to her cabin, which would feed the herd later in the year when the grass got eaten down.

From the look of the fencing, she'd been at it for a while, at least all day yesterday. So she was planning on making the move and had in fact already made it. Her cattle were here. She'd known the canyon was lost to her and she was making plans to survive without it. That meant she'd set the man-trap purely out of spite. It drove Gage's cool fury to white-hot rage.

He rode into the clearing, ready to make her sorry she'd ever come west.

Between the banging of her hammer and the horse walking on thick grass, he'd gotten within a hundred feet before a hoof clicked on a rocky spot.

She dropped the hammer, wheeled, her gun drawn, cocked and aimed. It was a motion so smooth it was stunning. Then she saw him and relaxed; she didn't shoot blind. Her reflexes, and her smarts—not to just start pulling the trigger because something spooked her—made his breath snag in his chest. She was good. So ready for trouble. So savvy. Bailey Wilde was too good to have done that to his men, so why had she?

Why had a woman with her strength and her skills reduced herself to sneaking around like a coyote?

Bailey holstered her gun and gave him a look of disgust. She picked up her hammer and started to turn back to the fence as if she intended to ignore him. Then those flashing gold eyes focused on the buckskin stallion he rode.

"You turn to horse thievin' now, Coulter? It ain't enough that you've stolen the grass from under my cows?"

Gage's boots hit the ground. He didn't trust the mustang to stay put, so he quickly lashed the reins to a scrub oak. "You're mighty bold talking about crimes, Bailey, when I just came from a whole stack of 'em, including three of my men who might as well have been killed, thanks to you."

The fire went out of Bailey's eyes, and she seemed to really see him. He was coated with dirt and hadn't taken the time to clean up or wash the blood off his face. "What happened to you? You had men hurt?"

Gage didn't even try to control his snort of disgust. "I shouldn't be surprised that you'd lie on top of everything else. But I thought whatever the trouble between us, you were someone with a code of honor. But if you'd try to kill my men, why wouldn't you lie about it?"

"If I what?" All the worry and concern vanished from her expression, and that fire in her eyes flared to life.

"As you can see, you didn't harm me. So the work goes on, and by the end of the day we'll have moved the cattle into the canyon."

"Gage, I didn't—"

"My men are doing it." He slashed a hand to cut her off, in no mood for more of her lies. "I should be helping, but I told them I was going to take care of you, and they were all for it. Get on your horse. I'm gonna make you watch my cattle move into my canyon. And when we're done, we're going to see the sheriff. There's law in this country now."

He expected her to yell back. Maybe run. Go for her gun in the worst case. Instead, she narrowed those eyes at him, slipped her hammer into a loop on her gun belt, dragged a pair of buckskin gloves off her hands, and tucked them behind her belt buckle.

"This happened this morning?"

Gage didn't waste his time answering. She knew exactly when it happened.

She sure enough didn't run, but instead took a step straight for him and jabbed a finger at his nose. "You've been pushing me as hard as a man can push ever since we've met, and you've won every fight we've had."

He leaned down just in case she wanted an excuse to jab him. He might just do some poking of his own. "Tell that to my bleeding men."

"And now on the day you're taking away the land I need, when you already own half the country, when you've gotten everything you want and left me with a hard winter ahead and hours of backbreaking work to get my cattle ready to live on this rugged ground, it's not enough for you."

"It's not enough if my men are bruised and bleeding.

54

Don't act like just because we got through it without anyone killed or seriously hurt, I'm going to look the other way."

Her eyes blazed. "On that day when you've won and I lost, instead of being any kind of decent neighbor and gracious winner, you come over here and accuse me of a crime and threaten me with the sheriff?" She shoved his chest. He didn't budge even an inch, yet he felt the force behind it.

He snagged her forearm. "Did you think being a woman would protect you?"

She shoved with her other hand, and he grabbed that one. This was the strong, direct woman he'd dealt with before. So why had she turned sneak on him?

Wrenching at his grip, she said, "I think that makes *you* the coward, not me."

"No one calls me a coward." Not since he left Texas. He'd learned to coat his feelings in ice. When he was frozen inside, he could handle just about anything. It was those fiery eyes that were burning him all the way to the core that melted his self-control.

She pulled at the hold he had on her, then stopped as if struggling was beneath her. But nothing was beneath someone who'd set those man-traps.

"Let me go." It was an order given with such command, Gage almost obeyed her by reflex.

He held on.

A cold wind buffeted them. The trees swayed. They glared at each other. Blazing fury flashed in her eyes. He fought for his usual icy control when her fire threatened to set his temper blazing, too.

Suddenly her chin came up. Her eyes cooled just a bit and met his directly. "I went straight from the meeting with you three days ago to scouting for new grazing land for my cattle."

"So you say."

Gage wasn't about to take the word of the little liar.

"Tucker and Shannon helped me find this grassland. We were days scouting out this place, and they stayed over with me at night."

"Tucker knows this land. He could've found it in an hour." But Tucker . . . Gage trusted Tucker with his life, and if Tucker had been with her . . .

"When we found it early yesterday morning, they, along with Kylie and Aaron, helped me build most of this fence and drive my cattle over here. And we all camped out here last night so we could take turns standing watch to hold the herd."

Gage looked away from her and saw how much fence had been built. Far more than one woman could build in a few days. But maybe she'd started it earlier. Maybe she'd been planning on adding this rough pasture to her holdings all along.

Except why would she when she had the canyon? No, she'd only found this when she'd faced defeat. Unlike the canyon and a lot of meadows a man could find with natural barriers, this mountainside had nothing that would keep a cow from wandering off. She'd needed this fence.

"I told them I could finish up this last stretch by the end of the day, so they rode off. They've only been gone a couple of hours. They can account for me every minute since I walked away from you. When was I supposed to have come over there and hurt your big strong men?"

A cool breeze blew down the mountainside, promising the approach of a long winter, yet it was no colder than Bailey's next words. "Get your hands off of me."

Gage let her go.

"I have another hour on this fence, unless you're determined not only to drive me out of my canyon—"

"My canyon," Gage interjected, but he lacked his usual conviction, because he was facing the fact that he'd been mighty hard on Bailey, and it looked for all the world like he'd just made a big mistake.

Bailey sniffed. "But also force me to leave my herd so they wander off and I'm days rounding them up—if the wolves don't get them. I'm not sure just what you've got against me, Coulter."

"I think you know." Though Gage knew that wasn't true, not now that he was forced to admit she hadn't set the deadfall trap for his men. "Listen, Bailey. You can see how I—"

"You've got how many acres under your control out here?" She cut him off. "Most of it you don't own. I did exactly what you did. I started using land that wasn't mine. I claimed water holes and pastureland and the gap into a lush canyon. Turns out you found a way into it, while I lost. Fine. Are you done harassing and insulting me?"

He was done, but she had to quit yelling at him so he could tell her that.

"If you're not, do you mind if I go back to fencing? No reason I have to lose work time just because you've got hired men to do all your chores. If you're still determined to insult me, speak up so I can hear you over the pounding."

And the need to make amends was almost driven from his mind, because he had something brand spanking new to worry about. "So if you didn't set that rockslide to fall on my men, then who did?"

He saw the concern flash in her eyes, but she fought it off. "Not my problem." She pulled her hammer out of its loop and turned back to the fence.

"Let me help." He could see exactly what she had left. If he pitched in, they could have it done fast. "Fencing is a two-man job."

And she wasn't even close to being a man, despite that close-cropped hair and the britches she wore—and her attitude.

"Get out of here, Coulter, and unless you've decided to turn horse thief, let my mustang go when you get back to my place."

"I'm sorry, Bailey." It had taken him too long to get those words out of his mouth. "When that rockslide came down, I didn't think you'd done it. It's not your way. But you were the only person I knew who wanted to keep us out of the canyon. So I came hunting you."

"My sisters have gone home with their husbands. If you want to check up and see if the story I told you is true, go and question them. You might decide all the Wilde women are liars and you might even doubt Aaron, as he's new to the country, but you've known Tucker for years. Maybe you'll decide you can trust his word. Besides, we'd have to be pretty organized to all tell the same story."

"I believe you." Gage sighed. "I'm going to help you with this fence by way of apologizing. And it isn't close to enough."

Bailey glared at him. "You're right about that." She shoved the hammer at him so hard, it amounted to a punch in the stomach. He figured he ought to be grateful she didn't try and outright hammer him. She bent to pick up a sturdy split log about ten feet long and handed him a little pouch. "I've got all the work done that can be managed without a hammer and nails. You do the hammering. It's harder work. You owe me that, too."

Gage gave a short, sharp laugh, then took the leather bag of nails and the hammer. "I really am sorry, Bailey. I should have known you wouldn't do that." He grabbed the end of the split rail, and as Bailey lifted her end, Gage turned to her. "But someone did."

Bailey looked up with a frown on her face. "Which means you've got an enemy, Gage. A man like you, I reckon it's not the first time."

He felt his temper snap. "What do you mean *a man like me*?"

She rolled her eyes at him and shook her head. "Start nailing."

6

That's the last of it." Coulter straightened from the fence.

Bailey didn't begrudge admitting he was better at this than her. Bailey was a skilled carpenter and took pride in doing fine work, but when it came to brute strength, well, a man surely qualified as a brute.

"And now I want you to come back to your place with me and help me usher my cattle into that canyon."

He took a step closer. Somehow when he got this close, things changed. Bailey couldn't quite understand it. Mostly she thought of her life as a battle, a fight to dig a living out of a rough land that, judging by last winter, was trying its best to kill her.

But when Coulter got close, she noticed the sky was an unusual shade of vivid blue that she'd seen nowhere else, certainly not back east on Pa's farm. The grass was an emerald green that nearly sparkled. The evergreens bobbed in a breeze that seemed bracing and fresh rather than painfully cold, as it had when she was working here alone.

She pulled the thin air deep into her lungs and felt her own good health and the strength of her muscles. A bald eagle soared overhead, and its screeching cry was like the music of the wilderness.

Her cattle, longhorns, looked like wild critters that were noble and strong, as rugged as the mountains, a perfect match for this life. It was a victory that she'd built this herd, and she felt that more with Coulter so near. It surrounded her with beauty and satisfaction.

She felt it all, let it soak into her soul, and loved her life. And all because a man stood too close. It made no sense to her. She should have been mad enough to chew up those ten-penny nails and spit bullets at this man. And honestly she was. But that didn't mean she didn't feel more alive right now than she had since, in a wasted effort to save her sisters, she'd signed up to fight in that horror called the Civil War.

"Why would I do such a thing?" She even enjoyed fighting with him.

Gage caught her arm as if he thought she needed saving. "I'm going to be in and out of that canyon every day."

"You are?" She swallowed hard.

"Yes, until the winter keeps me out. Don't you check your cattle daily?"

"Of course."

"If I'm not there, some of my men will be. And no matter how careful we are, my men are almost certainly going to see you. And because I hire men who are neither stupid nor blind, they're going to see right away that you're a woman."

"Gage, I don't want them on my place."

"Let's go together, right now. You can help us get the herd up that trail. Let my men meet you."

"No!"

"Yes! Right now they think you set off the trap that almost killed three of them."

"Well, straighten them out."

"No matter what I say, some of 'em might still wonder. Look them in the eye, let them know you're a decent, honest woman. That will put a stop to any hostility they feel toward you. I want to make sure they know I trust you. Whoever set up that rockslide might not be afraid to do harm to you too, Bailey. Good neighbors look out for each other. Come on back to the canyon with me and be a good neighbor."

She looked him in the eye. He was too close. Again.

He was right too, confound it. The word was out that she was female. Nev Bassett knew, Aaron's old friend from back east who'd come out here, half mad from his war experience, wanting to do harm to Aaron. Nev had come to his senses and stayed. And Nev had probably told Myra, his wife. And Myra's ma, Erica, ran the diner in Aspen Ridge and was the center of all town news. If Bailey's name ever came up, she was no doubt spoken of as a woman.

And Myra's stepfather, Bo Langley, was the law in these parts. He'd been involved when Shannon and Tucker had caught the man burning out homesteaders, so he knew

Tucker and Shannon well. Kylie and Aaron, too. There was no possible way he hadn't figured out Bailey was a woman.

Really, Gage's men were the only ones left who didn't know, and if they thought she'd tried to kill them, they might be forming a lynch mob right now. Keeping the fact that she was a woman a secret by hiding from them was a good way to get herself hung.

She needed to face them to convince them that a sneak attack wasn't her way. And if she did face them, Bailey knew her disguise wouldn't hold.

It worked during the war because she'd been passing herself off as a young man. But a homesteader needed to be at least twenty-one, and she'd been out here a year. The numbers didn't add up to her being a seventeen-year-old boy, as they had in the war. In truth, Bailey was nearing twenty-three. Any men who could do simple arithmetic would see Bailey didn't add up to a man.

She hated the weakness of fear, but was unable to control it. "I don't want to be bothered by your men."

Gage watched her, seeing deeper than she wanted him to. And yet she hoped he saw enough to believe her without asking more. "I'll make sure they understand that. But western men are loyal to their saddle partners. They'll only take my word for so much. They like seeing the truth with their own eyes. They'll cooperate better once they know you had no part in that rockslide."

As promises went, it wasn't much. Gage couldn't make his men do much of anything if it didn't suit them. And men could be monsters. Bailey knew that all too well. They weren't all monsters. She knew that, too. But you couldn't tell by looking which were and which weren't. Best to stay away from them all.

Right now it didn't look like that was possible.

She nodded. "I'll . . ." Her throat didn't work, so she swallowed and tried again, "I'll go then. I'll m-meet your men."

There was a roaring in her ears, and for a second the world turned dark around the edges.

A firm hand on her upper arm steadied her. "You're white as a sheet. Are you all right?"

It took her a minute, but Bailey didn't answer until she could tell the truth. Leaning too heavily on Gage's firm grip, she waited until her vision cleared and she could hear again.

Straightening, squaring her shoulders, she pulled away from him. "I'm fine. Let's go."

He held on. "Bailey, what's wrong?"

Turning, her eyes met his. All that gray, yet nothing cold about them at the moment. His eyes were washed with kindness and concern.

She managed to say, "I've been working too many hours without a drink of water. I just got weak-kneed for a minute." She'd been working long hours on short rations for a year now, and never for one moment had she gotten weak-kneed.

Gage looked hard at her. Then, holding her arm, he guided her to her saddle, which straddled a fence rail. He tugged a canteen off the pommel, twisted open the cap, and handed it to her.

While she leaned against the fence and drank, Gage made

short work of catching her mustang, staked out to graze in the pasture with her cattle. It was a blue roan mare wearing a halter. Gage led it over to where Bailey leaned. He saddled and bridled the critter, then handed her the reins.

She mounted up while he walked to the gate. Her other mustang, the one he'd ridden over, was tied outside the fence, grazing. He let Bailey ride out, closed the gate, then strode over to his horse, tightened the cinch and swung up into the saddle.

Together they headed for her place, and the canyon.

"Will your men have the cattle driven in already?" It made her sick to give up that grass, but she'd accepted it. It wasn't the first hard thing she'd had to take.

"I doubt it. Rowdy was going back to my place to tell the men to drive the herd over. Two of my men, Manny and Ike, were going to clear the last of the rubble on the trail. The herd will move slow, so even though I was a while working on your fence, I suspect we'll get there about the same time the herd does. There'll be plenty of work left to do."

Gage smiled at her. "You can help us. We'll swap work, just like good neighbors ought to. It might be best if you put on a skirt before you meet my men, though."

"I don't own a skirt, so whether that's best or not doesn't much matter."

He gave her a disgruntled look. "I should have expected that, I reckon."

He studied her for a long spell. She knew he wasn't satisfied with her saying she was dizzy with thirst. But he didn't goad her about her excuse. She hoped now that he'd started moving toward the canyon, he'd focus on that instead of the fact that his mentioning meeting the men had almost made her swoon.

✦

"So what is it about meeting a crowd of men that almost made you swoon?" Gage rode close by her side, ready to catch her if she toppled off the horse.

But he didn't expect that; what he expected was exactly what he got.

"I didn't almost swoon. That makes me sound like a delicate maiden in some parlor somewhere. I've never been close to such a thing. Let's make tracks. We're burning daylight."

Evasions. Distractions. Outright lies. Anything but the simple truth. It was perfect for a woman living as a man. A woman who'd done her best to run when he'd come close to her. A woman who'd pulled a rifle every time he came to her house.

He should probably just forget it, but they had a long ride ahead of them. "Bailey, I saw your face go pale. I saw your knees buckle. I know when a woman is near collapse."

"You don't know anything about women. You've hardly seen a woman out here."

She had a point. "All right then. I know when a *person* is near collapse, and you were. We were talking about you meeting my men."

Her knuckles tightened on her saddle horn until they went white.

"When you saw the right of it, that meeting them might

67

stave off a heap of trouble, you agreed to go and you went white as a ghost."

Despite the upset he saw in that grip of hers, she couldn't just quit fighting, not Bailey Wilde.

Turning those golden eyes on him, nearly spitting fire, she said, "I've had the same thought about you, Coulter—that you've got a haunted look in your eyes. What ghosts do you carry around? What haunts you?"

When evasions, distractions, and outright lies didn't work, he wasn't surprised that she attacked. But he was surprised that she picked a weapon that struck quite so sharp.

"We're talking about you."

"Hah! You don't mind poking and prodding at me, but you don't like being poked back. Just shut your mouth and ride, Coulter. Unless you want to tell me every little thing that upsets you, just keep your questions to yourself."

"Which means you have a few things that upset you, and I'm absolutely right about you almost swooning." Gage hadn't seen her be quite so vulnerable before. He just had trouble letting her get that tough buffalo hide back in place. This was his chance to figure out more about her.

"Tell me then, Coulter, why you left for the Rockies five years ago when most every other able-bodied young man in Texas signed on to fight in the war?"

Gage just about gasped out loud.

If he wanted her to tell him what bothered her so much, admitting his own ghosts might make her talk. Well, he didn't want to know about her that much.

Gage saw the rugged ground they'd been covering had finally reached an actual trail. Good excuse. "You're right, Bailey, we're burning daylight. Let's make tracks." Gage urged the mustang into a trot.

He thought he heard a low chuckle behind him, but he didn't turn around to check. He didn't want to know if she was laughing at him.

At least she wasn't threatening to swoon anymore.

❧

"You really don't own a single dress." Coulter wasn't asking a question; he was making a statement.

And he sounded tired and resigned. Bailey thought resigned was good. He must be getting used to her.

"No, I don't own a dress. Why would I?"

"At least leave your hat at the house."

"No."

"You won't leave your hat?"

"No, I won't leave my house. When you get in the canyon, you bring your men to meet me."

Coulter looked at the sky with those gray eyes. Bailey wondered if he might be asking the Almighty for patience. She was tempted to punch him. Then he could ask the Almighty for a new set of teeth.

"I thought you were going to help. I thought we decided to be good neighbors."

"I've got chores of my own. I don't have time to help my *neighbor* do his."

That provoked a little smile out of him.

"Come with me, Bailey. Face this. I'll make sure my

men know Tucker will vouch for you, and I trust you. But cowering here in your house won't impress them much."

Her shoulders slumped, but she rode on through the canyon. It burned to think of what a great setup she'd had in here. She saw where he'd blasted. "You really did it," she said. "You found a way over that peak."

"You doubted me?"

"I have to admit, I held out a bit of hope you'd fail, and the peak was a big part of the reason why. I didn't see how you were going to get a cow to climb it. It never occurred to me you'd just blow the whole thing up."

They reached the bottom of the canyon, right below where the giant bite had been taken out of the canyon rim.

"If you'd known I was going to make it in, would you have just let me cross on your land?"

"Maybe." Close to growling at him, Bailey added, "Probably not."

Coulter laughed again, then kicked the horse and started up the steep slope. Her horses were mountain-bred mustangs she'd caught wild and broke less than a year ago. This climb was nothing to them.

Bailey was riding her favorite mare. Coulter had picked the biggest of her brood, a tough stallion she hoped would breed a strong line in her horses. The surefooted pair went up the canyon wall and paused. The blasted-out rim was rough but flat for about ten paces before it dropped off.

They crested the canyon wall through what looked like a big old bear claw, then headed down where the trail was fairly easy. Even so, they came to spots so narrow that Bailey could brush the rocks with her fingertips as she rode along on one side. At the same time, her other foot dangled out over thin air.

They were halfway down the gut-twisting trail when a rider appeared at the bottom. From here, Bailey could identify Gage's C Bar brand. Gage was a ways ahead of her, and seeing the man below, Bailey couldn't help but slow even more. The distance between her and Coulter stretched out, and he reached the bottom long before she did.

He sat on his horse, talking with his cowpoke, waiting until Bailey reached him. She saw a young Mexican, whose black eyes flashed with temper when they landed on her.

"Manny, this is Bailey Wilde. You know Tucker, right?"

"*Sí?*" His tone was curt.

She saw a smear of dried blood on his shirt. He was one of the men who'd been hurt that morning. And he thought that man-trap was her doing.

"Well, Bailey is Tucker's wife's sister."

The fire went out of Manny's eyes, replaced with surprise, then confusion. "Sister?" He spoke decent, if heavily accented English. "Bailey Wilde is an *hombre*."

"No. I was told that, too. But Bailey Wilde is most certainly not a man. Bailey didn't set that trap for you. Once she gave up on keeping cattle in my canyon, she and Tucker and Tucker's wife spent every minute scouting new pastureland. Tucker's been with her the whole time. Day and night. I wouldn't necessarily take her word for it."

Coulter turned to Bailey. "No offense, but I don't know you that well. But Tucker is a good friend and a man I trust. I do take his word." He turned back to Manny. "That

71

means someone else is to blame for the rockslide, so be careful. Whoever did it is still running loose."

Manny nodded, though he gave Bailey a narrow-eyed look. Then his eyes flickered back and forth between her and Gage a time or two. He glanced at her britches and hair, then back to her eyes. The look seemed to be less than completed satisfied with Gage's explanation.

"Go on back and tell the others to be careful, too. And tell them that Bailey's not who we're looking for."

"Sí, boss." Manny turned and rode back the way he'd come. Only moments later, the first longhorn appeared on the trail.

Coulter directed his horse back uphill. "Let's head to the top. You go first while I let a couple of cows get ahead of me. If they follow along easy, I'll let more go. If they give me trouble, I'll fall in and start pushing them and be right behind you."

"I'm supposed to break the trail for your cattle?"

"Nope, we already did that when we rode down."

"You'd never done it before? When we rode up and down the canyon, we were the first?"

"Yep. Doesn't that make you feel like a trailblazer, Bailey?"

"It makes me feel like I've taken a hand in ruining my own ranch."

Coulter laughed. "Unless you want to stay down here alone with my men, you go on ahead up that slope, Bailey." He made it sound like a threat, even sitting there with a big smug grin on his face.

Bailey had no interest in what it took to get Coulter's

cattle into her canyon. Besides, the cattle were following along just fine. Coulter had held back to watch for a cow that didn't want to cooperate, but there weren't any of those.

Rather than stay and watch the invasion, she rode to her cabin and did her chores. That amounted to feeding the chickens and gathering eggs. She'd leave milking until later; she always put that off for as long as she could. She had ten horses she'd kept on a pasture close to her place. They were grazing, so there was nothing to do there.

Her herd was a long ride away and didn't need anything until tomorrow.

When she was done, she went to the mouth of the canyon. She hadn't been there long when the first critter skylined on that saddleback.

Bailey watched the invasion for a while. A mean part of her was hoping that when Coulter came over the hump, she'd get to watch a longhorn bull get testy enough to give Coulter a little poke in the backside. But no such thing happened, mainly because she couldn't see him.

Instead, the cattle marched over the ridge in a perfect row, cooperating as if they were part of a grand Fourth of July parade.

It seemed there wasn't anyone, man nor beast, who wasn't eager to steal her grass.

Bailey stood outside at the back door—closed to keep out the cold—and leaned against it to watch the cattle march single file down into what was supposed to be hers. Longhorns mixed with a few red-and-white-faced Herefords, and plenty of cattle that looked to be a cross between the two.

Talk about walking through the valley of the shadow.

Bailey about had her share of that. Her little sisters had been her friends and she loved them, but protecting them from Pa and Jimmy had been a weight on her shoulders that nearly crushed her, especially since she'd failed more often than not.

And then came the war. They didn't have a sheepskin diploma fancy enough for the hard schooling she'd earned fighting in the war.

The valley of the shadow of death.

I will fear no evil.

Was war what God had been thinking of in the psalm? That kind of fear? Or was He talking about the shadow of death of your spirit when you're separated from faith?

Either . . . or both, depending on who was reading it and the message they needed from God at the time. Bailey thought right now she needed both. Not that Gage Coulter was evil. But fear. Well, right now it was taking everything she had to keep from fearing everything.

She watched the first cow tear up a bite of grass with a dull chomp. Gage Coulter was stealing the dream she'd had for this canyon. It barely even knocked her back. Oh, it was upsetting, but Bailey would just find another way to get her ranch. Gage couldn't own the whole confounded Rockies.

Hundreds of cattle made their way down the trail. Bailey knew cattle often lined up and just followed the tail in front of them, and kept following with no thought to where they were going. Cows weren't the smartest critters, and in a case like this, it was for the best.

At least if you were Gage Coulter.

Bailey could have found work to do, but she allowed herself to be hypnotized by the steady march of the cows. Finally, a man came over the rim, and she instantly recognized Gage. Her stomach twisted at the sight of him. She stepped inside and closed the door before he could catch her staring.

She'd have ridden off to her own cattle where he'd found her this morning, yet he'd probably just come after her. He seemed determined that she meet his cowhands. She had a couple of stalls in her barn that could use fresh straw. Work helped her get through anything.

The half-wild longhorn needed milking, and the critter didn't care much for that, so Bailey was fully engaged with the effort. When she jumped away from the last lashing hoof, triumphant, her bucket half full, she turned to walk to the house and then stopped so suddenly she almost dropped the milk.

Gage started clapping, a smile like nothing she'd ever seen before on his face.

"What's so funny?" she asked.

"That's . . . that's . . ." Gage burst out laughing. In all the times they'd talked, and honest it hadn't been that many times, she'd barely seen him crack a smile. "That's the meanest cow I've ever seen." He stopped talking to laugh again.

Bailey took a threatening step toward him with the milk bucket.

He stumbled back, putting his hands up in self-defense, all without a break in the laughter. "I'm sorry. You did a great job of milking her. It's just, I've never seen . . ."

He was off laughing again.

She wasn't going to waste milk—not milk she'd worked this hard for, not even for the satisfaction of dumping it over Gage's head. So she started for the house, and he must have thought she was going to attack because he jumped out of the way when she got near him. She just stomped right on by, heading straight out the door.

Without a look back, she knew he was following her, for she heard the occasional chuckle coming from him. She smiled as she walked, knowing what a sight she must have been, but glad her back was to him so he didn't have to know she was enjoying the moment. And so he wouldn't know she was proud of herself. She'd like to see him milk that wild critter of a longhorn.

She went inside and swung the door shut. It never closed. That earned him a glance. He was right on her heels, a hard man to discourage.

Knuckling a tear from the corner of one eye, still fighting laughter, he said, "My men are probably in the canyon by now. Leave the milk and come on. I want them to meet you. I've told them you aren't responsible for the rockslide."

"That's good enough," she replied. "I don't need to meet them."

"These men are used to reading the measure of others. They need to hear it from your own mouth and look you in the eye. And the word is out you're a woman. I want to be standing right beside you to make it clear I won't put up with a one of them treating you wrong."

Put like that, Bailey didn't see that she had much choice. She set the milk bucket down with a metallic *clank* and pursed her lips in an unhappy scowl. "Let's go then." She yanked her gloves out from where she'd tucked them behind her belt buckle and stared at him.

He went to the back door, opened it, and swept a hand. "Ladies first."

"Boy, I haven't heard that much," Bailey said.

"Well, it's high time, Miss Wilde."

She growled as she walked out of the cabin, then stumbled to a stop.

Ten men, lined up on horseback, waited just yards away from her door. She shuddered, found it near impossible to move another step. Men in groups like this . . . she hated it. She had no idea how to handle it. Why couldn't people just leave her alone?

Gage came up beside her. She could swear that whatever reaction she'd had, she'd kept it inside. She'd stopped suddenly, but then there the men were. Of course she stopped.

And yet Gage rested his hand ever so gently on her back, and the warmth of it helped thaw the chill of fear. Then he moved his hand and stepped away, far enough that no one would get any improper ideas. She hoped.

"Men, I'd like you to meet Miss Bailey Wilde," Gage said.

Every man except Manny reacted. Most in small ways, but she saw their surprise one and all.

Maybe the word was out that she was female, but each of those ten men must have doubted. Narrowed eyes, hands clenched on pommels, arched brows. One man dragged his hat off his head. Another shifted his eyes between Gage and her. A horse shifted under reins that must have tightened.

"Miss Wilde?" A white-haired man who had a bandage on his forehead sounded confused. "I thought Bailey Wilde was Tucker's brother-in-law. I know for a fact I heard that."

"Well, the facts are—"

"I'll answer that, Coulter," Bailey said, cutting Gage off. She refused to stand by and let these men talk about her as if she weren't here. "I let my sisters say I was their brother, and I've lived as such because it suited me. I wanted to be on my own, and some folks have a problem with a woman doing that. I run my own spread and I fork my own broncs. You heard I was a man because I hoped that story would stand, but the truth is out now. And while I was willing to let folks believe what isn't so, that's not the same as telling a lie to a man's face."

"If Shannon said you were her brother, ain't no way that's anything but a lie." The older man rubbed his bandage.

"Well, the lie is over." Bailey thought of the rockslide. "I heard about that trap set for you this morning. I fight shy of people, but when I can't, I face my troubles head on. I'd never set a trap like that. You don't know me and you've no reason to trust me, and I've made no secret of wanting control of this canyon for myself, but I've spent the last three days and nights with my sisters and their husbands scouting pastureland. I need it to make up for losing this canyon."

Bailey shoved her hands in the back pockets of her britches and looked every man in the eye, one by one. "I don't blame you for doubting me, but Tucker will swear I've never been away from him until just before Gage found me this morning, over an hour's ride from here. If you've been around long enough to know Tucker, and you believe his word is good, go talk to him."

That swayed nearly every one of them. She saw it in the relaxed shoulders and a few faces that went from suspicious to confusion. It was clear to Bailey that they were now wondering the same thing she and Coulter were. If she wasn't the one who'd set the trap, then who was?

"Bailey, let me introduce my men." Gage started down the line. The old-timer was Rowdy, the man next to him Ike. The Mexican she'd met before, Manny, was next. The three of them looked the worse for wear, bandaged, blood on their clothes. They must've gotten caught in the rockslide.

Bailey took a hard look at each man, reading his eyes, looking for any sign of trouble, not that she believed she could see it coming every time. Besides, a perfectly decent man in the right situation could turn into a savage. The war had taught her that, too.

"Bailey hasn't given us permission to cross on her land," Gage went on. "The law is on her side, and unless she changes her mind, everyone riding in and out of this canyon will take the trail we just blasted. Like she said, she likes to keep to herself, and I expect each of you to remember that and not come onto her land, nor ask if you can."

Bailey glanced quickly at Gage, then away. She wasn't a pretty woman; she knew that. But there weren't many women around, and she could already see a few of the younger men studying her in a friendly way. Nothing dangerous or threatening about it, and yet Bailey felt badly threatened.

"That's it," Gage said. "Let's head home. Looks like snow tonight." He turned to Bailey. "Once the heavy snow comes, we don't get over here. One of the reasons I was so long in finding you was because this place is at the far end of my range. Between us, come winter, will be drifts deep enough to swallow a man on horseback."

He tugged on his Stetson. She noticed someone had brought his big stallion over. Gage had ridden her horse to get his cattle and brought it back, then released it with her mustangs.

He untied his horse as the other men rode off. Bailey knew climbing that trail sent them miles out of their way to Gage's spread. It wasn't just the climb up and down, it was also that they'd end up on the far west side of the canyon with a couple of extra hours to ride around it in order to get back to this side before they could head for home.

And that extra time on a hard trail was all her fault. She opened her mouth to tell them to just go on through, and then her eyes lifted to that stupid bite taken out of the top of the canyon ridge. How many sticks of dynamite had it taken to blast that away? How much had it cost? How many man hours had they spent doing it? And now, only hours after they'd finished, she would cave like an old mine shaft and tell them she wasn't serious about their trespassing?

She clamped her mouth shut and turned to Gage, who paused before swinging up on his horse.

"We're just a few days, maybe a few weeks, away from being shut down for the whole winter, Bailey. Once that happens, you won't get out until spring. How are you going to ride all that way to check your cattle?"

Bailey narrowed her eyes and refused to answer.

Gage looked at her, then at his cattle. "Listen, the canyon isn't that full. There's room for fifty more cows. Bring them on back and keep them here with mine."

Bailey thought of her scouting and the fence she'd worked so hard to build. "Thanks, but I don't want any favors from you, Coulter. I'll manage my own herd without any handouts from you."

"You mean you were willing to steal my canyon from

82

me fair and square, but you won't share it with me. Is that your idea of managing on your own?"

Bailey almost smiled at that. In fact, she must have quirked her lips, because Gage let go of his horse and took a couple of steps closer to her.

"Don't you get lonely out here?" he asked.

The question stunned her into silence. All she heard was the whipping of the autumn wind and the steady in and out of Coulter's breathing as he looked at her with those gray eyes.

"Your sisters are both leaving, aren't they? I thought they'd be gone already. Masterson has been waiting, worrying about his friend, but Nev is settled in with Myra, and they seem to be all right. Tucker, well, I can see him looking to the mountaintops. It's a wonder he hasn't headed up to his cabin before now. It's because of Shannon worrying about you, I think, but make no mistake about it, they will go. Are you really going to live here and not see another human being for six months? Because that's how long it'll be."

Bailey's throat closed as she thought of it. She lived a ways from Shannon and Kylie. Once the snow came down heavy, they didn't see each other until the spring thaw. And Pa's claim was higher up the mountain than hers. He might be snowed in already. He wasn't one to waste energy seeing his daughters, and Bailey had no interest in risking life and limb to go see him. She liked being alone, but she'd never been quite this alone before.

And the battle she faced this winter to get to her cattle didn't even bear thinking about. She'd do her best, and that was all any woman could do. Finally, because she wasn't about to show how upset she was, she sniffed and said, "Get along with you, Coulter. I like living alone. It suits me."

Coulter kept looking right into her eyes for a long stretch. He made no secret of showing his doubts, yet he said nothing more about it.

"Goodbye, Bailey." He swung up on horseback and faced her again. "Maybe I'll see you again. If not tomorrow or in the next few days, then maybe in May." He tugged on the brim of his Stetson and wheeled his horse to ride after his men.

Watching him go was the loneliest moment of Bailey's life.

8

Then Bailey found a new definition of lonely.

She rode in a new layer of snow to Shannon's. Tucker stood in the corral, yanking on a rope to secure a big bundle to a horse's back. They were leaving.

Swallowing hard, Bailey looked at the other fully packed horse. Shannon's favorite mare stood saddled alongside Gru. Tucker's gray mare wore no saddle, and she had a bridle with no bit. The horse stayed with Tucker because it wanted to. Tucker didn't try to tame the strange half-wild critter.

Shannon came out of the cabin pulling on her gloves. She wore a doeskin dress. Sunrise was showing Shannon how to survive in the mountains, as if they weren't high enough right here. Shannon also wore leggings and knee-high moccasins, so the dress didn't leave her legs bare and cold. Tucker was his usual buckskin-clad self.

Tucker noticed Bailey with a glance and a smile, then went back to work. Bailey figured he'd known she was coming for a long time. Tucker didn't miss much.

Pausing, Shannon turned to Bailey, who rode up and dismounted. They'd both known this was coming.

"We were going to ride by your place and say good-bye." Tears filled Shannon's eyes, and she swiped at them with the back of her wrist. "Tucker says if we don't go right now, we'll be snowed away from his cabin all winter."

Bailey didn't know what to say, which was just as well because the thought of Shannon moving so far away made her throat close up tight.

"Bailey, I—" Shannon stopped as the sound of hooves caught their attention. Kylie, the baby of the family, came riding in on a black mustang. Aaron was at her side on his huge thoroughbred, pulling two packhorses behind him, each loaded as high as Tucker's.

Bailey and Shannon turned to face their little sister as she rode up. No britches for Kylie, not even a pair made of sturdy doeskin. Kylie had on a dress, very pretty. It was a split skirt, though, so she could ride astride.

Kylie looked at Tucker packing the horses, then rode straight for her sisters. She swung down.

"You're coming here to say goodbye, too." Bailey didn't ask; she stated a fact. It was clear the Mastersons were set for travel.

Kylie nodded. Aaron reined his horse toward Tucker. Bailey thought he was giving them some privacy, and she appreciated that. Bailey and Shannon weren't real good with sad goodbyes. Kylie, on the other hand, seemed to favor them. She broke down and cried and threw her arms around both of them at once.

Bailey was glad because now she could pretend to cooperate without having to display how upset she was.

"W-we're riding south today. We were going to stop and say goodbye to each of you."

Bailey noticed that neither Kylie nor Shannon mentioned riding to Pa's homestead and saying goodbye to him. It would be a waste of time. Pa had barely spoken to either of them since they'd given up their homesteads and Gage Coulter had bought them.

Just wait till Pa found out Bailey had lost the canyon.

Kylie was crying into Bailey's neck, getting her shirt all wet, and for just one second, Bailey felt hot tears wash the backs of her eyes. The tears didn't fall, but her arms tightened on both her sisters.

"I'm going to miss you both so much," Kylie whispered. "I can't stand that Shannon and I are both leaving you."

Bailey laughed raggedly, glad for an excuse to break the hug. She rested one rough hand on Kylie's cheek. Strange business taking care of her little sisters all these years, protecting them from Pa. Of course, they'd all tried to protect each other from Pa and had precious little success, until maybe now. At least Shannon and Kylie were making the break.

Bailey thought grimly that she considered herself less under Pa's thumb than either of them. She ran her own ranch and didn't do anything that didn't suit her, no matter what Pa said. And yet here she stood in britches, as Pa wanted, living the life he'd set out for her.

Maybe she wasn't so independent, after all.

"All your life you've been fighting for the exact life

you're headed for, Kylie. You know nothing could stop you from going."

Kylie let the tears flow down her pretty face. Her sweet little sister. Light-brown hair shot through with a dozen shades of blond, with bright hazel eyes a lot like Bailey's. But on Kylie it was all so pretty, her cheeks dimpled, her streaked-up hair pulled back in a tidy bun with little curls escaping around her forehead and face. To make the picture perfect she pulled a lace hanky out of the sleeve of her pink calico dress and dabbed at her eyes, a vision of feminine grace.

"I'm going, but I want to take you both with me."

Shannon gave Kylie one more fierce hug. "Can you imagine Tucker taking the train to New York City?"

They all looked at Tucker, as wild a man as ever lived, and broke out laughing.

"Nev and Myra will be over later today." Kylie looked at the white balls of fluff that grazed in a pen next to Gage Coulter's cattle. Gage had built a fence to keep the sheep and cattle separate.

Shannon said to Bailey, "They're going to live here and tend my sheep through the winter."

A furrow of worry creased Shannon's smooth brow. "They'll take good care of them, won't they?"

"Yes, now stop." Kylie gave Shannon yet another hug. She turned her sister just enough that she could make eye contact with Bailey and roll her eyes. "You've done right to let them have the sheep. Myra seems interested in wool, so they'll baby them same as you did."

Bailey suspected that, unlike Shannon, the Bassetts would on occasion eat the sheep, too. No one said that out loud, especially Shannon, but sheep turned into nice lamb chops, and only Shannon was too softhearted to admit that.

Tucker and Aaron came over to where they stood, leading the horses. The men made it clear they were ready to go.

"I'd invite you in for coffee, Bailey, but everything is packed." Shannon's eyes filled with tears again. "And we need to get in as many hours as we can while the sun is up."

The days were short in the Rockies in October, and the cold, buffeting wind threatened more snow. Though Tucker should have headed out weeks ago, he'd stuck around because Shannon hadn't wanted to leave her sisters. Now with winter ready to slam down on them, they wouldn't see each other anyway. Tucker insisted they go.

"We're riding horseback to make the best time," Kylie said. "We're hoping to beat the worst of the weather. Aaron has a route planned for us to take us out of the mountains to the south before we ride east. Once we're out of the Rockies, we hope for much milder weather than this." Kylie nodded toward the sky, pure white, as if it were loaded with snow.

"You'd both best get on, then. I'm glad you were coming to my place to say goodbye, but this will get you on the trail hours earlier." Bailey found the inner toughness that had gotten her through so much and didn't do one thing to slow them down. Neither did she shield herself to the point she couldn't be kind. That would bother them, as well. She gave them each one last hug. Then she smiled at Aaron and said, "Don't let Kylie run everything just her way. She's a tricky one."

Aaron smiled. He looked like he knew just how badly she felt, but he wasn't going to make it worse. He pulled her into his arms and yet made it quick. Bailey didn't like it, and Aaron seemed to understand.

"Nev and Myra have been living in the house I built near Aspen Ridge. But they're moving into Shannon's cabin, so remember you have friends close by."

Friends? With a man who tried to kill Kylie and shot Shannon? With a woman who tried to steal Kylie's land? Not likely.

Nodding, she didn't comment on that pair. She'd be switched if she'd ask them for help.

She backed away from Aaron to look at Tucker. "And you, be careful or Shannon will be making pets out of the grizzlies and trying to move them into your cabin."

Shannon gave Bailey a good-natured slap on the shoulder, and Tucker laughed. "We'll be back in the spring, Bailey."

They would, but what was unspoken was that it would be for a visit only. With the homestead signed away to Coulter, they had no home here anymore, nothing holding them here. Coulter would let them live in the cabin, though, with Myra and Nev taking Aaron's place. Tucker worked for Coulter in the summer, so they'd be around, but never again would Shannon live nearby for any length of time. Her life was taking her away.

"And Sunrise is living in Kylie's old homestead cabin. She'll help you if you can get word to her."

They both knew once winter started dumping snow by the yard, no one could get word to anyone.

Kylie was never one to pass a chance to be affectionate. She hugged Bailey one last time and whispered, "We're expecting a baby. I'll write you all about it." Then Kylie let her go, crying hard.

"I love you, Bailey." Kylie shoved a package wrapped in brown paper into her hands. "I know how much you've done for me. Thank you." Kylie turned to Shannon and hugged her too, but with no package. "Thank you both. I love you, Shannon."

Aaron's arm went around Kylie's waist. "Let's move out." He supported her as they turned to the horses.

Bailey should have moved out too, just mounted up and ridden away, but she couldn't. She stood there and watched the four of them leave, Shannon headed up, Kylie headed down, separating from each other just as surely as her. And a baby, a baby Bailey doubted she'd ever meet. It felt as if her heart was being torn out of her chest as both sisters turned back and waved before they curved around their separate trails and vanished from sight.

She stood alone in the blustery wind, as cold in her heart as she was in her fingertips. Finally, moving like an old woman, she got on her mustang and started for home.

A home without enough grass.

A home with cattle so far from her cabin, it would be a life-and-death struggle to get to them through the winter.

A home so lonely that Bailey, a woman who didn't cry, let the wind cry for her.

She was home before she gave another thought to the present Kylie had tucked into her hands. Setting it aside while she unsaddled her horse, she did her chores, ate a quick noon meal, then rode out in the growing cold to check her cattle.

When she returned, she noticed a pair of riders amongst the cattle in the canyon, neither of them Gage—even from a good distance, she was sure of it. It was only when she saw them that she realized somehow, foolishly, she'd thought he would come.

Despite her rudeness, she thought he'd make it a point to check the cattle himself and then come in to say hello.

The sun was setting. The wind started howling louder, the snow coming down more heavily by the minute.

She watched the riders climb that trail. She should just let them ride through her place. She had a fight on her hands not to run out and yell for them to come on through, cut hours off the ride in the nasty weather and not attempt the treacherous trail Gage had blasted open.

She won the fight to keep her mouth shut as the men skylined themselves in what was left of the setting sun, then dropped over the rim for that rattlesnake of a descent.

The snow kept falling. How long would they take to reach the safer parts of the trail? Their lives might be in danger.

She felt like the worst kind of coyote for not calling out and was determined that tomorrow she'd go out and tell them they could use her property to gain entrance to the canyon. That would make them climb in on that ugly path one more time, but then she'd put a stop to it.

Her quiet prayer followed them while the snow grew heavier and she tried uselessly to guess if they'd made it to safe ground.

9

*T*he snow came and came and came. She never had a chance to make things right with Gage's men, because they never got back into the canyon.

She battled her way to the cattle about once a week, and by the end of November, she risked her life with each trip wallowing in the deep snow.

She'd look over her shoulder the whole time she made the trek, afraid another snowstorm would start up. It seemed to be a worse winter than the one she'd survived the year before. But she couldn't quite decide if it was worse or if she just found it harder to endure, knowing how alone she was in the world, with her sisters long gone.

The stream that flowed along the edge of the grassy woods where she'd left her cows kept flowing, though she wondered what would happen when the really brutal cold settled in. Would the water freeze over and leave all her cattle to die of thirst?

Bailey fretted through the long nights as November stretched toward Thanksgiving. Finally, when the weather had cleared a bit, remembering Gage's offer, Bailey herded her cattle back home and shooed them into the canyon. With the high sheltering walls, the snow didn't get so deep the cattle couldn't find food. And the stream in the canyon was much deeper and faster moving and wouldn't freeze over.

She'd bide her time, and then the first chance she had in the spring, she'd get her cattle moved out and Gage would never have to know she owed him.

Bailey forced herself to make a special dinner for Thanksgiving. And she forced herself to spend time counting her blessings.

She even thought of a few that weren't pure lies.

As Christmas drew near, she had a few longing thoughts of Pa that told her just how lonely she was. She considered risking the long ride to his cabin just to break up the relentless monotony of winter. Surely by now even grumpy old Pa was lonesome.

If the weather looked good, she decided, she'd ride over on Christmas morning. At least she'd set out. If the travel got too difficult, she'd turn back.

Then, midafternoon on Christmas Eve, the snow started up with a vengeance. Riding to Pa's was out of the question. She was worried about making it the fifty paces to the barn.

Weeks ago she'd tied a rope between the house and the barn to help her make it there and back in bad weather. She

bundled up and stepped outside into a wind so bitter cold
it stole her breath. Each step was a fight, but she battled her
way onward. The chores wouldn't do themselves. After
what seemed like hours, she knew the barn had to be just
ahead, yet she couldn't see it in the blinding blizzard. Then
the rope snapped and tore out of her hand.

Leaping for the rope, clawing the air, she stumbled and
fell into a drift. The rope vanished in the white.

All around her was nothingness. She could die out here.
Alone. It hit her hard and deep that if she died, no one
would even know for months. Wolves might find her and
drag her off. Her family wouldn't miss her until spring,
when Shannon came back . . . if Shannon came back. And
would they ever grieve? Yes, Kylie and Shannon would feel
bad that she'd gone missing, but how much could anyone
love you if they got married and rode off with little more
than a hug and a backward glance?

For a moment, lying there so utterly alone, it was all
too much to bear. She was brutally tired of the fight for
this rugged life. But Bailey didn't know how to quit. Her
fighting spirit roared through her harder than the whipping wind.

"I'm close to the barn," Bailey yelled into the teeth of
the storm. She was no more alone right now than she had
been a few minutes ago in the house. Bailey stayed on her
knees where she was less likely to get blown in the wrong
direction.

The wind came from the north, of course, yet it swirled
around until it was hard to be sure from which direction
it hit her the hardest. She pivoted in the snow until she

thought the wind blew hardest against her back. She stared forward, and prayed. She thought she saw a darker patch in this direction.

Inching forward on her hands and knees, she didn't find the barn where it was supposed to be. It couldn't be this far ahead, could it? If she kept crawling, she might crawl straight out into the forest where she'd freeze to death for certain.

That's when she realized she carried her milk pail with her. It was still hooked over her arm. An inspiration that seemed to be whispered in her ear straight from the mouth of God had her grab that pail, face again the direction she thought was right, and throw the bucket forward as hard as she could.

It banged into something solid. The barn was the only solid thing on this side of the house, not counting the canyon walls, but she couldn't have gotten that far off course. She crawled forward eagerly toward the sound, until the wind mixed her up again.

The bucket landed under her hand, and right ahead was a log. She'd found the barn. Grabbing the bucket, she scrambled to her feet, never losing contact with the building. She edged along in the direction of the door and almost fell into open space.

Shuddering with fear, she realized she'd gotten blown farther to one side of the barn than she'd thought. Rather than being centered with the building, somehow she was far to the left. Only a foot or two more and she'd have missed the barn completely and ended up out in the open where she'd never survive the harsh weather.

She moved back down the wall until she found the door, undid the latch with gloved fingers, clumsy with cold. She stumbled into the barn, then turned to shut the door behind her, struggling against the howling wind.

Once inside, although the cold was still so sharp she felt her eyes and nose freezing up, at least the wind was blocked. With her heavy coat and a scarf wound tight around her neck and over her head, high boots and thick gloves, she soon got her shivering under control.

Panting, she tried to figure out what she was going to do. She couldn't stay out here overnight. The temperature had to be below zero. She'd never make it through the night. Her eyes then came to rest on her milk cow. Its wide spread of horns seemed to gleam in the dim light.

She'd milked this cow morning and night for almost six months and never worried overly about it. But now she was worried. What if that animal killed her? Or worse, what if it maimed her and she lay on the barn floor slowly freezing to death? Maybe she'd live long enough to die a slow, painful death of thirst and starvation.

Disgusted, Bailey tossed the bucket down, and the cow lashed a hoof at her. The cow just won, because Bailey wasn't about to milk her. She was close to calving, probably three months away, and Bailey planned to dry her up in about a month's time. Well, the cow wouldn't mind a bit more of a break.

She turned to her chickens. Earlier, she'd moved them from the coop into the barn. The chickens she could handle. She gathered eggs and then sat on the floor to figure out how to get back to the house.

There was rope coiled on a nail. She could tie that to the barn door and lash it around her waist. She might fight for her life for a while, but she should find her way to the house eventually.

If the rope was long enough . . . and it didn't snap.

The soft whicker of her horse drew her attention. The cow was a killer, but she'd kept one of her gentlest horses penned in the barn, with the remaining horses in Gage's canyon along with the cattle.

Her eyes settled on that friendly horse, and Bailey made a decision. She wasn't leaving this barn until the blizzard ended. Her horse was warm enough to keep her alive through the night.

She was spending Christmas Eve sleeping with her horse.

Bailey fed her animals and cleaned out the stalls, leaving a pile of old straw by the barn door to be tossed out later. By the time she was done with that hard work, she was comfortably warm. The night would be a hungry one, but she'd missed a meal before. She hunkered down on a pile of hay. While she sat there pondering the mess she was in, the light waning but the blizzard as strong as ever, her eyes landed on a bit of brown shoved under the railing of her cow's stall and mostly buried in straw. It didn't match the rest of the barn.

Curious, she stood and got down on her hands and knees to reach the item. As her hand touched it, she remembered exactly what it was.

Kylie's present.

Laughing quietly, Bailey realized her little sister had managed to give her a Christmas present. Bailey hoped it was something useful, like a tightly wrapped package of beef jerky, though it was doubtful that would have survived her pecking chickens.

She got comfortable and made a ceremony out of the parcel. First a prayer; then she spent time remembering the first Christmas, also spent in a stable. Strangely, her choice to stay in the barn seemed fitting. The smell of the animals, the musty straw, the occasional cackle of a chicken or rustle from her horse and cow as they crunched on hay. This was how it had been for Mary and Joseph as they awaited Christmas and their baby's birth.

That first Christmas had included gifts of gold, frankincense, and myrrh. Bailey grinned, wondering if Kylie had given her one of those. Not likely.

Finally, when she was calm and in a mood of peace, with her faith clear in her mind, she decided she'd delayed the pleasure of opening the gift long enough. She reached for the string that tied the parcel closed. The knot had tightened and didn't want to give. Bailey could have cut the string with the knife she always carried in her boot, but she enjoyed drawing out the unwrapping.

The sun was setting, and the barn was getting murky by the time she pushed back the brown wrapping and narrowed her eyes at the bright blue fabric. Had Kylie given her a length of cloth for a gift?

Bailey lifted it. It unfolded and took shape. She was a long minute figuring out what in the world it was—and why wouldn't she be confused? It was nothing she'd ever had before, or at least not for so many years it seemed like this was a first.

A shout of laughter broke the silence of the barn as she stood and held the Christmas bounty up by its shoulders. The hem reached the floor.

Kylie had made her a dress. The most useless piece of clothing ever invented, and almost certainly invented by man.

A note dropped to the floor with the unfolding skirt. Bailey grabbed at it. A worthless gift and now a scolding note to tell Bailey she needed to start dressing and acting like a woman. Kylie had given her that little sermon any number of times.

Tossing the dress over her shoulder, she sat again and read:

Dear Bailey,

You might consider trying on this dress. I think you'll be surprised at how fun it is to feel pretty. I know if you're reading this note, I was successful in my escape attempt, so you wouldn't be able to throw the dress right back in my face.

As much as it has been my dream to live in a civilized place, I find my heart is breaking to leave you and Shannon. I am going to miss both of you terribly.

Please wear this dress at least once. Being a woman is a wonderful thing, and I hope and pray for you to learn to enjoy that part of yourself. You're a beautiful woman. Always remember your baby sister loves you.

Kylie

Bailey laughed aloud, then was shocked when her eyes burned with tears. She sat there alone, except for her animals, with this note and these words of love.

For a woman who had just decided her faith was solid and there was pleasure in sharing a barn with the animals to celebrate Christmas, she, a woman who didn't cry, was fighting tears.

The loneliness of it was deep. Her soul seemed to cry out for someone to share her life with. She prayed that God would be with her in this dark, cold place.

She read the note again, then another time. She read it until she had it memorized.

Was she a pretty woman? Kylie was kind and would say such a thing, true or not. One hand went to her hair, and Bailey realized she hadn't cut it since before winter had closed in on her. Her fingers clenched in her hair, and she pulled until she forgot her tears. But the loneliness! Nothing could make that pain go away.

Bailey had chosen a miserable life, but she had no idea how to change it. Her sisters had done it by getting married. The idea made Bailey nearly sick with fear.

The darkness deepened and pressed down on her bowed shoulders. She sat and listened as the wind and snow blew against the barn roof and walls. The storm seemed to grow claws that reached out to dig through the walls and drag her into the cold night. Right now, outside the barn, from every direction, she was under attack from a desperate, raging lunatic.

And she had no choice but to face that raging lunatic alone. Always alone.

10

Only a raging lunatic would consider what Gage had in mind.

He slammed the side of his fist against the front door and waited. Just as he was about to start hammering again, the door swung open.

He blinked, wondering if he'd truly lost his mind. Then he leaned forward—honestly he lurched, as if he'd lost all control of his muscles. He stared until he thought his eyes might pop out of his head.

"Bailey Wilde, is that you?"

It was impossible but for the golden eyes. It was her, like he'd never seen her before.

"Howdy, Gage. It's a little early for you to be over here, isn't it? I can't believe you got through the trails." Her fiery eyes shifted in a way that struck Gage as devious, but then that was his Bailey all over again. A sneaky woman. That's why he thought she'd cooperate.

He'd figure out what she was sneaking about later; he didn't have time now. Plus, she was probably doing something that would make him furious, and yelling at her was a mighty poor idea, all things considered.

"Bailey, I . . . Your hair is long." Not *long* really, but the woman hadn't cut her hair since last fall.

"Almost as long as yours." That was definitely her sassy mouth.

"Why'd you stop cutting it short?"

The corners quirked up on her pink lips, which made Gage aware of just how closely he was watching her.

"I did it for a stupid reason. Shannon always cut it, and when she moved she not only took her barbering skills with her, she also took the only pair of scissors around. I don't own a pair, so it was either hack it off with a knife or leave it alone." She ran a hand deep into the pretty curls that were about three inches long all over her head. "Honestly, I sort of forgot about it. Heaven knows there's not a mirror anywhere around."

It was the prettiest yellow blond he'd ever seen, and it curled around her ears and highlighted those bright flashing eyes. It was also a tousled mess, like maybe Bailey didn't own a hairbrush. Maybe she combed her fingers through it much like she'd done when it was short. That's what Gage did with his.

He looked down the length of her body at the blue calico dress . . . and completely forgot what he'd come over for.

Bailey shrugged her shoulders. "Come in. You're letting all the warm air out."

And then he remembered. He went in so fast he was

embarrassed, but his plan was starting to look like it just might work. Her hair had really worried him.

"You're wearing a dress? I didn't know you even owned one. In fact, I think I remember you boasting that you didn't." He closed the door behind him.

"You want some coffee?" She almost smiled. He'd've never called it a smile on anyone else, but considering how rarely Bailey smiled, he could tell that's what it was supposed to be.

"Coffee sounds fine." He pulled off his gloves, shook the snow off, shoved them in a coat pocket, then shed his coat and hung it on a peg by the front door. He removed his Stetson and snagged it on another peg. Then he followed her to the table and sat down. He'd never once taken his eyes off of her while he did all that. She turned away, her blue skirt twisting and turning around her ankles, the messy blond curls bouncing with every move.

He was still staring when she slid a cup of coffee in front of him.

The look on her face was hard for him to understand. She was staring at him just as hard as he was staring at her.

"Bailey, what I came over for . . ." His voice faded. He wasn't sure he could force himself to say it.

She broke the silence. "Were the trails passable?" Her voice sounded a bit rusty, as if she hadn't used it . . . maybe not all winter. "I suppose they must have been because here you are. But I've ridden out daily since the first of April and found drifts so deep I was turned back every time."

She curled her hands around the tin cup in front of her and savored the coffee's warmth.

Gage wanted to talk about the weather and the trails and how the long winter had lingered up here in the higher elevations while spring had come to his ranch. Truth was, he wanted to talk about anything but what he'd come for.

Which was why he couldn't put it off—it was too cowardly. He shoved one hand into his own untrimmed hair. "There's no right way to say what I need to say." He gave her a long, level look. "Bailey, I need help."

"Is your horse hurt?" She half stood from the table. "I saw him outside." She was no doubt ready to go carry the horse to safety, on her back if need be.

"No, no, my horse is fine. I need help." He raised his eyes to meet hers and watched her sink back into her chair. "Please just let me get it all out before you interrupt."

"Just say it, Gage. You're scaring me."

"That's probably just as well. Fear is called for, I'd say. I know I'm scared to death."

Her eyes grew wide. "Well, what is it?"

"Bailey, I . . ." he began, sliding his hand forward to grasp hers. He also knocked her coffee aside. It skidded, but even with her hand in his, she used the other to snag the cup before it spilled into her lap.

Great idea, douse her with boiling hot coffee! Oh, this was going all wrong. And he'd been rehearsing the whole way over, ever since he'd gotten to town to find a letter that had been sitting there waiting for him since last October. No one had brought any more mail to Aspen Ridge because of the weather, so who could tell how many letters might be out there waiting to jump up and bite him in the backside?

"What is it?" she asked again. Her hand tightened on his.

She'd be tightening that hand on his throat in just a few minutes, so he firmed his grip for his own protection. He also took just a second to grab her coffee cup and move it out of reach. Scalding hot coffee in the face would sting.

"Bailey, I . . ." He'd given this part of the speech before. He couldn't look her in the eye when he said it, so he stared at their clasped hands and forced the words out of his mouth. "I want you to marry me."

She inhaled at just the wrong time and started choking. She got her hands loose and stood, hacking, and tripped over her chair when she backed away.

He jumped up and slapped her on the back. That was heroic, right? Keeping her from choking to death. He tried not to be too rough about it. No sense making her wonder if he was a ham-handed brute. Other than in how he proposed, of course.

Through the coughing she managed one word. "Whaa-t?"

The choking was keeping her from talking but not from hearing. He'd better not miss his chance. "This is a desperate situation, Bailey. I'm in need of a wife, and honestly you're the only single woman I know—not counting the ones who work in the saloon—unless some married man around these parts died over the winter."

That wasn't part of his prepared speech. And her eyes grew wider, the cough easing. She'd start talking any second. He needed to get down to business.

A bright idea came to him. "If you don't want to marry me, you can just move in with me and stay until you've served my purpose."

"Until I've served your *purpose*?" He ducked just in time to miss her swinging fist.

He'd never thought of Bailey as a screamer, but she was mighty good at it. "I mean, of course, the offer to marry is good, but if you just wanted to live with me, we could pretend to be married. That would be good enough for me. I'd even pay you." He smiled. How generous did a man have to be?

Her next punch landed square in his mouth. He staggered back from her surprisingly solid hit and was only kept from falling because he backed into the wall. He sure hoped he healed quick. "I must be saying this wrong."

"No, I think I understand your offer exactly right." Bailey came at him again. He was ready this time. He caught her fist in one hand with the slap of skin on skin. Then he grabbed a second fist. He was ready when she tried to kick him, too.

This was getting them nowhere. He lifted her off her feet and used his weight to turn her around and pin her to the wall. He had her hands and he was too close to kick. "Now you listen here, there's no call to go to beating on me. That's no way to start a marriage."

That brought a solid kick to his shin. "Ouch!" Maybe not too close to kick.

"You expect me to live with you until I've served your purpose?"

Yep, definitely a screamer.

"You offer to pay me as if I'm one of the ladies at the saloon?"

Gage was so offended he could barely answer. "Good grief, where'd you get that idea?"

"I got it from you! You had such a lonely winter, you waded out here to . . ."

Gage wrestled the slippery little woman's two hands into one of his.

". . . through neck-deep snow, at risk of your own life . . ."

He had to get this proposal back on track, and he couldn't do it with her screaming.

". . . to insult me and act like I'm the kind of woman who—"

He clamped his hand over her mouth. She tried to bite him, but he was properly cautious now and held her jaw shut.

"That is *not* what I meant." He sounded shocked, even a little prim and proper, which wasn't a sound he could claim for himself real often. But honestly he *was* shocked. So shocked he regained the icy control that usually got him through tight spots. Although that usually involved slashing horns and wicked hooves, but he'd never been in a tight spot quite like this before.

"What sort of man do you think I am?"

Her golden eyes narrowed from behind his hand. She quit struggling, though the burning eyes told him exactly what kind of man she thought he was, and it wasn't good.

He was suddenly aware of just how close he was to her and jumped back. It wasn't just her eyes that burned.

Her skin was hot. He rubbed his hands on the front of his shirt, hopefully to rid himself of the feel of her. He stood watching her, trying to figure out what to say, how to get what he wanted—what he had to have.

"I didn't mean anything sinful when I spoke of *my purpose*. My purpose is keeping a big old heap of trouble from ruining my life. A wife will save me, and I want that wife to be you. I am willing to marry you and live with you without . . . without . . ." Now he was furious. "Blast it, Bailey, the saloon girls? You really thought that's what this was about? How *lonely* did I get over the winter?" He crossed his arms and nearly growled. "I'm ashamed of you for saying such a thing, Bailey Wilde."

He'd honestly never been so insulted in his life, and he was a man who'd been called a coward so often it had driven him out of the whole entire state of Texas.

And the reason he'd refused to fight was the exact same reason he needed a wife, and he needed her fast. "My offer of marriage doesn't even include the . . . the rights of a husband. At least not until you are fully ready."

She stared at him, her head shaking in such a tiny way that he didn't think she was saying no exactly; it was just that every instinct deep in her soul was saying no. Well, he felt the same, but he had his instincts under control and was acting against them. Except, since he'd seen her with her hair longer and wearing a dress, some of his instincts had thrown in to agree with marrying Bailey. Which no doubt spoke poorly of a man's instincts.

"If we find we suit each other, then that's good. If not, you can walk away, come back here to live on your own.

I never saw myself getting married. It's a man's life out here, and I was content with the idea. So I can be content with a married state that doesn't allow me to take another wife, even if I'm living apart from you."

In truth, he'd been so glad to get away from his mother that he'd washed his hands of the very thought of women entirely.

"I will leave you strictly alone until the day you wish it otherwise."

Bailey opened her mouth, then closed it, then opened it again. She had something to say, but she wasn't getting the words out.

"Just say yes, Bailey. I need help. You've never shown much inclination to marry, either. We'll be a good team. How can this be a bad deal for you?"

"Marriage isn't a *deal*." Bailey suddenly moved. He tensed, thinking she was going to attack again, but instead she sank into her chair. Then her head sank onto arms folded on the table.

Still, she hadn't said no.

Gage dragged a chair around so that he was closer to her, not *close* precisely—his mouth still hurt from being punched—but closer.

"Why?" Slowly she raised her head, and those eyes, pure fire, liked to burn him straight to death. "What happened that made you need a wife so confounded bad?"

He was really dreading this question, because for as much as he'd messed up the proposal, he hadn't begun to get to the hard part yet.

"I need a wife and I need her quick."

"Yes, you've made that clear, Gage, but why?"

Gage ran both hands through his hair and added to his list of things to do. He needed a wife and a haircut.

"I need a wife because . . ." He paused, knowing he sounded as weak as water. Then he shrugged and went on speaking because there was no avoiding it. "Because my mother's coming to visit."

$\mathscr{B}$ailey stared at Gage and saw a man who hated to admit the truth. Hated it, was embarrassed by it, and trapped by it. With his icy control wiped away, she saw all those things so clearly she couldn't help but believe him. He'd have never said it if it wasn't true.

Yet none of that changed a thing.

"Your mother is coming." To her own ears, she sounded like the voice of doom. "That is the reason you want to marry me?"

She really should have hit him harder when she had the chance. He was on guard now. Of course, her hand hurt so maybe she'd given him her best. But she'd never been so happy to see anyone in her life—so how hard could she be expected to punch? She'd been so desperately lonely for so long she'd been more tempted to throw herself into his arms than punch him, until he'd started talking.

"Ma is going to turn up any day in Aspen Ridge, and I mean *any day*. Trails are passable now."

Bailey shook her head. "The snow is still too deep."

"Up here it's deep. I barely made it, that's true, but Aspen Ridge and my place are lower, and it's warm enough the trails are opening. That's how they got the mail through. I just got her letter today, first mail of the spring. And she's coming with plans to"—Gage cleared his throat—"to meet my wife."

"You told her you were married?"

"Yep." Gage braced his elbows on the table and buried his face in both hands. "Last fall, I told her."

"Why would you do such a stupid thing?"

Gage shrugged and slid his hands down and clenched them together on the table, not unlike a man who was begging. "I never dreamed she'd come for a visit. Now I've got to find a wife or she'll think I lied to her."

"You *did* lie to her." Bailey slammed the side of her fist on the table.

"I know. But she never stops begging me to go home. She wants me back there. She's so desperate, she threatens to move up here and put my life in order."

"Threatens? Your ma threatens you?"

"Offers," Gage said too quickly. "She *offers* to come. And if I'm not real careful, she'll stay forever." He paused, studying her. "So I told her my life was in good order, that I had a wife and was happy and settled. Then this letter comes, with her all eager to meet my wife and tell me she is headed up here. And in Texas there's precious little winter, and I suspect she can't quite imagine the winter

114

up in the mountains. When I got her letter today telling me she'd set out, it had been sent weeks ago. She's going to show up here any day and find out I lied—unless I do something fast."

"Like present her with a wife." Something strange happened inside Bailey then, for as unthinkable as being married to anyone was, this proposal hurt her feelings.

"Please, don't look at me like that," Gage said.

"Like what?" Bailey wondered what showed, because she thought of herself as someone who kept her thoughts to herself real well.

"Like this is an insult. I don't mean it to be. It's just . . ." Gage threw his arms wide. "I don't know nuthin' about women, Bailey. I've hardly ever even been around one 'cept Ma, and she'd so easily get upset that she wasn't much good for teaching a man how to behave."

Bailey studied on that for a while. "Is that why you left Texas, not because of your pa and sharing the ranch—I'd heard that somewhere—but because of your ma?"

"There was more than one reason," he replied. His eyes went cold, and she saw the ghosts that haunted him. "But the one that matters most is why I'm here proposing. I need a wife and I need her bad. If you're there, she'll be satisfied. If you're not, she'll be so hurt by my lie. She'll cry. And that I can't bear to watch. Then after she's done crying, she'll decide she needs to run my home. She might never go back to Texas." Gage got a stubborn look on his face.

Bailey could out-stubborn him any day. "I'm not going to even consider your proposal if you won't talk to me

115

about what brought you here." She crossed her arms and squared her shoulders.

Gage sat up straighter. "You mean you're considering it?"

"I might be." She absolutely was not. "Why did you leave Texas?"

The idea of putting herself in the clutches of any man was out of the question. She couldn't bring herself to risk it, not even to cure a loneliness that ate away at her soul. "And what makes you think a wife will be enough to make your awful ma go back to Texas?"

But what about just pretending? She could see now what he meant by that. Could she possibly do it? Now that she knew his purpose wasn't . . . what she'd first assumed. She massaged her sore hand, and confound it, she *was* considering it.

"First off, my ma isn't awful." Gage sounded offended. "She's the sweetest woman who ever lived."

Bailey laughed. "You're willing to marry me to drive her off, and you left Texas because of her, but she's the sweetest woman who ever lived?"

Agitated, Gage shoved himself away from the table, grabbed his full cup, and walked the few steps to the fireplace to get the coffeepot. Bailey was pretty sure he didn't need more coffee; he was just too worked up to sit still.

"The reason I left Texas was because I was burning mad at the Union for dictating to the states, especially a state as fine as Texas. They had no business setting laws in Washington, forcing us to mind them. President Lincoln wasn't elected king. I was crazy to go join the Confederate Army."

"Gage, President Lincoln didn't issue any laws that drove them off. The South was just afraid he would. The South seceded."

"Lincoln should have let them go."

"The South fired the first shot." Bailey watched him take a few desperate sips of his coffee, probably to make room in the cup. Then he fell silent as he poured. He brought the pot over to the table and refilled her cup, which was also mostly full. The man was thinking up excuses not to look at her.

He hung the pot in the fireplace. Rather than come back, he stayed by the fire. He was probably chilled, but he wasn't over there to warm up.

"Let's not refight the war right now, Bailey. You said you wanted to know what brought me to the mountains. I'm trying to tell you."

Bailey decided he had a point and stayed quiet.

"Pa was all for me signing up. He was as stirred up as I was. But Ma . . ." Gage crouched by the fire and jabbed at the burning logs with the poker.

He was quiet for so long, she finally asked, "What about your ma, Gage?"

"She agreed with secession, but she hated war."

"Everyone hates war." Bailey sure did.

"Not like my ma." He turned to look over his shoulder at her, then went back to poking at the fire. "She seems like a sturdy enough woman, but she's got a fragile side, nerves, especially when it came to me and war. Her parents died at the Alamo. She was a half-grown girl, and they sent her and most of the other women and children away, but her ma refused to leave her pa. They both died. She got taken in by some folks, who made her life a misery, and she blamed it all on war. She got hysterical when I said I was going. Every young man around us left to go and fight. I was the only man under forty and over fifteen left in the territory. But Pa was afraid Ma might lose her wits, maybe even take her own life."

Bailey tried to imagine cool, controlled Gage Coulter with a ma so fragile. Of course, Bailey knew precious little about mothers. "So you agreed not to fight."

Gage stood and came back to the table, as if the part he couldn't talk about while facing her was over. "The pressure to go was fierce. A few of my neighbors had sons die. I was branded a coward to the point I didn't leave the ranch, didn't even go to church anymore. It got so bad I was afraid someone might come gunning for me. Finally, Pa admitted I had to get away from Texas. He gave me a herd to push west, and I kept pushing until I got here. Winter was settling in, and I found grass for my cattle and built a small cabin." Gage took a long pull on his coffee. "I've been here ever since."

"And now your ma is coming and you need a wife because . . ."

"Ma cost me everything."

12

*G*age's eyes locked on hers, his gaze as cold as a Rocky Mountain blizzard.

"I shamed myself because of her," he said. "I've been driven from my home, and I can't ever go back because of her. The only good thing that came of it was being on my own, being able to stand on my own two feet without Ma's fussing over everything, always in tears and half mad with worry. And it's only me, too. She's a good ranch wife. A great cook. Her and Pa get along fine in everything else. I can't believe she's coming out here. But I shouldn't be surprised. I was her only child, and she's always doted on me. She's just desperate to"—Gage swallowed hard—"to take care of me. From her letter I can tell she's imagining a harsh life for me up here."

"You did just ride halfway up a mountain on treacherous trails and risk your life. And the winter *is* hard; she's not really imagining anything."

Gage shrugged one shoulder. "I don't mind the cold, but she won't see that. I'm sure she plans to take charge of the house and . . ." Gage glanced at Bailey, then away. "And my wife . . . and me."

Bailey had to fight not to laugh at the usually so cool Gage.

"And if I object she'll start fretting and crying, and I'll end up doing almost anything to get her to stop. I suspect her real plan is to persuade me to go back to Texas, and I'm not going. No one will have forgotten. And besides, I like it here. I like having my own spread torn out of the mountains with the strength of my own back." Gage reached across the small space on the table between them, trapping Bailey's hands in his.

"You've got to save me. I'm a desperate man." He tightened his grip.

Bailey didn't try and pull away as she studied him. She saw more than she wanted to.

It was a nice side of him. He honestly didn't want to hurt his mother by having her find out he'd lied to her. And he was fretting about telling her to get out of his house and go back to Texas. At the same time, it appeared he didn't think he could bear living with her.

He really was a desperate man.

"Maybe we could pretend," she said.

Gage shook his head almost frantically. "I said that on the spur of the moment, but we can't pretend."

"Why not?" That was the only way she could imagine doing this.

"Because that makes us both liars, and I have learned my lesson about lying to my mother!"

Bailey had made it through four years of war keeping her thoughts to herself. She tried not to lie, but she could sure behave in such a way that folks believed something that was completely untrue. She veered her mind away from that, because she didn't want to test it against God's Word.

"I'm sure we could convince her."

"No, you don't know that woman. She'd catch on right away. And besides, you have to stay with me, in my room, and you can't do that if we aren't married. I've only got two bedrooms. If you don't sleep with me, then you sleep with Ma, and she's sure to notice if you're sharing her bed."

"You can wait till she goes to bed, then sneak out to the barn to sleep," Bailey said in an arch tone that seemed to calm him down a bit.

"Nope, we have to be married. But, Bailey, is there someone else? Do you dream of someday finding the right man?"

"No, absolutely not." She said it with too much fire.

"Why not?" He was paying real close attention.

"I'm not going to marry you, so if we can't pretend, then we can't do it." She thought of the long, miserably lonely winter and how his pounding on the door had been like God sending her manna from heaven. The bitter loneliness of the winter had been almost too much for her. It had started the day her sisters rode away, but from the time of that Christmas Eve blizzard when she'd slept in the barn beside her horse, she'd ached from the isolation.

"Please, Bailey. I'll be good to you. We can make a marriage work." He sounded like a man hanging on to the knot at the end of his rope.

She knew how that felt.

Last winter she'd known her sisters were close, even if she couldn't get to them. And she'd needed the quiet, for she had deep healing to do from what she'd seen in the war. Being alone for months, with no possible way anyone—any man—could get to her, had given her a feeling of safety that she'd treasured.

But this year the solitude had almost broken her. And right now she'd agree to almost anything to keep Gage from riding off and leaving her.

"You have nothing to fear from me," he added.

That jerked Bailey out of her weak moment of self-pity. "I'm not afraid of anything, Coulter." She tore her hands free, and almost as if it was part of his promise, Gage let her go.

"That's not true. I've seen it in you a few times, mostly when my men are around." His eyes narrowed. "What are you afraid of? I promise I'll protect you from whatever it is."

"I can protect myself!" She clamped her mouth shut. She'd just as good as admitted she was saying no out of fear.

He watched her intently. She'd never had attention paid to her like this before, never thought she wanted it. But something swelled inside, right in her chest, to have a man focus on her so completely. It was as if he could see every tiny ripple of feeling, as if he was trying his best to read her thoughts.

"Tell me, is it something to do with the war? Were you . . . hurt? Did some man see through your disguise and harm you?"

"No!" The shout was another mistake. He was poking at her and opening up wounds.

"Tell me, Bailey. I swear to you I'll listen. And whatever you're scared of, I'll see to it you never have to face it, at least not alone."

That he'd speak of her fears and of being alone in the same sentence—it was like he saw exactly what was roiling inside of her. It drew her to him so hard that she could barely stop herself from standing from the table, wrapping her arms around him and holding on.

With a wry smile, he said, "My most fearful trait is my temper, and that doesn't seem to bother you overly."

Could she do it? The temptation was almost overwhelming to let it all pour out—what she'd seen, the horror of men it had given her, especially a crowd of them. She'd never talked of it. Shannon and Kylie had known there was something, but they'd never pushed her to share it. They'd let her be the mannish rough-talking sister, though she knew they'd listen if she wanted to talk. Even so, they had their own burdens, and she'd die before she added to them.

No words came out. In fact, the very idea of saying out loud the worst of what she'd seen was unimaginable. And that she was even considering it scared her to the bottoms of her booted feet. If she could only have some kind of promise that if things didn't work out . . .

And then it hit her, harder than that punch she'd thrown at Gage. "I'll marry you, but I have some conditions."

Gage recoiled as if her words almost knocked him over. His eyes darkened and sparked with gray fire. A smile broke out like sunshine after a long, dreary winter. Leaning forward, he grabbed both her upper arms.

"Really? You'll marry me?" He dragged her to her feet to face him, sounding like the happiest man alive, almost like a man might sound who'd talked the woman he loved into marrying him, rather than a man arranging his own marriage because he'd trapped himself with a lie.

The big idiot.

She slapped both hands flat on his chest. "I said I had some conditions, Gage, and I'm not one bit sure you'll agree to them."

"Name it." He held her solid in front of him, a firm grasp on each of her arms. He was so happy, she almost hesitated to say what her conditions were.

"If I don't like being married, you let me leave."

His grip loosened. "What?" He sounded a lot like she had when she'd first heard his proposal. "Marriage is forever, Bailey. You can't just leave."

"Of course I can. But that's not my only condition."

His brows arched almost to his hairline. "There's more?"

Nodding, she gave him a few seconds to get used to the idea she might leave. Because leaving was the only way she could even consider this. The idea of signing on to sharing a home with him, with any man, forever, was impossible.

"I'll agree to marry you if, before we get married, figuring you'll buy my homestead when I give up the claim—"

"I intend to do just that."

"First, once you own it, you have to sign *my* homestead over to me."

"Now, Bailey, I don't think—"

"Along with," she said, cutting him off, "the title to this canyon."

Gage's eyes turned to pure ice. "You want my canyon in your name?"

"Yes." Bailey knew he'd never agree.

"No." His smile shrunk away.

"And I want the title in my hand before I speak a single word before a parson." Now for sure he'd leave, and without forcing her to tell of all the things she feared, the things she'd seen. And if Gage leaving in a fury made her heart lurch with regret, well, so be it.

"That canyon belongs to me," he said.

"Indeed it does, and you don't need my land to get in and out. I know. But you can run your ranch without that canyon. You may need to cull your herd a bit, although you'll still be the biggest rancher around. But I need that land, Gage. If I can't have it, I might as well give up and leave the territory right now, because after a winter of trying, I know I can't make a living or run a ranch the way I want to on the land I have left. For the security of owning that canyon if I find myself unhappily married to you—*that* is the kind of thing that would make me take a chance on marriage."

"You fully intend to marry me." His frigid eyes stabbed her with icicles. "And at the first sign of trouble, light out with the canyon signed over to you."

That quieted her, because she did have something about exactly like that in mind. And that wasn't the deal he was after. Finally she said, "I promise I'll stay until your ma heads for home. After that, it'll depend on how we're getting along."

She expected to head down the trail for home before Mrs. Coulter's dust settled.

"I don't want you to plan on leaving." His eyes warmed up, his voice coaxing as his hands slid up and down on her arms. "I think we'll suit, Bailey. We'll make a good team. You'd be a great rancher's wife."

"No, I'd be a great *rancher*. Truth is, I'm already a great rancher."

That seemed to stop him from talking for a while. At last he said, "I'll treat you right."

"Which means there should be no problem, and you'll hang on to that canyon. So why not agree to sign it over to me?" Bailey knew she would be leaving Gage just as soon as was humanly possible. Only having his mother around—no matter what kind of odd character she was—made the idea of living with him bearable.

"Bailey, no."

"You told me you were a desperate man." She wrenched free from him and stepped back. "But when it comes down to it, you're not willing to give up a single thing, are you?"

"A single thing?" His voice rose in anger. "That canyon is five thousand acres!"

"You probably control forty thousand."

"None of it as prime as that canyon. Isn't it enough I give you my name and my own ranch to live on, and my protection? And if you leave me, we'll still be married, but we'd both be alone with no chance to marry anyone else."

"It's a big risk for you. Yet no matter how desperate you say you are, you don't want to take it."

Gage opened his mouth to respond, and she braced herself for him to yell a few choice words before storming out of the cabin.

Well, she didn't feel like getting hollered at. "Just go, Gage. I hope you and your ma have a happy life together."

Silence stretched between them. It was so profound, she thought she heard her heart beating. A roaring filled her ears.

"It's a deal." He spoke as if his mouth were full of gravel.

"Really?" Her heart beat even faster.

"Really, Bailey." He wasn't happy about it, so he must indeed be desperate.

Bailey went to a shelf and pulled out a piece of paper, an inkwell, and a pen. "I want it in writing. Signed and witnessed."

Gage looked between her and the paper. His jaw tensed, and for a moment Bailey thought he'd balk.

Finally he said, "I agree to put it in writing, but we can't show it to anyone. I don't want word getting out about our deal."

Now it was her turn to get tense. She didn't particularly want anyone to know about their deal, either. "If one other person knows, the whole world knows."

"And the paper's worthless, anyway. It's only as good as my word, because under the law I will own everything."

Nodding, frustrated, Bailey said, "I do think your word is good, lying to your mother aside. Fine." She wrote fast.

Gage read every word, then glared at her for too long

before signing it with a heavy, slashing hand. "Now, let's get ourselves to town and get married."

She'd own that canyon again. Then she remembered saying only minutes ago that marriage wasn't a *deal*. And now here she was bargaining over it. It was shameful.

Before her conscience could goad her into telling him to forget the whole crazy idea, she said, "Get on out so I can change into britches." Bailey had taken to wearing her dress inside, but she still wore her manly clothes to do chores.

"No!" Gage gasped. "You can't wear britches in front of my mother!"

She decided then and there she'd get along fine with Ma Coulter, who no doubt had realized long ago that her son was a half-wit. She most likely worried herself sick about him for perfectly good reasons. Bailey was going to team up with her and worry about him too, and maybe the two of them could torment Gage into leaving off idiocy at least part-time.

"Go on with you, Gage. I need to change."

"Just pack up what has to be taken. Riding out of here is going to be hard work for our horses. The snow is shoulder-deep in places, and the only trail through it is the one I broke. I don't want to be loaded down. Besides, my cabin has most of what you'll need. I'll go deal with the livestock. Your lunatic milk cow will be happy to go into the canyon with the rest of the herd."

"She's already out with them. I gave up milking her."

"Glad to hear it. I'll put out enough grain that your chickens can live for a month. By the time the food runs out, we'll be back checking the herd regularly and we can bring them over to my ranch. Maybe they'll hatch chicks in that time. I'll get your horse saddled for you. Are my cows dropping their calves?"

"Yep, most of them are done birthing their babies. You've got a nice spring crop."

"How about your cattle? Did your herd do well wintering over in that pasture we fenced? Do we need to bring them over here?"

Bailey realized then the first thought she'd had when he came in, at least after the pleasure of seeing him had calmed a bit. Her cows were still in his canyon. She'd intended to sort them out before anyone showed up here this spring.

"Well, uh . . ." She didn't know what to say. Gage was sure to check his herd, any responsible rancher would, and he'd never overlook fifty extra cattle with the Double W brand. Whatever her differences with Gage, she knew he was a good rancher.

With a weak jerk of one shoulder, she said, "My cattle are already in the canyon."

That startled a smile out of him, followed by laughter. "You moved them in there the minute my back was turned, didn't you?" He laughed louder.

"I waited awhile." About a month. "And you offered to let me." An offer she'd slapped back in his face.

Gage walked up to her, real close, and placed a hand against her cheek. His fingertips were rough, the palm of his hand callused. She respected hard work, and his hands were proof he did his share.

He tilted her face up and leaned down. "Bailey, we've got more to clear up. I told you about my ma, but you've yet to tell me why the thought of meeting my men scared you last fall."

She'd hoped he had forgotten that.

His hand, so gentle, seemed to hold her in place without any effort. His forehead furrowed as if he genuinely cared.

"I'm not afraid of anything, least of all a man."

Gage ignored her bluster. "I hate thinking what must have happened to make such a brave woman afraid." He arched one brow, and his worried expression eased. "But have you noticed that no matter how bad we squabble, you never seem to be afraid of me?"

She hadn't noticed, but it was true. She'd never imagined letting a man so close to her, and yet Gage had been this close several times. He'd made her feel a lot of things. Most of them weren't good, but none of them was fear.

"I wonder why that is?" Gage sounded curious.

A loud thud shook them apart. Gage's hand flew to his pistol. He rushed to the door and threw it open.

Bailey snagged her rifle from over the door and stepped beside him.

There was nothing.

His stallion stood there patiently.

"What was that?" Gage studied the quiet, snow-covered terrain.

Bailey poked her head around the door, frowning. Then she pointed at a huge icicle that'd been hanging from the eaves. "That icicle fell, I suppose."

"It didn't sound like an icicle hitting the ground. It sounded more like someone slammed the icicle into the side of your cabin." They exchanged a look of concern.

The ground was too churned up to show tracks. There was nothing else out there.

Standing close by in the doorway, Gage turned to her. "We'll be married today, Bailey. Only hours from now." He looked at her long and hard, then almost ran out the front door as if he wanted to get away from her. A cold blast of air wasn't enough to shake her out of the strange confusion she felt.

She had a time of it, gathering her wits. Finally, knowing Gage didn't have that much to do, she closed the door and forced herself to get moving.

Looking around the cabin, she remembered Kylie trying to put up curtains. Bailey had refused. Her windows weren't nice ones with glass like Kylie had. They were slits built to slide a rifle through to ward off intruders, with tight wooden shutters built to stop a bullet.

And Shannon had put real skill into the table and chairs, but those couldn't be hauled through snowdrifts on horseback. Maybe when the snow was all melted, she'd come back for them.

What did she have here she even wanted? A few pots and pans. Bedding. Surely Gage had his own. Her manly clothes, which she'd gotten tired of wearing once she'd spent some time in the pretty dress Kylie gave her.

She had long woolen underwear on beneath her dress, and that's what she wore to sleep. Some days she even wore the dress to do chores. Of course, her only real chores required a short walk to the barn to feed the chickens and gather eggs. She'd turned her horse into the corral by the barn so that no stalls needed cleaning.

Gage had told her she couldn't wear her britches, and the truth was she didn't want to—especially not in front of his mother. Maybe he'd see leaving them behind as an act of obedience from his wife.

Possibly when things came along she didn't want to agree with him on, he'd remember the abandoned britches and decide to give her a turn at having her way.

She didn't even collect the food from the cupboards. It would keep just fine in the cold cabin.

Her fire . . . she hesitated because it seemed so final, but she forced herself to take the mostly empty pot of coffee and pour it on the smoldering kindling. Thanks to Gage's poking at it earlier, breaking up the bigger pieces of wood, it had burned low. The coffee went a long way to putting it out. The last of it would burn out harmlessly.

Grabbing a canteen, she filled it with water. There was half a loaf of bread left from breakfast. She wrapped the bread in a towel and stuck it, along with the jerky left over from a deer she'd brought down, into her saddlebags. She reached for her holster. She always wore it when she ventured outside, over her dress. Gage wouldn't like it.

Fuming, she stuffed the pistol into a saddlebag, added the bullets, then grabbed her rifle. She'd put that in the boot of her saddle. Surely that wouldn't offend Gage's desire to have a ladylike wife.

That was the end of her packing. It was time to go.

Leave her homestead.

Take vows before God to love, honor, and obey a husband.

She suspected she was incapable of doing any of that, so

132

she tried to gather her courage, strengthen her spine to go and tell Gage to head down the trail without her. But the thought of letting him go, and staying here by herself . . . a scream built inside her.

The winter had been unbearable. Literally unbearable. And because she could not bear it, not for one more day, she turned to her coat.

It was as if she watched from a distance as a woman, nearly addled from loneliness, pulled on her heavy buffalo robe and wrapped a scarf around and around her head and neck.

It was sad that there wasn't a single thing in her cabin special enough to take along with her—not a keepsake, not a pretty doily crocheted for a hope chest. Bailey had none of those things, and what's more, she'd taken pride in never wanting them. But now it struck her as sad.

She peered out one of the narrow windows and saw Gage leading her saddled horse toward the cabin. It wasn't a bitterly cold day, as spring had definitely come, but there was still deep snow everywhere.

And although Gage had broken a trail to get here, the trek down to Aspen Ridge was sure to be an exhausting one.

13

"I can't believe you rode out here through this snow," Bailey shouted from behind.

Gage glanced back. They were on foot, descending from higher elevations, his horse belly-deep in snow. Gage, who was leading the poor, tired stallion, was waist-deep. As for Bailey, she was just plain floundering. But she kept moving forward, so Gage did too. He was determined not to help her unless she absolutely needed it.

And this was on a trail he'd already broken coming up here.

"I told you I was desperate," he shouted back, then turned and plowed on. If the snow had been hard, they might've been able to walk right over the top of it. Yet it was more like powder.

"This drift is only a little bit longer." About a hundred more yards, which seemed like ten miles to him. He was trying to keep her spirits up. "Then it's clear the rest of the way to town." Gage would plow through, tie his horse, then go back and haul Bailey out if he had to.

"I know exactly where we are." Her voice sounded like she was talking through gritted teeth. She'd always had a deep voice for a woman. And heaven knew she could turn a phrase in a cranky way. But this was so grouchy he was afraid that Bailey was coming to her senses, and by the time they got to town, she'd have changed her mind about marrying him and would turn around and flounder her way back home. And he'd have to go with her, blast it all, and talk her back into it again.

The snow was thinning out on the lower part of the mountain where the little town of Aspen Ridge sat. His ma could show up anytime now.

Aspen Ridge was tucked in along the Oregon Trail. The town had grown up to serve as a location for a land office for homesteaders. It was nothing but a small collection of houses, still raw from being built over the heads and under the feet of the settlers as they opened one business or another. In the year since the war ended, Aspen Ridge had sprung up from nothing. The town survived mainly because there was nothing else for miles.

Bailey didn't speak again, and Gage didn't try to cheer her up. He quit goading her into continuing on. Both took too much energy.

At last the snow was knee-deep on him. He was through the worst of the drift. He reached a spot in the trail swept clear of snow by crosswinds. Nearly staggering as he stopped, he led his horse to the side, thinking to tie the stallion to a scrub pine and go back for Bailey. Before he could knot the reins, he looked back and saw she was almost through it.

He didn't want to talk to her because he figured the more tired she was and the farther they got from her land, the less likely she was to turn around and go home. So he mounted up and headed on down.

A second glance told him she was riding after him. He was still stunned that she'd agreed to marry him, but didn't question his good luck. Instead he picked up his pace. Even his big chestnut must know the worst was over, because he stepped out eagerly.

About the time they reached the edge of town, the trail was wide enough they could ride two abreast.

Bailey caught up to him. "There's a parson in town?"

"I saw him this morning," Gage said. "First day my men and I have been to town all winter. Parson Ruskins is here. His ministry is to folks on the mountain, up where Tucker lives. He didn't mean to spend the winter in town, but he got snowed in. He's the same man who married Kylie and Shannon."

Bailey gave Gage a rueful smile. "A family tradition."

***

"Yep, you three girls sure are sentimental about such things." Gage grinned back, teasing. He probably knew, just as Bailey did, that the Wilde women were about the least sentimental family in the whole country.

"Parson Ruskins marrying all of us, and each under strange circumstances." Kylie had married Aaron because she was afraid of snakes. There'd been more to it than that, but the snakes had prompted Aaron's proposal and Kylie's acceptance.

Shannon had married Tucker because they'd been trapped in a cave and spent several nights alone together.

Now Bailey was marrying Gage because . . . she wasn't one bit sure why. For the canyon? To save him from his mama? To spare herself terrible loneliness?

Despite the strange starts to Kylie's and Shannon's marriages, they looked like happy ones. Bailey held out no such hope for herself.

"I reckon this counts as strange, all right. But I appreciate it, Bailey. Let's go. See there, he built his own church." Gage pointed to a tiny building that looked as raw as the rest of the town. Above the front door, two short pieces of sapling had been fashioned into a cross. Beyond that, nothing set the building apart as a church.

"Ruskins has been sleeping in the church and it's only one room, so I reckon he'll be there. If not, in a town this size, we'll find him quick."

Did the man stand next to his bed to hold Sunday services? That seemed improper, Bailey thought. She hadn't been to town much. She'd been content with her manly disguise, but she knew that avoiding people to the extent she'd done was an admission that her disguise wasn't good enough.

Gage led the way to the livery. He swung down and turned as if he'd help Bailey down, but she was already dismounting. She didn't need a man to help her on and off her horse.

Gage turned back. "Sandy, you here?"

"Howdy, Gage." An old codger limped out. His knees must hurt him, but he had the powerful arms and chest of any blacksmith.

"Can you feed our horses and rub 'em down? They've had a hard time of it, and I need to head on for the ranch right away."

"Sure enough." Sandy gave Bailey a curious look.

Gage said, "We're getting hitched, Sandy. This is Bailey Wilde. Sister to the women who married Aaron Masterson and Matt Tucker."

"I heard they had a brother."

"You heard wrong. We won't be long." Gage took Bailey's hand, and they headed for the general store where they bought supplies, including the only bolt of fabric in the place—a dull blue wool, probably meant for men's shirts.

"Elijah, can you run this over to the livery and pack it on my stallion?"

"I'll see it's done right away, Gage." The man running the store began wrapping up the fabric and the other things they'd purchased.

Bailey wasn't all that sure she even knew how to make a dress. She could probably figure it out, though.

That errand done, they walked to the land office, where Bailey rescinded her claim with the new land agent, Bo Langley. He'd been given the job, along with sheriff of Aspen Ridge. Gage bought the land, then glared at her a second.

She crossed her arms. "I can stand here waiting just as long as you can."

With a scowl, Gage brought out the title for the homestead land and the canyon.

139

"Bo, I need a witness for this."

The land agent studied the paper. "A man can't give title of his property to his wife. All holdings go in the man's name."

"That's only true if I want to fight over it in front of a judge. Just sign it, Bo."

Bailey thought that sounded like she was on mighty shaky ground.

Bo glanced between the two of them. "This is highly irregular."

"A witness is someone who admits he saw something happen. That makes you a witness, even if you think you're witnessing nonsense. Now sign it." Gage thrust the paper at the land agent and part-time sheriff, who shrugged and duly signed his name.

Gage retrieved the paper and handed it to Bailey. "Let's get married."

He took her hand, and together they strode to the church. He reached for the doorknob, then hesitated. "I don't like barging into a man's home, even if it is a church.

He knocked instead, and the door swung open.

"Howdy, Parson Ruskins."

The man was in his shirtsleeves, wearing buckskin pants like Tucker favored. He was a preacher to the fur trappers and the Shoshone. Staying in Aspen Ridge was probably as trying for him as it was for any mountain man.

"I'm Gage Coulter. I met you at Aaron Masterson's wedding to Kylie Wilde." Gage's introduction didn't bode well for his own church attendance. Of course, he probably couldn't get to town all winter, and Ruskins was gone more than here most of the time.

"I remember you." Parson Ruskins extended a hand, and the men shook. The parson turned his eyes to Bailey.

"We're here to be married, Parson," Gage said.

Bailey did her best not to appear as if she'd been bribed into marrying Gage.

"Fine, come on in." The parson looked past them. "Nev, fetch Myra. I need someone as witness to a wedding."

"Nev tried to kill my sister . . . now he's attending my wedding?" Bailey gritted her teeth.

"Kylie forgave him," Gage reminded her. "And he helped save Shannon's life when Hiram Stewbold was after her."

Bailey appreciated Nev's help with Stewbold, but she wasn't so quick to forgive him for nearly killing Kylie.

Patting Bailey on the shoulder, Gage added, "Nev's calmed down considerable."

"I know that," she snapped. There were some things about the Wild West that Bailey really didn't like. A man saying he was sorry and getting out of jail on that alone was one of them.

And here came Nev and Myra, hand in hand. "And Myra and her brothers tried to steal Kylie's homestead."

"She's sorry, too." Gage rested a hand solidly on Bailey's back and guided her, just short of a shove, into the church.

Nev and Myra stepped inside, as well.

Nev gave Bailey a friendly smile. "Howdy, miss. Welcome to Aspen Ridge." He pulled off his hat and narrowed his gaze. "You look familiar."

Bailey scowled at Gage, who said, "You've met Bailey before. She's the oldest of the Wilde sisters."

The color drained from Nev's face, and the smile shrunk away. "Hi, Bailey. I remember you."

"I'll just bet you do." After his attack, Bailey had kept such a close eye on him that they might as well have been lassoed together. He'd probably even figured out she was a woman, though he'd never seen her wearing a dress, and with a head full of curls.

"Nice dress." Nev looked confused, and Bailey would have liked to slug him.

Myra clutched Nev's hand with both of hers and watched Bailey as if she might attack her. Which was an idea with merit.

14

"Now then, let's get on with it." The parson picked up his Bible. "You two come and stand in front of me."

Bailey was having a hard time doing anything, while Gage seemed willing to do all the thinking for both of them. So when he firmly took her arm and hauled her to stand squarely in front of the preacher, she went along because she didn't have a better idea of where to go or what to do.

"Dearly beloved . . ."

The words distracted her, for there was no one in the church that was dearly beloved to her. Then she thought the parson might be talking about things from God's point of view, so fine, they were all dearly beloved to Him. Good thing this wasn't about her.

"To have and to hold from this day forward . . ."

Honestly, she was sure Gage had said there'd be no holding. Maybe Bailey should speak up and ask for a different set of vows.

". . . for as long as ye both shall live."

Bailey backed up a step from that, since she had no doubt a marriage lasted for as long as she lived, but that seemed like longer than it had before, now that they were standing in front of a parson . . . and before God. Gage caught her and pulled her back to his side. He didn't even look at her, and he did it smoothly as if he'd been expecting an escape attempt.

"Gage Coulter, do you take this woman . . ."

Bailey heard Gage swallow hard before he forced out, "I do."

Well, at least he wasn't all that excited about this foolish idea of his. She'd have worried about him if he was.

"And Bailey Wilde," the parson said, and that got her full attention, his speaking her name aloud.

It was like a light flaring bright, blinding her as she realized what she was about to do. These were vows to God. Vows she was taking with full understanding of what they meant. "Until death do us part" did not mean *Until your mother falls for our act and goes back to Texas, and by the way, thanks for the five thousand acres of grassland.*

She couldn't do it. She just couldn't take such a vow in full knowledge that she didn't mean it. *"Let your yes mean yes and your no mean no."* That verse applied to her right here, right now.

It was barely noticeable that Gage rested his palm on her back and slid his hand up and up and up. She opened her mouth to put a stop to the whole thing just as Gage's hand gripped the back of her neck. And tightened and tightened and tightened.

She gasped, "I do."

Gage's grip relaxed.

Even though she wanted to punch him, she had to admit the man knew her pretty well. Maybe he was the sensitive type.

The parson said, "And now a reading from the thirteenth chapter of First Corinthians, beginning with verse four." With great emotion he read, "'Love is patient, love is—'"

"No time, Parson." Impatient, Gage cut him off.

Did he not want to hear the verse because he didn't like this whole pack of lies, or was he just in a hurry to get home?

"We got a long ride ahead of us." Gage caught her hand and towed her out of the church without another word.

That left out sensitive, she reckoned. But the parson's advice on the married state was probably a waste of time, anyway. Almost for sure, the Lord disapproved of what had just taken place. Bailey started praying, aware she was far too late with it.

As they rushed down the wooden steps to the dirt street, the parson said sarcastically, "I now pronounce you man and wife."

Bailey looked back to see the parson had tagged after them and now stood, disgruntled, in the church doorway. He must've wanted to give a good long sermon. He glared at them and added, "You may kiss the bride."

"Maybe later, Parson. We'll be riding in full dark before we get home as it is."

Nope, definitely not the sensitive type.

Gage hustled her toward the livery, where the sound of banging iron rang out.

Again she glanced back at the church. Myra and Nev stood right beside Parson Ruskins. They both waved rather weakly, as if glad to see Bailey go.

Well, the feeling was mutual. "I suppose those two make decent witnesses. Not much chance they'll ever forget they saw me get married."

"Pretty short service. Why would that be memorable?"

"Because they came face-to-face with me and lived to tell of it."

Gage snorted. "In that case, we were mighty lucky to get them."

Sandy paused in his work as they came in. He nodded toward where Gage's horses stood saddled. "They ate some oats and hay, had a good drink and a rest. They're ready to go."

Gage flipped a coin to the hostler. "Thanks, Sandy."

"Elijah from the general store brought your supplies over. But your horse wouldn't let him do any packing." Sandy nodded toward a small stack off to the side of the horses, slipped the money into his pocket, and went back to the forge.

Bailey knelt beside the supplies to split the pile into two smaller packs to tie behind the saddles.

Gage crouched near her. "Are you okay?"

Turning, she arched a brow at him. "What if I wasn't? What would you do about it?"

"We could eat a warm meal."

That she hadn't thought of, and it was a decent idea because she hadn't eaten since breakfast. "I don't like eating in the diner."

"It's closed after the noon meal anyway. Has been all winter. Summertime, Mrs. Langley opens up for supper. But we could find something somewhere else."

"I've got jerky in my saddlebag." She was slipping Elijah's supplies into her saddlebag, so she dug around until she found the strips of meat and handed Gage a few of them.

"Thanks." He stuffed them in his coat pocket. "But it was a long, hard ride. If you're too tired to go farther, I could find a place for you to stay in town. You could rest up, and I'd come back for you tomorrow or the next day, whenever I could get away."

"If you can make it, I can make it, Coulter."

"Try and get used to calling me Gage before my ma gets here."

She looked at him and grinned. "I'll work on it."

"You need to learn your way around the cabin and maybe sew up another dress or two real quick. I want my ma to think we're well settled." Gage glanced around the livery. Sandy was banging away, not paying them a bit of attention. "I don't want her to get any notion that we're newlyweds. She'll know I lied. And I surely don't want her to know I married you because of her."

"I doubt she'd believe a man could be that stupid."

Gage's eyes narrowed, but he didn't respond.

"Let's go. I don't want to stay in Aspen Ridge. Never had much use for a town, especially one full of men."

"You've never told me why you don't like crowds of men."

"You mean there are people who do like crowds of

men?" She took what wouldn't fit in her saddlebags, bundled it with the pretty fabric wrapped around it, and hoisted the pack onto her mustang's back.

Gage chuckled. "Still not talkin', eh?" Well, that was better than his insisting she talk.

"Let's head on out to your place." She tied on the pack while Gage readied his horse.

"Our place," Gage said, falling in beside her.

His words drew her attention in time to see a wince of pain, as if he was remembering all he'd given up by marrying her. He'd lose his canyon if she left, and his privacy if she stayed, and his chance to marry for love should some woman come along that captured his heart.

"Fine. Our place." Bailey just wanted him to quit looking at her and ride.

They led the horses out of the livery just as a stagecoach came rattling into town from the south. At this lower altitude, spring was more in evidence, but Bailey was still surprised a stage had made it through. Yet a supply wagon had made it here with the mail, so why not a stagecoach?

They kept walking as they watched the coach slow and stop right in front of them. The livery supplied fodder for the horses, so it was the usual stopping place in town.

The door swung open, and a woman poked her head out. Gage stopped so suddenly his stallion plowed into him and knocked him forward.

"You're here!" the woman cried out in a piercing voice that caused every horse within earshot to prance.

The coach horses reared, fighting the brake. The driver had locked the brake by tying off the reins on the brake lever. He fumbled to tear the leathers loose before the horses broke their harnesses. The coach lurched.

Leaning out the coach's open door, the stout middle-aged woman screamed. Gage's horse started dragging him backward. Why didn't he let go of the reins? Bailey dropped hers when her horse skittered.

The woman toppled. Bailey dove for the coach.

Though she was about half the size of the plump passenger, Bailey, who wrestled thousand-pound steers for a living, caught the woman. Bailey then staggered and went down under billowing gray silk skirts. The lady landed hard on top of her, shrieking even louder.

Batting the skirts away from her face, she looked up at the woman sitting on her chest. A big woman, tall and round, with eyes of a color Bailey had only seen once before in her life. The color of icy gray clouds.

The woman on her chest was lifted away. Bailey scrambled to her feet to see Gage had her in his arms.

"You're alive!" His ma shouted loud enough, both the riding horses trotted away. Sandy rushed out of the livery. He must've heard her shrieks over his banging.

The land office door flew open, and Bo charged out with his gun drawn.

Nev and Myra stepped out of the general store, Elijah peeking out from behind them. Parson Ruskins stuck his head outside to see what all the racket was about, most likely prepared to pray over the dead.

Bailey and Gage noticed all the attention, but the woman clinging to Gage was too busy. She'd buried her face in Gage's neck and sobbed.

The coach driver climbed on top of the stage and started hurling trunks and bundles to the ground. No one else stepped out of the stage. Bailey stared at the mountain of packages. Were they all Ma Coulter's? The driver met Bailey's gaze and nodded, pointing from the parcels to the crying woman.

Bailey compared it to what she'd packed to move from her home to Gage's place. She wondered how many other stark differences there'd be between her and her new mother-in-law.

Settling into Gage's house wasn't going to happen now. Getting to know each other privately was definitely out. Forget a few weeks to adjust. So how were they supposed to act now? From the way Ma Coulter was near to strangling her son, they weren't going to be allowed to step away so they could cook up a plan.

"My baby boy!"

Gage flinched.

The woman clung to Gage like a burr, her sobs wrenching her whole body.

Slowly, he lifted his shocked gaze from the woman in his arms to meet Bailey's eyes. The dull red that crept up Gage's neck to his cheeks was riveting. And behind the embarrassment, Bailey saw those ghosts in his cold gray eyes.

*I*t looks like you're planning a long stay, Ma." Gage couldn't believe the stack of trunks and bundles piling up on the ground. The stage driver was throwing them off with undue roughness.

Gage wondered how difficult Ma had made the journey for the poor man. Considering the way the man cast the load to the ground as if he were on a sinking ship and needed to lighten the load to survive . . . Gage figured it had been a long trip.

Ma affected most people like that, Gage included. After all, he'd moved to the ends of the earth to escape a woman who loved him until he could barely breathe. With a sigh, Gage admitted it wasn't far enough, and he mentally kicked himself for letting the ocean limit his thinking. He wondered if she'd have followed him all the way to China. Did they have ranches in China?

"Ma, I didn't bring a wagon to town. I've got no way to haul all these trunks home."

Bailey flinched. He wasn't sure why, and looking over Ma's shoulder, he tried to ask what her trouble was.

Bailey rolled her eyes heavenward, gave the mountain of packages a disparaging look, then came up and rested a hand on Ma's back. "Mrs. Coulter, welcome to Aspen Ridge." She sounded so cheerful and friendly, Gage was tempted to call the marriage off. It might not be too late. They could march into the church and tell Parson Ruskins to undo the whole thing. The parson's feelings had been pinched when Gage wouldn't listen to his sermon, so he might be inclined to save Bailey from Gage. And Myra and Nev were present still. Bailey could probably scare them into denying they'd witnessed anything.

Ma's sobs turned to wailing, and Gage remembered exactly why he'd gotten married. He was in desperate need of a wife.

"Gage is so happy to see you after so long a time," Bailey said to Ma.

It was his turn to flinch. He probably should have said hello before he started complaining. He patted the weeping woman on the back.

"How long's it been since you've seen your baby boy? Five years?" Bailey went on in her perky tone.

Gage lifted his hand off Ma's back and reached for Bailey's throat. She backed up a step and smirked at him.

He pointed at her in a way that would have been threatening if he hadn't had his hands so full. He scowled, then went back to holding his mother.

"Howdy, Ma. It's nice to see you." When he said it he realized it was true, mostly. He loved his fussy, nervous mother, and it *was* nice to see her. He tightened his hold into a genuine hug.

He held on for a few long minutes and let himself get good and soaked with salt water, then finally relaxed his hold. "Let loose, Ma. I want to look at you. Leave off your crying now."

He thought it sounded kind, lighthearted. Of course, Ma was crying so hard he could've probably told her flames were shooting out of the top of her bonnet and she wouldn't have paid it much mind.

Finally, probably from pure exhaustion, her crying eased along with her strangling grip, and she let him pull back a step.

He smiled. "Ma, I want you to meet my wife."

Ma jerked her head back like a horse getting ready to rear up. "You told me you got married, but you never mentioned her name."

Gage hadn't been able to come up with a name so he'd left it out. He slid his arm around Ma's shoulders, noticing she'd gained some weight, which meant things must be prosperous back in Texas, and turned her to face Bailey. "Here she is, my pretty little wife, Mrs. Gage Coulter. Bailey Coulter, this is my mother, Sarah Coulter."

Ma sniffled and dabbed a kerchief at her overly pink nose. "Bailey is a man's name." She looked Bailey in the eye, and Gage was glad his wife was wearing a dress and had her hair at a more reputable length. Though few women wore their hair cut short. Still, it beat the manly cut she'd had last fall.

"My pa picked it." Bailey extended a hand and took one of Ma's. Not a handshake exactly, she just pressed her hand to Ma's, held on and smiled. "I'll admit the name's unusual, but I'm used to it. I've found it suits me."

Gage tensed up, waiting for his wife to say something outrageous.

"We don't have what we need to haul your trunks home, Mrs. Coulter." She turned those shining golden eyes on him. "Gage, are the trails open enough you can send a wagon to town tomorrow?"

"A wagon can't get through, but I can send a pack-horse." Gage looked at the baggage and added, "A string of packhorses."

"Good. Let's pick out what you need for overnight, ma'am. Gage, see where you can stack these things until tomorrow. Maybe Sandy will let you store them inside the livery, out of the weather."

"Now wait one minute!" Mrs. Coulter's tone froze both of them in their tracks.

"What is it?" Bailey asked. She gave Mrs. Coulter her full attention.

"I just think we need to spend a few moments introducing ourselves. Heavens, it's so nice to meet the woman my boy married."

"I'd like that too, but if we don't move quick, we'll be riding in the dark. It's a far piece to Gage's . . . uh, our ranch. We can visit on the trail. It's mighty lucky we were even in town or you'd have needed to send a rider out for us and then find a place to sleep in town. And there isn't a place, except maybe the boardinghouse, and that's packed high to the rafters with men."

Gage jiggled her shoulders with the arm he still had around her, hoping to brace her up. "Let's find you a riding horse and head home. It'll be past suppertime before we get there. It's been a long day for Bailey and me."

"And for you too, I'm sure." Bailey still held on to Ma's hand, and though his wife didn't glare at him, considering Ma was watching real close, he could tell his wife thought he was a thoughtless lunkhead. Which was no more than the plain truth, so he took no offense. Good chance that Bailey already knew he wasn't the sensitive type.

Ma steadied herself and slipped out of Gage's grasp to reach for Bailey. "Welcome to the family, dear."

Bailey liked the sound of that and moved closer to Mrs. Coulter. The two of them stood facing each other, holding hands as if they were going to start dancing around the Maypole.

This was going to be good. Ma would pay attention to Bailey and ignore him. Maybe she'd even be more cheerful, quit all her worrying and crying. Bailey was a strong woman. Ma might toughen up just from being around her.

"I've always wanted a daughter!" Ma's voice rose to a wail, and she threw herself into Bailey's arms so hard that Bailey staggered backward.

Gage caught her in time to prevent her falling down under Ma again. With wide eyes, Bailey stood there with her arms extended at her sides, staring at Gage. As if he was going to be able to help her.

It looked like Ma wasn't going to cheer up; she was just

going to spread her crying around even more. Gage felt bad for Bailey, who was in for some hard adjustments.

Under any circumstances she'd shown signs of finding marriage to be a trial. But marriage to Gage, with his ma living in the same house, was going to be a nightmare.

At least Gage wasn't in it alone. "You two go ahead and hug while I haul these things into the livery."

Bailey nearly burned him to a cinder with those fiery eyes.

His turn to smirk.

Until he picked up a trunk.

"No, not that one!"

Gage had forgotten Ma had a squawk that reminded him of a large bird. Her gray silk added to the feathery image. She let go of Bailey and flew toward him, and he half expected her to lay an egg.

"I can't leave anything behind." She slammed into Gage and clutched his arm. He was pretty sure she was going to turn on the tears again.

"Like I said, Ma, Bailey and I have had ourselves a long day. We're tired and hungry, and there's no food closer than my place, which is an hour's ride on hard trails. We don't want to be caught out after dark."

The tears started pouring. Gage knew then he was done for. He just couldn't stand up to her when she was crying like that. "Why didn't Pa come with you?"

To help tend her. Pa always handled her better than Gage. Everybody handled her better than Gage.

"He couldn't leave the ranch, not in the spring. He's busy with branding."

"But doesn't he need you there? I'm surprised you took off on such a long, dangerous ride. I'm surprised Pa allowed it."

Ma sniffled.

Gage braced himself for more tears.

"I've been after him to come for a visit almost since you left," Ma said.

"You lived in Texas, and the war was going on. It wasn't easy to get across the Mason-Dixon line."

"That's what he kept saying." Ma sounded baffled, as if the ways of men were a mystery. "He wouldn't even consider a trip. And once the war was over, he still wouldn't budge."

"Maybe because it's fifteen hundred miles of bad roads with miserable, long hours of discomfort, harsh, sometimes deadly, weather, dangerous river crossings, and trails thick with hungry animals, gunslinging outlaws, and restless Indians."

"Your pa never wants to have any fun."

Bailey laughed, then quickly covered her mouth and started coughing to hide the laughter.

Ma wasn't paying attention. "He finally agreed to let me go on my own."

Gage couldn't imagine his pa agreeing to it. Ma must've made his life unbearable. Now it was Gage's turn to put up with her for a while.

He sighed as he surveyed the heaps of trunks and baggage. "I can rent a couple of horses from the livery, but we'll have to break open the trunks and make more bundles. A trunk isn't going to ride easy on a horse's back. And even if I do that, we won't be able to get it all loaded. When we head for home, you'll see the trails are impassable with a wagon and rugged going for a horse. Now, you and Bailey get busy picking out what you need to take, Ma, while I arrange for the pack animals."

Gage took Ma by the shoulders, gently but firmly pried her off of him, turned her, and although he was gentle about it, he pretty much threw her at Bailey. This was what he'd married her for, and he'd paid for it with five thousand acres of canyon grassland. Well, she could just start earning her ranch right now.

16

ailey's shoulders slumped, and she struggled to keep her eyes open. She was so tired, she considered lashing her wrists to the saddle. She was so hungry, her stomach thought her throat had been cut. And she was so weary of listening to her mother-in-law fuss, she was tossing two ideas around in her head: gag her new ma; cut off her own ears.

Neither was a good idea, but contemplating it was better than doing it, and only the daydream was keeping her from whipping out her kerchief and silencing Ma Coulter.

There was jerky, but she'd strapped several of the bundles behind her saddle, and the saddlebags were buried among them. Since food was impossible and so was assault, and since she was bringing up the rear, leading a string of three heavily laden packhorses, maybe she could sneak in a nap.

In the full dark, Gage led the way and had a packhorse

of his own in tow. He'd tried to take two but found his ma didn't like being that far back from him.

Ma Coulter had proven to be a woman of Texas when she swung up on her horse. No matter how fussy, it seemed that a woman couldn't spend her whole adult life in Texas and not be a skilled horsewoman.

Bailey's head bobbed low, and her eyes drifted shut. She grabbed for a lasso to tie her wrists.

A wolf howled and sent a chill up Bailey's spine. As often as she'd heard it, she still thought it was the eeriest sound in the world. It came from the dark woods that lined the narrow, drifted-over path. The trail had been broken by the riders who'd come to Aspen Ridge with Gage and then ridden home. And it wasn't nearly as deep as the snow on the way from Bailey's. But they were still plowing through drifts deep in the black belly of the woods, because packing Ma's things had made them very late. It was colder with each passing minute.

The wolves howled again, this time several of them. It must be a pack, and they sounded closer than they had just minutes ago.

"What were you thinking to live so far from town, son?"

Bailey slid her hand to the pistol she always wore. It wasn't there. It was in her saddlebag, shoved beneath one of the bundles tied on behind her saddle. Her rifle was gone, too. She'd paid only passing attention to Gage stowing it somewhere out of sight. It sure as certain wasn't in grabbing distance.

"The town wasn't even here when I moved in, Ma. And I was just looking for a nice patch of grass." Gage's voice, deep and raspy, had taken on a tone that made Bailey nervous. He was sounding like a pouting five-year-old. She figured the way he talked to his ma, and she to him, must be how they always acted toward each other.

Bailey needed to fix that before she started whining and nagging like Ma, or pouting like Gage.

Before Gage could say more, the wolves howled, this time even closer. He drew his gun.

"What is that?" Ma Coulter shrieked.

"Gage, my gun's in my saddlebag. I can't get to it." Forgetting to keep her gun within grabbing distance was so stupid, she wanted to punch herself. "Give me your rifle."

She could act ladylike when it didn't matter, but if wolves attacked, she wanted a gun at the ready.

"They're not that close," he said.

They howled again, an unearthly sound.

"Gage!" Bailey's voice cracked like a bullwhip. "They're close enough! You can't handle two guns at once. Give me one of 'em." Bailey rushed her horse, dragging the packhorses along, past Ma Coulter. The trail was just barely wide enough to get past.

One more howl, closer than ever. Gage jerked his rifle free of the sling on his saddle and pulled his horse to a stop just as Bailey caught up to him. He thrust his rifle into her hands.

"Keep moving." She checked the load in the long gun. "I'll get back to bringing up the rear."

"We're less than a half hour from home," Gage said, speaking low for her benefit only. "We may have a fight on our hands."

"They shouldn't attack a group of riders like this."

"Nope, it's strange they're coming."

Sniffing, Bailey said, "What's that smell?"

Gage, who'd been acting baffled since his mother showed up, suddenly was himself again. Tough, trail-savvy. "Dead animal. Blood. I wonder if that pack made a kill around here. They may be hungry. It's been a long, cold winter."

"If it's about an animal they brought down, once we're past it, they should leave us alone."

With a nod, he glanced back at his ma and said sharply, "Ma, we've got to move faster. Keep up with me."

Gage tried kicking his horse into a run. But with the packhorse to drag along, he was slow getting going.

Bailey pulled her horse to a stop and let Ma Coulter pass. She gave Bailey a fearful look. "Why do you live in this savage place?"

As if there weren't a thousand ways to die in Texas.

"Hang on tight, Mrs. Coulter. We've got to make a run for it." Bailey slapped the old nag on the rear—the old nag meaning the horse, not Ma Coulter, although Bailey was sorely tempted.

With three packhorses to convince, Bailey was slow picking up speed.

The wolves helped. Soon they were trotting, closing the space between her and Ma Coulter with every stride.

She had the rifle cocked and pointed straight up. Her eyes never rested on any one spot. It helped to catch any unusual movement if she looked back and forth, always moving, studying the woods. At last their horses had all broken into a gallop.

"I think we're losing them," Gage called out.

The howling did seem to fall back some. They kept up the pace, and Bailey judged they had about fifteen minutes at most until they'd be home and done with this long, strange day.

They reached a stretch where the trail narrowed and thick underbrush came so close, a wagon would scrape its sides on the trees getting past. Not much moon shone in the dark, thick woods. Ahead, Bailey saw lighter sky and hoped that once they were done with this tight stretch, she could relax.

With a shout, Gage's horse went down. Barely visible in the dark, she saw Gage fly over its head. The horse screamed as if in pain.

Bailey couldn't see if his horse landed on Gage or not. The packhorse behind skidded to a stop, nearly sitting down on its haunches to keep from running over the horse ahead of it.

"Stop, Ma!" Bailey spurred her horse and caught Ma's reins. They slid on the frozen ground. Ma's horse ran into the packhorse ahead.

"Gage! Oh, my baby boy!" The packhorses, Ma's and Bailey's mounts, all twisted and reared up as they collided. Bailey grabbed Ma's arm to keep her from falling to the ground.

In the midst of it, Bailey saw Gage's horse neigh in a terrible way that wrenched Bailey's attention to the animal as it surged to its feet. She wasn't sure where Gage was.

God, please don't let him be under the stallion's hooves.

Ma started to dismount. Bailey still had her arm and

kept her in the saddle through sheer grit. The stallion, still tied to the packhorse, twisted sideways.

Gage lay facedown, unmoving on the ground.

"Don't get down." Bailey used a voice that could make a whole army of Union soldiers snap to attention. She leapt to the ground, rifle in hand, dodging the nervous horses. "You're safe from wolves up there."

Safer.

Not safe. But maybe it would keep Ma from getting down and getting in the way.

Bailey sprinted toward Gage. Her ankle hit something. She tripped and went flying. There was a tearing pain in her shoulder and side. She shoved at the ground, and her hand came down on something sharp.

Gritting her teeth to keep quiet and not add to the turmoil, Bailey moved her hand and found the ground, gingerly, realizing she was lying on something that spiked out all over. A fallen tree with broken branches maybe?

She found space between the spearing objects, regaining her feet. She saw her rifle that had flown a few feet ahead and grabbed it, then picked each step carefully until whatever was in the way was behind her. What had she landed on? She remembered the horse's cry. It'd been a cry of anguish. The stallion had been stabbed by the same thing that'd gotten her. Had Gage gotten stabbed, too?

Ma made some new squawking noise and drew Bailey's attention. The woman looked like she was swinging down. "Stay up on that horse! There's something sharp in the path." Bailey hoped her mother-in-law had at least one obedient bone in her body.

It was too dark for Bailey to see if Ma was annoyed or obedient or both. Bailey didn't have time to worry about making a good impression on her new mother-in-law.

She dropped to her knees beside Gage just as he groaned.

"Where's my gun?" Gage rolled onto his back, dazed but still moving, ready to fight.

"Shh, quiet . . ." Bailey heard rustling in the woods. She reared back on her knees and braced the gunstock against her right shoulder.

❦

He looked right down the barrel of that gun and saw death.

The gun didn't fire. The man holding it hesitated and just knelt there, a black shadow against the black night. Only a glint of moonlight off the barrel of the rifle told him the gun was there.

No other detail was visible. But it didn't matter, because Coulter wasn't alone. He tried not to make a sound, but pure fear made him move fast, even if there was noise.

A few trees between him and the rifle and the worst of his terror faded, until he felt safe enough to be angry.

He'd missed again.

Lucky for him, a coward held that gun without the guts to shoot. It'd saved his life. Knowing how close he'd come to dying built his anger until he regretted not just standing in the shadows and shooting Coulter out of the saddle.

But he'd never done it before. He'd never committed cold-blooded murder. He'd hoped the fall from the horse onto those spikes would be enough, and if not, well, he'd have done what he had to do. But he didn't want gunplay. He wanted it to look like Coulter had died in an accident.

Fuming, he wondered why Coulter wasn't alone. All his men had ridden back to the ranch; it should only have been him.

He kept moving away, no sense going back now that there were three of them. He didn't like those odds. In fact, as he strode toward his horse, he realized he couldn't handle this alone.

And he didn't have to. A few people in Aspen Ridge had ridden the outlaw trail and still knew how to get ahold of the right kind of men.

He picked up his pace, eager now to get to town. He was a long way from defeated.

She steadied the gun with her left hand, which caused a tearing pain in her shoulder. She was sure she was bleeding. Her right hand ached as she steadied it on the trigger. She was in pain from every direction, but she ignored it and aimed for whatever—or whoever—moved in the woods.

Gage's eyes sharpened, and he looked around, saw his six-gun and stumbled to his feet to grab it and aim. "That's not a wolf."

"Nope." Bailey knew what a wolf acted like, and this wasn't it.

She knew exactly where she'd put her bullet if she took a shot. But she didn't fire. Only a fool pulled the trigger when they weren't sure what they were shooting at, and Bailey was no fool.

In the moment of taut silence, Bailey felt hot liquid course down her right side, and her left arm throbbed and burned. Her hand burned with pain. She was bleeding from at least three places, but the wounds weren't bad enough to slow her down. She'd tend to them when she didn't have someone to aim at. She didn't stand, as Gage had, because she didn't want to turn her attention for even a second.

The rustling stopped. The only sound was the restless movements of the horses. Even Ma had fallen silent. Gage reached down, and she let go of her rifle barrel for a single moment to slap her left hand in his and let him yank her to her feet. It ripped at the wound on her arm, but she stowed the pain away for later.

They stood side by side. Aiming at the woods. Neither fired.

The wolves yipped and snarled now instead of howling, and they weren't getting closer. They'd found something, no doubt that carcass Bailey had smelled, probably from an earlier kill. And now they were content to feed on that. Although who could ever be completely safe when there was a pack of hungry wolves nearby?

Gage wobbled, and Bailey ignored her own pain to grab his arm and steady him. Once his knees stiffened, she went back to holding her long gun two-handed, but there was a certainty in Bailey that whoever or whatever had been there was gone. Whether she knew that by sound or sight or smell, she wasn't sure, but she knew it just the same.

Bailey spared a glance at Gage and saw a black streak running down his face. Blood. "They're gone. And I'm not chasing into those woods after them."

Gage nodded and lowered his pistol.

Bailey followed suit with her rifle. A glance back to the trail told her something dark was across it, barely visible, mostly buried in snow.

Had Gage been stabbed, too? He'd propelled over his horse's head; she hoped that'd thrown him past the sharp object in the road.

"Is my horse hurt?" Gage turned and almost fell.

She caught him again and looked at the flowing blood on his face. "Your stallion sounded hurt. There's something across the trail that's sharp, a downed tree maybe." Bailey knew that whatever stretched across the path had to be connected to whoever hid in the woods looking on. It was no accident, no tree that fell at random. And whatever had poked her had been sharpened to a point.

"Your horse jumped right up. He may be injured, but he's standing. He'd have probably run off, except the pack-horse tied on stopped him." She pulled a kerchief out of her pocket. "You're bleeding." She dabbed at the head wound.

Gage took the cloth away from her and pressed it to his temple. "I took a knock on the head. If you can help me get to my horse, I can mount up and stick a saddle. What happened? My horse went down at a full gallop."

"Let's get you mounted up, Gage. Whatever's across the trail is dangerous. I'll have a look, see about getting the packhorse across that barrier."

The stallion tossed its head with a panicky whicker as she approached. She untied the pack animal, then ground-hitched it and hoped it was well trained enough, or tired enough, not to run off. With wolves behind them, the barrier in the trail ahead of him and the woods too thick to enter, she thought he'd stay put. And if he didn't, right now, she was in too much pain to care.

She led the stallion well away from danger. The normally well-trained horse was so jumpy she lashed it to a scrub tree rather than trust it to stay hitched. A horse this nervous might take it into its head to run for the barn.

When she reached Gage, she hesitated. They had to get home, but he was so unsteady. It shocked her because she'd never seen Gage show one bit of weakness, unless she counted when his ma was crying and he looked desperate and at a loss for words.

She dropped her voice. "Can you ride?"

"Yeah, I can do it," Gage said. He sounded confident, yet staying in the saddle . . . well, she'd believe it when she saw it.

He grabbed the stirrup.

She saw his Stetson tossed aside on the trail. "Hold still." She let go, retrieved the hat, and handed it to him.

"Son, are you all right?" Ma sounded tearful, but at least she hadn't dismounted and gotten herself stabbed.

"I'm fine, Ma. Let's get back to riding. My horse just tripped over something."

Leaving Gage, she went to the spot where she'd fallen. "There's a thick branch across the trail." Bailey crouched beside it, her hand tightening on the gun. "It was buried in snow; there aren't any hoofprints on it. This wasn't here when your riders went through."

She slid her hands carefully along it and found a second length of wood studded with sharp points, sticking out

169

straight into the trail. In the pitch-black she couldn't make out what exactly she was dealing with.

"It couldn't have been." Gage's harsh voice came out of the dark. "And it didn't fall and get buried in snow on a day when it wasn't snowing. Someone put it there."

Bailey went back to his side. He made slow work of putting his Stetson on. With his voice low to keep his ma out of their conversation, he said, "That's why my horse went down?"

"Yep, someone set a trap for you."

"Like they did last fall on the canyon slope."

Bailey hadn't thought of that. "You never figured out who did that?"

"Winter shut us in hard after the last day I came to the canyon. I haven't done a thing to get to the bottom of it."

"You reckon whoever set off that landslide did this?" Bailey remembered how the chestnut horse had fallen, and she slid her hands along the animal's body and found one bleeding wound. It didn't seem to be life-threatening, just as the pokes she'd taken to her shoulder, arm, and hand weren't. But she hurt something terrible, and she was sure the horse did, too. She felt a deep scratch in the horse's saddle and hoped that had protected the critter from worse harm.

"It very well might be. The first day we're away from the place in the spring, we get another man-trap sprung on us? What have they got planned for us next?" Even though Gage was barely walking, he crouched at the horse's neck and ran both hands down his legs. "One foreleg is cut, but not deep."

Pivoting on his toes, still hunkered down by his horse, Gage looked up at Bailey. His hat shaded his eyes, but the cold rolled off his voice. She didn't have to see those icy eyes to know he was furious. "Maybe I should go into those woods. My prize stallion could have broken a leg over this."

"We don't have time for that." Bailey didn't even tell him about her stab wounds. She was light-headed, her wounds still bleeding. They had to move while she still could.

"We've got to get on. Neither of us wants a shootout with your ma smack in the middle of it."

Gage's jaw tightened, and the muscles in his cheeks were so hard that even in the deep shadows of the woods, Bailey could see it.

"Let's go." Gage rose from his crouch, using a grip on the stirrup to pull himself upright.

"Can you get up there and stay up?"

Sounding offended, he said, "Not counting breaking wild mustangs, I haven't fallen off a horse since I was four years old."

"Good, don't start now." Bailey wasn't one to worry much about a man's feelings. Most men didn't treat each other that way, and she was used to acting like a man. "Mount up and let's head out. But move careful. There could be more traps like this one."

She decided not to stand there like a hand-wringing maiden to catch him if he fell. Instead, she headed back for her mount. She'd have offered to help him climb onto his horse but figured he could manage, and she had no desire to get her ears scalded with his refusal. And anyway, she wasn't sure she had the strength.

171

Bailey made short work of dragging two branches off the trail, one of them crossing lengthwise to trip a rider, and the second with the sharpened pegs stretched down the middle of the trail right in front of the first.

Next, she grabbed the loose packhorse and led it over to tie it back on Gage's horse. She led Ma Coulter's horse through the small drift, then untangled reins until she got her own horse and the pack animals all in line.

Gage was on horseback by the time Bailey mounted up.

"Are you ready, Ma?" Bailey decided that unless the woman forbade it, she'd be called Ma. Who had time for Mrs. Coulter all day every day?

"Is Gage going to be all right?"

"Yep." She hoped. And she didn't mention her own injuries. "He got bumped up some. Your baby boy will be stiff and sore for a few days, but he'll be fine."

"Let's ride." Gage urged his horse into a walk. No more galloping.

Anyone who'd set such a yellowbelly trap might set more than one.

Bringing up the rear, she listened for anyone who might be following them while she pressed against her wounds. The one on her side she could control by pressing her left arm against it. Her right shoulder, though, was trickier. And with her right hand, wounded but not too badly, controlling the reins, she had to satisfy herself that she wasn't losing much blood and just leave off tending it until she could get home.

*T*he rest of the journey was slow, but there was no more trouble. Bailey's tension finally eased as they rode out of the dense woods into the open space around Gage's house. The moonlight made everything visible for the first time since the accident. And when her tension left, it stripped away the grit she'd used to get home.

Now the pain pulsed from her wounds. Her stomach swooped. She fumbled with the buttons of her coat and saw the front of her shirt was soaked in blood.

"Hang on tight. I'm going to get my men out here." Gage drew his gun and fired into the air. The noise made her horse jump, and Bailey grabbed at the saddle horn to stay upright. Her head spun.

Armed men came boiling out of the bunkhouse.

Gage snapped orders. "Ike, see to my horse. He's hurt."

A skinny cowpoke Bailey vaguely remembered meeting

came fast and reached them just as they got to the house. He caught the reins. "What happened, boss?"

"He went down on the trail. Someone put a big branch across the road. His foreleg is cut, and I'm not sure what else. Look him over careful." Gage dismounted.

Several of his men had come close to listen.

"You're bleedin', boss." An older man, the foreman named Rowdy, stepped closer. He raised his voice, "Manny, fetch a lantern out of the house."

One of the men ran into the house and ran out with a lantern, which he lit and brought over to Gage.

The oldster took the lantern and lit up Gage's face. The man said, "You all right, Gage?"

"I'm fine. I just took a hit to the head. Ike, you tend my chestnut, the rest of you, lend a hand with the baggage."

The men split up, heading for the packhorses. Someone lit a second lantern and carried it onto the porch. All the men milling around worked on Bailey's nerves. She could handle almost anything except large groups of men.

Rowdy stayed by Gage, and they talked quietly. Ike stripped a pile of supplies packed behind the stallion's saddle, dropped them to the ground, and led the horse away.

Bailey dismounted, tied her horse to the hitching post, then headed straight for Ma, thinking it would help keep her from fretting to be with another woman. She helped Ma down.

"Let's go on inside." Bailey watched Ma abandon her and rush to Gage's side. "Someone help my boy. He hurt himself when he fell off his horse."

Gage froze in midsentence. In the moonlight, with the help of the lanterns, Bailey saw Gage's face turn so red it nearly shined in the dark. No man liked to admit he'd fallen off his horse. A horse going down and taking the rider along was completely different.

His men, working over the packs, stopped to look at Ma, then turned back fast to unstrapping and hauling. Bailey thought she heard a few snickers.

Rowdy rubbed his hand over his mouth. Then with a somewhat unsteady voice, like he was fighting not to laugh, he said, "You get your ma and your wife settled, Gage. We'll get these things inside."

So Gage had mentioned he got married. Had he told Rowdy before he'd come to Bailey's or just now? And did Rowdy know Gage was supposed to have been married for a while now?

She shook her head, but only once. The motion made her dizzy. The cowhands ignored her, so did Gage and Ma. Everyone ignored her, which gave her the perfect chance to get out of the crowd. Something she needed to do while she could still walk.

"Let's go inside, Ma." Bailey thought her bleeding had stopped, but she was weak and in pain. She could probably use a woman's help. She went to Ma.

The woman barely spared her a glance. "I'd better oversee the unloading."

A heavy trunk landed hard on the ground.

"Be careful! Some of my things are breakable." She rushed away from Bailey toward the trunk. Manny jumped aside to avoid Ma running over him.

"Now, you men handle my things gently," she said.

Normally, Bailey would have pitched in and helped, but with all the men surrounding her, and her wobbly knees, she gave up on Ma.

Most likely the woman would be worse than no help, anyway. She'd find a chair out of the way and sit down awhile, gather her strength, then find bandages and heat some water for herself. She walked toward the house, slowly.

She was none too steady as she mounted the porch steps empty-handed and listened to Ma squawk about breakables. She realized then that she was about to face her darkest fear.

Not a frightening cluster of men, though that was bad.

Not moving into a house, knowing she had to face a wedding night with Gage, though that should have been it.

Not giving up her land to marry a stranger, though she knew the papers Gage had given her were only as good as his word; no court would let a married woman own land separate from her husband.

Not her pa finding out she'd turned her homestead over to Gage. That would come, and Pa would be loud about his complaints, but Bailey had heard it all before.

Nope, her darkest fear, the one thing that drove all the other fears to the back of her mind . . .

What if Ma's visit was permanent?

◦❀◦

The ride had cleared Gage's head . . . mostly. As he turned to protect his men from his mother and help with the hauling, he watched his wife step up onto his porch. She was moving wrong, not her usual fast, take-charge way.

Of course, she was exhausted and half starved, but he didn't question the reflex that sent him rushing toward her.

Bailey reached for the post at the top of the two steps. The lantern light gleamed on the bare skin between her coat sleeve and her leather glove, bright red. Blood. That scarlet hand grabbed at the post and missed. Her knees buckled.

She toppled backward off the stairs. He sprinted the last few steps and caught her before she fell to the ground.

"You're bleeding." She didn't respond. He looked down into her face, eyes closed, skin as pale as ash. Unconscious.

He roared, "Rowdy!"

Swinging her up, he carried her inside and went straight to his bedroom at the back of the house. He called over his shoulder, "Bring a lantern, Rowdy. The rest of you men, let Ma tell you where to take her things."

So much for protecting them.

That was the last thought he gave to anything but his wife.

He laid her down right on top of the blankets. Rowdy rushed in, boots clomping, lantern in hand, to light up the room. Gage stripped Bailey's gloves off, and the lantern flared on vivid scarlet. Her right hand was coated in blood.

"She didn't even tell me she'd been hurt. She said something sharp had stabbed my horse. It must've stabbed her too, and all she did was take care of me and get us back on the trail." Purely ashamed of himself, he added, "She even lifted that branch out of the way while I sat on my horse."

He tossed her hat aside and unwound the scarf from

around her neck. Next, he took off the heavy buffalo robe and found her shoulder was bleeding. The whole front of her sleeve was soaked in blood.

"Get her uncovered, Gage." Rowdy had the best healing skills of any of them.

Gage reached for the buttons that went down the front of her dress and hesitated. He looked up at Rowdy, who only tore his eyes off the sleeve when Gage stopped.

"What's the matter?"

"I think you should step out while I undress her. It ain't fitting that you should see my wife's . . . uh, my wife's . . ." Gage shrugged. "And tell my ma to come in here. The men can get her things to her room without my help."

Rowdy blushed, something Gage had never seen before. The old man nodded and hurried out. "When you're down to the wound, cover the rest of her up and I'll come back. I'll heat water and get bandages while you make sure she's decent."

Gage went back to unbuttoning and knew he shouldn't be doing this. If she was conscious, she'd probably punch him in the mouth. She'd already proved herself capable of that.

When he got her dress open, he heaved a sigh of relief. She had woolen underwear on. Spikes on that branch had to pierce her tough buffalo coat and long-sleeved dress and long underwear, lots of protection and still she was bleeding.

She'd been stabbed in the hand, at the base of her thumb.

There was a hole poked in her arm a couple of inches down from her shoulder. He drew the knife out of his boot and carefully cut the sleeve away.

A puncture—he had no idea how deep—but it hadn't gone all the way through. He pulled up her shirt at the waist and found an ugly cut, as if the spike had raked along on her skin but hadn't stabbed into her. He shifted her around to pull the blanket over her up to her neck, leaving her injured arm outside.

As he tucked the blanket around her neck, he saw an ugly red scratch right below her ear. It was only a mark. The scratch hadn't bled. He could imagine one of those spikes scraping along her neck, inches from an artery that would have left her bleeding to death.

A deep and abiding rage filled him. Whoever had done this was going to pay.

He looked her over more carefully in case he'd missed other wounds. There were none he could see. He called, "She's ready."

His foreman came in fast with a basin of steaming water. "We had some hot by the fireplace. Figured you'd need to wash up." Rowdy went to the far side of the bed and set the basin on a table, his eyes examining the puncture on her arm first.

"She's got a cut on her waist on the other side, too." Gage carefully exposed her as little as possible by pulling back the blanket.

"That's an open wound." Rowdy sounded grim. "It'll hurt, but it should heal fast. The hand and the shoulder are punctures. That's the kind of thing that can bring on a fever."

"These three are all." His eyes went to the scratch on her neck. "I didn't see blood anywhere else." Lifting his eyes, he knew the blazing fury must show, because Rowdy was paying real close attention.

"Someone set a trap for us out there. It just might be the same varmint who was behind that landslide last fall."

Rowdy's eyes narrowed. "This was a lot closer to home."

"I want you to ride out at first light and study that trail. Backtrack them if you can. I heard someone in the woods tonight. They were waiting, watching for us, but they didn't take the chance to attack when I was down." Gage remembered how fast Bailey had gotten there and knelt over him, gun in hand. She'd saved his life.

"Whaddya reckon they're up to?"

Shaking his head, Gage turned back to Bailey. "I don't know, but they hurt my wife, and they hurt my horse. They could've killed someone. I aim to find out who's behind it."

Ma stepped into the room. "What happened?"

"She got hurt on the trail. Same place I fell."

"I saw her fall on the steps." Ma came around the bed and stood beside Gage. "I thought she was just tired or . . ." Ma's hand came to rest on Gage's shoulder. "She didn't say a word."

"Nope, she was too busy taking care of both of us. She cleared the trail." It was making him crazy to think of her bleeding, lifting that trap, straightening the horses' reins, getting them all moving again. Something hard trembled deep inside him to think of the caliber of woman he'd married.

And Gage knew that even though Ma had a strange way of treating him, she'd stood at Pa's side through some mighty hard times. He needed to find a way to make Ma see that he was in good hands with Bailey as his wife.

Rowdy handed Gage a cloth. "Keep pressure on that arm until the bleeding stops. I'm going to bandage her side."

"I should be tending her," Ma said. "This isn't proper to have your cowhand do it."

"I know you're good with those who are hurting, Ma, but Rowdy has some mighty fine healing skills. I want him to take care of her. With your help."

Her hand tightened on his shoulder, and he was glad for her support.

"Say a prayer for her, Ma." Gage pressed firmly on the puncture wound, and Bailey moaned in pain. It was the first sign of consciousness she'd shown since she collapsed. But that one sound was the only one she made.

Rowdy dipped a cloth in the steaming water, wrung it out, and went to work.

18

Bailey's eyes flickered open. A lantern turned down low showed enough of the room to make her sure she'd never seen it before. This bed wasn't hers. Nor did she recognize the thick blankets covering her. She swept her hands out, and pain hit her hand, her side, even her left shoulder and she hadn't moved that an inch.

She forgot about the pain when her hand collided with something. No, not something . . . some*one*. Someone was in bed beside her. She squeaked.

"Bailey, you're awake."

She snapped her head around . . . and went back to thinking of the pain. Breathing hurt. Thinking hurt. Moving sure enough hurt. Everything hurt.

She looked right into the gray eyes of . . . oh, good heavens, she'd gotten married. To Gage Coulter, of all people. Remembering that hurt worst of all. Well, maybe not hurt, as in pain . . . more like dread.

The whole long, strange day came rushing back. But finding Gage in bed with her was the strangest part yet.

And where exactly did you think he was going to sleep?

Gage rose from the bed so quickly she wondered if he was just remembering what they'd done, too. Maybe he was a little unsettled to be so close to her. He adjusted her blankets until they were pulled up to her chin, and she wondered if he was tempted to pull them all the way over her head so he could deny he'd married her.

"You fainted. You lost a lot of blood."

Fainted? Bailey hated such weakness. "How are you?" She hoped he was the kind of man to talk about himself.

"I'm fine. You're the one who got hurt." Gage leaned close, focused on her, his attention not turned one speck. "Your right hand and waist and your left shoulder are bandaged. Maybe we should have sewn you up, but we didn't."

Bailey remembered being hurt, but she'd never gotten a chance to see what all had happened.

"Rowdy does the doctoring around here, and he said there was no cause for stitches."

More about the day came back to her. "Did you warn your men about the trap? Whoever did it may strike again."

"They'll ride out at dawn, try to pick up a trail. They know to be on their guard."

"Have them check that carcass the wolves were after. If there's anything left of it, they might find tracks or proof the animal was killed and staked out by the trail to draw that pack."

"Good thinking," Gage said.

"How long have I been unconscious?" She hated the thought of how vulnerable she'd been.

"There's a lot of night left yet. We rode into the place before midnight, and you haven't been out that long. Rowdy said it's a mercy not to be awake during his doctoring. He's none too gentle."

"Rowdy tended me?" How exposed had she been?

"We kept you covered except for the places he had to work," Gage said. "We were careful of your privacy."

He'd read her mind, and she didn't like that her face must've given away so much. Probably she was weak from her wounds. She'd toughen up come morning. "How's your ma?"

Gage flinched. "She's asleep."

Had Ma stayed and watched over her during the doctoring?

"She came in and saw to it there was a woman present. She was a while settling down, but then she came back to look in on you."

Bailey was glad for that simple decency. Except, of course, Ma thought Gage was her husband. Well, Gage *was* her husband, but that didn't quite seem real.

"Getting all her things up to her room kept the men busy awhile."

Bailey nodded, wondering just how long the woman intended to stay. "I need to get up. I'm thirsty and I need a . . . a moment. Outside." She reached for the covers, and pain struck from all sides. Fighting not to make a sound, she forced herself to lift the blankets. A wave of relief swept through her when she saw she was still dressed in her bloodstained woolen underwear. They were ugly and uncomfortably stiff, but she hadn't been undressed. It lifted some of the feeling of being defenseless.

"Take it easy."

Since she was inching out of bed on the side away from him, he came around and reached for her, then hesitated. "Which'll hurt the least, my arm around your waist on the side that's wounded or on the side with your hurt shoulder?"

Bailey sat on the edge of the bed while the room swayed. She wanted to shoo him off, yet she wasn't that sure she could stand up, let alone walk out to the privy. Things steadied. Mostly.

She tried to identify the pain, which seemed to come from everywhere. "The right side so your hand closes on my waist on the left. But be careful of my shoulder."

Gage slid his arm across her back and caught hold at her waist. She lifted her arm thinking to loop it around his neck for support, but lifting her arm pulled at her wounded shoulder and waist so she gave that up. As she stood, her vision blurred and her ears buzzed.

"Wait, let my head clear." Her voice sounded far away. Gage stood still. Bailey was surprised how sure she was that he'd keep her from falling. She trusted him.

Finally the room came back into focus. "I'm ready."

They took two steps, and her knees sagged. Gage swept her up in his arms.

"No, I need to walk, clear my head."

"You can do that later." He carried her to a door, probably the back because the kitchen was there, though she remembered nothing of being brought inside. "Let me fetch your coat."

"I'm sure it's cold, but I don't want to fuss with a coat." This made Bailey look down and realize her boots were still on. They hadn't done a thing to her they didn't need to.

Gage swung the door open and made a sound of disgust. "It's snowing."

"Bound to happen, even this late in the spring."

"But it's going to cover the tracks left by whoever did this to you."

That hadn't occurred to her. "So no chance you'll be able to pick up a trail." Bailey looked at the snow sifting down, at least a couple of inches already covering the ground.

It was beautiful, silent and soft. Bailey shivered, partly from the cold, but also because now their mystery had just gotten harder to solve.

"You want your coat, after all?" Gage stared down at her.

"I can make it. It'll be a good reason to hurry."

When he got her to the privy, he opened the door for her. "Can you manage all right?" Gage sounded as uncomfortable as she felt.

They were nearly strangers and now they were married and forced into a situation far too intimate, one that neither of them particularly wanted. Bailey expected the next few weeks would be an adventure—and that didn't count if someone kept coming after Gage.

"I can make it," she said.

He set her on her feet.

She took a solid hold of the door with her left hand,

letting her heavily bandaged right hand hang idly. She got herself inside . . . and out.

Gage had stepped away, but when she emerged he rushed to her side and plucked her off her feet again. "Let's get you back to bed. A good night's sleep will help more than anything."

"I need a drink of water, and Gage?"

He headed toward the house. "What is it?"

"I think we need to talk. And now, while your ma's asleep. This'll be our only chance."

Gage swallowed hard as he swung open the back door. His voice dropped to a whisper. "You mean concoct a lie about how we met and when we decided to get married and such?"

"No, I think we should just tell her the truth."

Gage shook his head frantically. "I'm not telling my ma I lied to her last fall, and I'm sure as certain not telling her I was afraid she'd never go home so I married a stranger who barely likes me and bribed her into it with a five-thousand-acre canyon."

Bailey felt a headache coming on. "I mean tell her the truth except for that."

"That's a big exception. Pretty much covers the whole thing, don't you think?"

"It does not. We met when you wanted your canyon back, true. We got married, true. We don't have to say a date. And besides, since you wrote to her, she thinks she knows that. So what we say saves us from having to make up a story, and later trying to keep it straight."

"What do you want to talk about, then?"

"I want to talk about who hates you enough to want you dead."

❦

Gage looked at the ceiling—his ma sleeping right above them—and listened before settling Bailey in a rocking chair in front of the fireplace, which glowed with dying embers.

He fetched logs from the woodbox and laid them on the floor beside the fire. Next he used scraps of bark to get a flame going from the embers. As the fire caught, Gage laid kindling on it, then added a few logs. The fire crackled and grew, soothing her tension. Her eyes rested on the leaping flames.

Gage left her to rest, coming back a few minutes later with a tin plate in one hand, a tin cup in the other. He set them on a small table, pushed up against the wall by the fireplace, picked the whole table up and brought it over to sit in front of her.

"There, go ahead and eat. I can get you more if you want it. I didn't have supper, either. I'll get myself a plate."

After a bit of food went down, her hunger blazed to life.

Gage returned with his own meal and pulled a second rocker close enough to use her table. He must've been as hungry as she, because they dug in and ate in silence for a while. Her full belly and the crackling fire relaxed her until she thought she might fall asleep where she sat.

"You said you wanted to talk?" Gage's deep voice broke her out of the drowsiness.

Bailey looked at Gage. In the flickering light, his unusual gray eyes reflected the flames and replaced the cold so often found there with heat.

She couldn't help but smile. "We oughta talk about so many things it's hard to know where to start."

Gage managed a smile over that.

"But what I wanted to talk about"—she dropped her voice to a whisper—"is who wants to hurt you?"

"Someone had to see me in town to get ahead of me and set that trap."

"What's more, it wasn't set for a group of men. Whoever set it would've known he was as good as asking for war with a crowd of tough gunmen ready to fight. Anyone have a grudge against you?" She leaned closer, barely able to hear his whispers over the crackling logs.

He leaned in, too. In the room, lit only by firelight, there seemed to be a cocoon around them. Like they were the only two people in the world. Bailey couldn't help leaning even closer.

"There are a couple of area ranchers who've never been friendly. Some of 'em are men who've never impressed me with their hard work. Rance Boyle is one, and he saw me in town."

"So you think it's him?"

With a shrug, Gage said, "Mo Simmons has a good-sized spread, and I'm not sure how he hangs on to it. He's a poor cattleman. He's made no secret of being jealous of my ranch, even though he could have a good herd and a nice house himself if he'd just spend his time working instead of complaining."

"Are there other big ranches around?" Bailey asked. "I've always heard you were the biggest."

Gage's eyes rose to catch hers. "I am the biggest *and* the best. But that's only because I've worked my heart out for five years. I left my home and my family, my friends and a good chunk of my self-respect behind when I came out here. I've been working to get back my self-respect because none of the rest of it is possible."

He sounded so grim, Bailey decided their time for talking was over. So she pointed out the obvious. "You may have left your family, but your ma is right upstairs. I think she wants to take care of you."

Gage rolled his eyes heavenward. "And if she has to move in here and live with me forever, well, that's what a loving mother does. And I'm a brute if I disagree."

Bailey was afraid Gage had his mother figured about right. "I'd like to have a look at those tracks, too. I'm not as good on a trail as Tucker or Sunrise, but I do a decent job. If I saw a familiar track, I'd recognize it."

"You're not up to riding." Gage made it sound like an order, which pinched. "For now, my men and I are going to handle it."

Unfortunately he was right. "I think I'm going to fall asleep where I sit. We've done enough talking. We'll need to be on our guard."

"I always post a sentry, and my men ride out for miles all around. If there are more man-traps, someone could die. I've warned them, but I've got to figure out who's doing this." Gage stood and moved the table to the side.

He reached for her good hand, which hurt her shoulder, then for her waist and stopped.

Picking up her right hand with its thick bandage, he turned it over and ran his fingers over the white wrap. "I'm sorry my trouble got you hurt, Bailey. A man's supposed to protect his woman, and I've failed you after less than a day."

Bailey thought of her pa sending her off to war. Not much protection there, either.

He raised her hand and pressed his lips to the bandage as if he could kiss the hurt away. It was so sweet, so at odds with the man she thought he was.

"Instead, you protected me. You were kneeling over me with your gun drawn before I could pick myself up, and that was after you got stabbed in three places."

Bailey brushed the dark hair off his forehead and ran one of her winter-chapped fingers over the goose egg on his brow. "You were knocked witless. The second your head cleared, you were helping me. And I hurt, but I didn't have time to worry about it at the time. Kind of like you climbing back on that stallion when you could barely stand."

His eyes came up to meet hers. She'd never expected to like a man's eyes so much. Never thought of such a thing.

Shaking his head, he went to her side and eased her to her feet. The whole room wavered, and Bailey's knees turned to liquid. She sank, but before she could hit the floor, Gage had her cradled in his arms again.

Again his eyes met hers. She saw the good man beneath his hard ways. Strong and warm. The tender care he'd taken of her, his confused love for his mother. Their gaze held.

The moment stretched on. His eyes flickered to her lips. Then Gage lowered his head an inch at a time.

She raised her mouth just as slowly. The kiss made her think of her wedding vows. She had no plans to stay here, to be married. But as the kiss deepened and his strength surrounded her, Bailey realized she felt safe for the first time in a long time.

Not that she'd ever felt like she was in danger exactly. At least not since the war ended. She knew how to take care of herself. But this safety was more than the absence of danger, or someone strong enough to stand between her and danger.

It was safety for her heart—safety that included a man. And after all she'd seen, she never expected to feel that again. She couldn't explain it; she just knew it felt wonderful.

He broke the kiss and looked down at her, somberly. He carried her to their room and sat her on the bed.

"You should get clean clothes on," he said.

"I'm too tired to do anything but fall asleep." A troublesome thought hit her as she looked at her wretched, stained woolen underwear. Her dress couldn't be in any better shape. "I don't have any clothes."

"Ma's good with a needle. She saw what happened to your dress and said she'd find something of her own and make it fit. And we bought fabric, so you can make yourself a new dress as soon as you feel able." Kneeling before her, he unlaced her boots and slid them off, then helped her lie back and settle in. "She said a lot of those bundles we hauled out here are full of wedding gifts for us."

"That's sweet of her." Bailey needed to at least give Ma

a chance to be more than the weepy woman who embarrassed her son. As for clothes, Ma Coulter was about the size of two of Bailey, though they were close in height. Bailey would look foolish, but then she wasn't going to look all that good in tattered long johns, either. They'd figure something out.

He covered her to her chin, then rounded the bed and got in beside her. He turned on his side and raised himself on one elbow to look down at her.

"Good night, Mrs. Coulter." He brushed her hair back. "So far I'm thinking being married to you is a fine idea indeed." He kissed her again, then rolled onto his back.

For some reason, that bit of kindness helped her forget all her aches and pains. She took Gage's tenderness and his kiss with her into sweet dreams.

Ma fussed over Bailey owning only one dress, but she immediately took charge of the situation. She took charge so thoroughly it made Bailey nervous.

If Bailey wasn't careful, Ma would take over everything, and Bailey was too weak from her injuries and blood loss to do much about it.

Ma's help was a relief, but it was also humiliating because her dresses were frilly with ribbons and lace. Something had to be done, yet every time Bailey sat up she got light-headed. Sewing was beyond her.

Bailey had barely stirred all morning. Ma brought her breakfast and helped her sit up to eat it. Then Gage had come in and helped her out to the privy again.

"Why don't you have more than one dress?" Ma asked as she came in the bedroom carrying a dark purple dress weighed down with flounces. Gage was just done pulling the covers up.

"It was the trail, Ma." Gage had that pouting tone Bailey didn't like. "Last fall the winter landed hard on us right after we got married, and we couldn't get back to pick up more clothes for her."

Ma shooed Gage from the room, pulled a chair up and settled in, needle in hand. "Now, dear, tell me about yourself."

Bailey had no idea what to say. She stuck to the truth, in case of a faulty memory.

Whatever oddities were in Ma's character, she was a fine seamstress and had the dress pared down to size before an hour had passed.

"Let's get you out of those dreadful woolens. Goodness what woman would even wear such things?"

"I reckon it makes more sense to someone who doesn't live in the Texas heat."

With Ma's help she shed them and saw for the first time her real condition. Beneath her clothes she had three bandages. One thick pad at the top of her arm. A bandage wrapped several times around her middle, with blood seeping through at her waist. A third on her hand. She never saw that spiked trap in the dark woods, but she sure felt it. She could imagine falling on it, poking herself in just these places. She was lucky she hadn't had a spike stab her in the face, put an eye out.

Ma washed Bailey, and it made her cringe to be handled like a child. But she endured it and felt so much better with all the blood washed away. The wounds were bandaged again with strips of clean cloth. Ma took a few nips in the waist to a chemise of her own and slipped it over Bailey's head. It hung loose, but Bailey didn't think it mattered since it wouldn't show. It was cold, though.

"Women have to wear woolen underwear in the mountains, Ma." At least Bailey hoped they did, and how would Ma know? "It's just too cold out here. We have learned to be sensible."

Ma gave Bailey a long look, then nodded, which might mean Ma would see to figuring out warmer underclothes. She helped Bailey don the purple dress and then started to fuss with Bailey's hair.

It was so unusual to take time over her appearance. Bailey wanted to swat the woman's hands away. Instead, lucky to have the excuse of exhaustion and pain, she sat quietly and allowed Ma to comb her cap of blond curls and tie a purple ribbon in it.

She endured it by daydreaming about whether Gage would let her help around the ranch. She liked breaking wild mustangs a lot more than she liked sitting still to get her hair combed. And she couldn't see herself busting broncs in a dress.

"Well, not much can be done with such short hair, but you're as presentable as I can make you." Ma sounded cheerful, except her words cut just a bit. Bailey had a feeling that was Ma's exact intent.

"Let's move to the kitchen. We can visit while I set the kitchen to rights and get a meal on." Taking over. Gage had said his ma liked to be in charge. If she had more energy, Bailey would insist Ma sit down while she ran her own household, but when Bailey stood, even leaning heavily on Ma, her head wasn't steady and her vision darkened.

They barely made it to the kitchen, where Bailey sank heavily onto a chair. Not much chance Bailey was going to take over anything.

~❦~

Bailey was sitting at the kitchen table, drinking coffee and eating bread and cheese while Ma got a meal, when the back door banged open.

Gage stormed in muttering furiously under his breath. He slammed the door so hard, plates rattled in the cupboard.

"Gage, for heaven's sake," Ma said.

Gage skidded to a stop, looked at Ma, and flinched. He swiveled to look at Bailey. "Uh . . . sorry. I forgot you two were here."

Ma clutched her throat and in a wobbly voice said, "You mean you forgot your mother came to see you for the first time in five years?"

That drew his eyes back to Ma. Unlike her, Bailey was tempted to laugh at the dumbfounded look on Gage's face. She couldn't resist adding dryly, "And that you have a wife?"

He'd been staring at his ma, but when Bailey spoke, his eyes lost their wide-eyed surprise and became sharply focused—on her. He blinked and looked Bailey up and down . . . and up. Then he walked into the cupboard.

"Doesn't Bailey look lovely in my dress, son?" Ma started fluttering her hands nervously.

Ma hadn't been like this when the two of them were alone. She had a bit of a critical way about her, but she'd worked hard. Bailey didn't like the way Ma took over, but Bailey just plain wasn't up to it.

Now with Gage here, Ma was a different woman.

"She looks real pretty." Gage didn't even look at his mother. "Real, real pretty." He smiled in a way that made her remember his kiss from last night. Remember it fondly.

Bailey's cheeks heated up in what had to be a blush. She hadn't blushed in years. Maybe never. What was happening to her? If she wasn't so battered, she'd go brand a steer just to remind herself of who she was.

It was time to distract Gage from staring. "What made you come storming in here madder than a rabid polecat?"

Gage's warm eyes turned to ice. "My men are just back from the trail. They couldn't pick up any tracks—the snow's too deep—but they sure enough found the trap set for us."

Gage yanked his gloves off his hands. "You're lucky to be alive, Bailey."

"Don't forget I want a chance to study that trap and examine any tracks you find. You never know what might be familiar. Everyone you trust should examine it."

Gage didn't respond to that. Instead, walking over to her, he touched her neck with one finger.

Bailey felt a raw spot she hadn't noticed before. "I've got a cut there, too?" She touched her neck, his warm fingers intertwining with hers.

"You could have died, Bailey." He quit touching her where it was sore and ran a finger around to the front of her neck along the ruffled collar of her silly purple dress.

Except the way Gage was looking at her didn't make her feel so silly.

"It's not serious." She found herself wanting to ease his upset.

"I know. It didn't even bleed." His voice dropped to a whisper. "But it was so close."

He was silent for a long moment.

"The only reason I didn't get stabbed was my horse threw me over its head. And my stallion . . ." He closed his eyes and nearly growled when he said, "You knew he was bleeding on his side, and I found that cut on his leg, but he's also got a wound on his flank. And there are two ugly gouges in his saddle or he'd be a lot worse. He's got some healing to do."

"Maybe I can get to know him while we're both mending." Bailey smiled to lighten his mood.

His fury eased into grim resolve. "I'm going to find out who did this, and I'm going to stop them. They're not going to hurt my wife and get away with it. What's worse, it's a sloppy way to try and kill someone. It amounts to vicious mischief. They're only trying to cause harm, like they're taking pleasure in hurting me and my men, and for no purpose."

Bailey knew he was wrong. "If I hadn't been with you, Gage, it could have been a lot worse than mischief. They had no way of knowing you'd have company riding home. In fact, they *expected* you to be alone."

Gage's eyes narrowed, and she saw he'd already thought of that.

"There was someone in those woods, Gage. Someone

lying in wait, expecting they'd kill you with the trap, and if that failed, they'd finish it and make it look like an accident."

His hands fisted. "Like a landslide looks like an accident."

"Right." Bailey's eyes shifted to Ma. Last night they'd planned to protect her from this kind of worry. Gage was upset enough, he wasn't thinking of that, and it wouldn't hurt Ma to know the truth.

"That day of the landslide was the first time I wasn't up there ahead of my men. And Rowdy only survived because Ike pushed him. Normally I'd have been up there alone. If whoever set that trip wire was watching before he set the trap, he'd have figured me to be the one to set off the avalanche. I'd have been right in the path of those boulders and with no help close by."

"What avalanche, Gage?" Ma rushed to him and grabbed his arm. "Someone is trying to kill you?"

Gage, facing Bailey, went wide-eyed. He'd forgotten to speak carefully around her. Bailey saw the effort he made to reply calmly.

"Ma . . ." He turned and pried her hand off his arm. Not that easy because she seemed to have sunk her fingernails in. "I shouldn't have mentioned it. It was clear last fall. Yes, someone has been up to no good, but we're ready for trouble now. My men are always on guard. I'm doubling the posted sentries, and I've got my best men scouting, watching for intruders. The snow is covering the tracks but not erasing them. When it melts we'll find the trail the coyote left and put a stop to this."

"But he could strike anytime. Shoot you in the back."

"Not now that I'm on guard against it." He sounded so sure, Bailey almost believed it. Except she didn't.

"Whoever did this won't get within ten miles of us without being spotted."

Bailey thought of the endless miles of forest and how someone could slip around, get off the trail, and sneak in without being seen. She knew Gage was plenty worried, but he wasn't going to let his ma know it.

He had to watch his words, and she suspected Gage was a man who hadn't done that much. He said what he meant and did what he said he'd do. He was a man used to straight talk, with little regard for what people thought of him. It was a trait Bailey possessed, and it suited her. She liked honesty, maybe more because she'd spent years living a lie.

So it wasn't going to be easy remembering to mind her words to protect Ma's feelings.

"But, Gage—"

"Ma, did you say you had some food? I'm starving."

Ma looked nervously from Gage to Bailey, not satisfied with the change of subject. But her cheeks had pinked up, and her expression lightened when Gage asked her for food. It was clear she was delighted at the thought of feeding her son.

"Yes, I made a meal for you. It's such a pleasure to cook for my boy again."

Flinching at the word *boy*, Gage turned from his mother to Bailey and asked, "Are you ready to eat?"

Gage looked at her, sitting at the table as if she were

always ready to eat. He didn't notice his mother's slumped shoulders as he paid attention to his wife. Bailey wasn't sure what was upsetting the woman. Gage had hoped being married would make her see he was getting along fine. Was that it? Did Ma for some reason want Gage to be struggling? Did she think it would prove he missed her and needed her?

Bailey could see Ma's hurt and tried to cheer her up. "Ma has been taking good care of me. I slept through breakfast, and she got a dress ready for me—one of her own. Then she got me a bite to eat, but I'm hungry enough the stew would be welcome and it smells delicious. Thanks for cooking, Ma. I wasn't close to having the gumption to prepare a meal today."

"Go ahead and wash, Gage," Ma said. "Then come and sit up to the table. I'd love to serve you both."

"No, Ma. You're not serving me. You're a guest in this house. Bailey needs to take things slow for a few days, and your help is greatly appreciated, but I've been running this house as a bachelor for five years. I can set plates out and lift the heavy stewpot."

"Now, Gage . . ."

Gage pulled her into a long hug. He let her go and smiled, and she practically glowed with the pleasure of being so close to him. "Let's work together. How does that sound?"

Ma was silent awhile. Bailey thought she was probably stirring around to protest, but Gage's kindness was too much for her. "I think that sounds fine."

Bailey felt like a slug for not helping, but she just barely could sit upright at the table, so there was no use trying to do more.

Ma had baked biscuits to go with the stew, and there was milk. For dessert she made an apple cobbler with apples she'd packed in from Texas. Apparently there was food in some of those bundles of hers.

As Gage and Ma took turns putting savory food in front of her, Bailey tried to remember anyone treating her like this in the past. She was determined to put a stop to it the first second she was able, of course, but in the meantime she decided to enjoy it. It was so much different from what she expected from any man.

Pa was the worst of the bunch.

The front door slammed open. It was behind her as she sat at the table, and Bailey clawed for her gun. It wasn't there.

She stood and turned to fight . . . and waves of dizziness swept over her and she almost fell. Gage rushed around the table, his broad shoulders blocking her view as he stood between her and danger. He didn't catch her, but he was handy to grab hold of.

Blood left her head, her vision narrowed, and her temples gave a sickening throb. She held tight to Gage's waist to keep from pitching face-first to the floor.

"You got married?" The roar of anger told her no gun was necessary. That was a relief, but something to plug her ears might be good.

"Hi, Pa." She steadied herself and let her head clear, then leaned to look around Gage.

Shaking her head in disgust, she ducked behind Gage

again and stretched to whisper in his ear, "Your ma is a dream compared to my pa."

Gage grunted and crossed his arms, though the rigid set of his shoulders eased some. "Come to congratulate us, Wilde?"

Bailey stepped up to Gage's side, mindful of what Pa might say to give away the wedding date. Pa stormed straight for her, his eyes bulging, his face red with fury. Honestly, Bailey wasn't sure if it was red with fury. He was always red-faced, but he was always furious, too. Pa had grown a beard over the winter. He'd lost weight. He was more stooped and gray-haired than she remembered. His clothes looked like they hadn't been washed in months, and he got close enough for her to notice he smelled none too good, either. The winter hadn't been kind to Cudgel Wilde.

"You betrayed me." He shook a fist so close to her nose, he almost punched her.

Like a striking snake, Gage's hand shot out and grabbed Pa's arm.

Pa wasn't one to hit. All his damage came from his yelling. But Gage didn't know that. Bailey had her arm along Gage's waist, mainly to keep herself steady, but she patted him on the back, hoping to head off a fistfight. Pa wasn't worth that.

"Gage and I fell in love, Pa."

She said it with such confidence, Gage glanced down at her. She smiled. He arched one dark brow, then smiled back and let go of Pa's arm.

"I had to follow my heart." She sounded as perky as the injuries that were gnawing at her would allow.

Gage slid his hand along her waist, careful not to touch any wounds. "Yep, Cudgel, I'm a mighty lucky man. You brought three beautiful women into this country, and I married the pick of the litter."

Bailey pinched his back, but she didn't put much force behind it. "Sorry about that dynasty you wanted to build to honor Jimmy." Bailey remembered more about Jimmy than her little sisters because she'd worked more closely with him. Jimmy had been no great hero. He was cut from the same cloth as Pa.

"How'd you get here, Wilde?"

"That's a good question, Pa." Bailey realized it was a really good question. "The pass between my place and yours can't be open yet."

"I got a different way out." Pa didn't elaborate, but Bailey knew the trail to Pa's. Although truth be told, she'd only been there a couple of times, when they first moved here and were scouting homesteads. And she'd never seen a way around one gap that snowed in deep.

Of course, she hadn't thought Gage could find a way into her canyon, either.

"I came to your house and you were cleared out, but I thought maybe you'd just ridden into town for supplies, so I rode on. I stopped by Shannon's house and it was empty. I finally got to Aspen Ridge and heard the news of Shannon heading for the high hills, Kylie heading back east, and you getting married, which means Coulter now owns your spread. All of you betrayed me."

"A grown-up woman finding a good man is usually her father's fondest dream, Wilde," Gage said coldly. Bailey looked sideways at him and saw those eyes turn to ice. She hadn't seen so much of that look lately.

Pa didn't yell back. Instead, he stroked his whiskered face. "You're part of my family now, Coulter. Maybe I finally have a son who knows how to build something out here. Maybe I can finally take some pride in my family. But Bailey's brand oughta be on your cattle. The Double W could come to mean something out here. It's Bailey's name, but it stands for Jimmy too, and also me. All the Wilde family. Wilde would make a fearsome name for a ranch."

Bailey's brand was two Ws, one on top of the other.

Just the thought of her husband giving up his C Bar brand made Bailey want to laugh. To name his cattle after his wife was real unlikely, but after his cranky father-in-law and an unknown, long-dead brother-in-law?

Bailey couldn't control a grin when she said, "Double W means Wilde Women, Pa."

Pa recoiled like someone had laid a whip across his back. "No, it don't. That second W is for Jimmy. I've said it plenty of times."

"And I've heard you say it, Pa, but your words don't mean much to me. I registered that brand at Fort Boise as the Wilde Women Ranch. Double W. Do you really want a ranch named after your daughters?" Bailey wondered if Pa had ever said the word *daughters*.

"What is the meaning of this?" Ma Coulter came up beside Gage on the side Bailey wasn't on. Her tone and eyes were as icy as Gage's. Maybe the two of them working together could cool Pa down.

Pa was still blubbering over the Wilde Women Ranch when he turned to Ma. "Who are you?"

At least Pa didn't come up with some phony manners that he'd never shown before.

"This is my mother, Mrs. Coulter." Gage sounded like he didn't want Pa knowing his mother's first name. "Ma, this is Bailey's pa, Cudgel Wilde."

"And you are interrupting our meal, Mr. Wilde. Your manners will not add to our ability to digest the food, so you are not invited to join us. Please be on your way."

Bailey had never heard such a politely delivered insult in her life.

Pa scowled at Ma Coulter. "I will *not* be on my way. I let the others give up, but not Bailey."

He turned to her, and she saw something in his eyes she'd never seen before. A desperate man who'd been . . . hurt. Pa with hurt feelings? Bailey couldn't quite imagine it. Pa was always angry. Selfish. Even his grief over Jimmy was laced with rage and a need to strike out at the world. Bailey had always thought that under her father's unkindness was just a hint of madness.

But hurt? It kicked over something deep inside her, and love for her pa spilled out.

She'd never seen him in a state where she had any hope that he loved her. But right now she hoped.

It was useless, but even so, Bailey pressed a hand to Gage's chest and said, "Let me talk to him, please."

Gage grunted, but he let her take Pa's arm. She gently turned him, and they walked the few paces to the door. "Pa, I liked the idea of building a ranch together out here.

You know I did. But I can't live my whole life building something for my brother. I have to build something for myself. And marrying Gage is a kind of building." Bailey almost choked on the words, yet she forced herself to say them. "Can't you be happy for me, Pa? I'd like that because . . ." She swallowed hard and forced the words out. "Because I love you, Pa."

Pa lifted his eyes to meet hers. She couldn't remember ever saying those words before, and it felt like the greatest risk of her life . . . and that counted her time in the war. "We're family, and Gage is our family too now. He's got this big well-run ranch, and you're part of that. We did it. We're part of something grand. Can't you be satisfied with that? Why not make friends here? Jimmy's been gone for nearly five years. Why not enjoy the living and put aside your grief?"

Pa's eyes, so much like her own, seemed to lose the anger he carried like stones. He looked at her, really looked at her. He seemed to notice her longer hair, her feminine clothes.

It might well be that Pa had truly gotten to thinking of her as another son. Of course, not the son he wanted. Jimmy was dead. But for a second she thought he saw her as she was and had, buried somewhere deep, a father's heart for her.

Then he shook his head as if to shed any weakness. His eyes flashed with such rage, Bailey backed up. "You've betrayed me, girl. You're a coward who won't do what needs to be done. You picked Coulter over your brother." He leaned close so that only she could hear him. "I regret every day my son died in that war and the rest of my young'uns made it through."

"Pa!" Had her own father just told her he wished her dead? She was speechless. And to call her a coward for marrying. When marrying Gage had taken every ounce of her courage! When even now she was in terrible pain, which she'd endured to protect Gage.

Pa had no idea what she'd been through in the war. Of course, he'd never asked, and when she'd tried to tell him, he'd told her to stop whining.

Bailey didn't know how she looked, but Gage noticed how hard the words had hit, because he was at her side instantly and he had no trouble speaking. Sounding strong and far too calm for how fast he moved, he said, "If you want a dynasty in honor of your son, you're going to have to build it yourself."

Pa glared at Gage with pure hatred. Next, Pa's rattle-snake eyes turned to Bailey. She braced herself for whatever hurtful thing he threw her way. "I saw the way it was going to be last fall." Pa jabbed a finger in her face. "Just you remember, there are more ways than one to build a dynasty." He stormed out and slammed the door behind him.

The love she'd just realized she still had for her pa turned into something dead and gone. She didn't know how to handle the ache in her heart.

He saw the way it was going to be last fall? What did he mean by that? Could Pa . . . ?

Gage ran a hand up and down Bailey's back, drawing her out of her painful thoughts. "You and your sisters turned out mighty good for being raised by him," he said.

That shocked a laugh out of her. Bailey shoved away

her pa's unkindness and made a silent promise to herself never to risk letting him hurt her again.

"I reckon we did." She looked across Gage's broad chest at Ma, fuming with indignation, still staring after Pa. "Thank you for helping us put an end to that. I apologize for my father, but I have no control over him. Let's just hope he's gone for good."

Bailey was struck by her father's last words about more than one way to build a dynasty. What had he meant by that? She shuddered to think.

21

It'd been a week since Gage had gotten married, and in that time he'd never seen his bride outside, except for necessary things. And she'd healed up mighty fast, so she was staying inside for her own reasons. Gage had a feeling it concerned his hired men being close at hand.

So it surprised him when Bailey stepped outside in a swift, furtive way that made him think of an escaping prisoner. She opened the door and closed it quickly and silently behind her.

His wife was making a break for it.

She wore a dress in a dull blue shade. It looked good on her. Great, in fact. Gage remembered buying that cloth at the general store. His wife was wearing a dress he'd provided for her. For some reason that made his chest swell with pride.

She had a matching ribbon in her hair, which fluttered in the spring breeze. There was little snow left and the weather was mild. She wore no coat, so he could enjoy how her dress fit. She moved well. Ma had watched over her all week and fussed like a hen with one chick. Of course, Ma fussed over him the same way, so the one chick wasn't quite right. And Bailey had barely lifted a finger. Ma had seen to it. Whether she admitted it or not, it was exactly what Bailey needed to heal.

And now she'd jumped the fence and was on the loose. She must've been watching for him, because he'd just come out of the barn and she headed straight for him.

She looked around. Even from a distance he could tell she spotted the sentries he had posted. She made note of Manny and another man on horseback, riding toward the far end of the pasture. Then she studied two cowpokes, who ducked into a shed on past the corral. Gage had sent them there to work on a worn-out wagon.

He knew she was wary of the men, and he wondered if she'd waited for them to scatter before she'd come out. What he didn't know was why.

She must've decided they were far enough away, for she started toward him.

Rowdy walked out of the barn and up to Gage.

Her steps faltered.

"Mrs. Coulter is healing up good." Rowdy watched her come as if he were inspecting his doctoring. Bailey had refused to let Rowdy have another look at her wounds.

They'd just come from checking a mare who was about to birth her first foal. Several of them had been in the barn, but Ike had kicked them all out. He said they were making the laboring mama nervous.

214

Ike stayed behind to soothe the skittish filly.

"Can you see if the men need help on that wagon, Rowdy?" Gage didn't look away from Bailey. The blue dress brought out the gold of her eyes. Gage hadn't given much thought to a woman's eyes before, but Bailey's were unusual and so pretty they were worth considerable thought.

"Call me if Ike needs help." Rowdy touched the brim of his hat as Bailey came close. "Howdy, ma'am. Glad to see you up and around."

"I've never thanked you for bandaging me up." She didn't quite manage a smile, but her expression wasn't openly hostile. "Thank you, Rowdy."

He nodded. "Best get to work." He headed for the shed.

Gage waited until he'd gotten out of earshot, then turned to Bailey. "You look really pretty today."

"Don't waste your time with sweet talk, Gage." She crossed her arms.

Gage had to remind himself she'd worn britches and lived as a man most of her life. He'd very much like her to learn to take a compliment as her due.

"No sweet talk, just the plain truth. Did you need something?" He tried to move along the talk so she'd let his compliment stand.

"Yes, I want to talk to you about several things. First of all—"

"Gage, I've got trouble." Ike's voice sounded from inside the barn. "There's only one leg. And the mare is so small, my hand . . ." Ike stepped into view and noticed Bailey. He clamped his mouth shut as if he couldn't speak of such topics in front of a woman. "Sorry, ma'am." Ike had no hat on, but he made a gesture to his head like he'd intended to doff one by way of apology. He had his shirtsleeves rolled up and a frantic look on his face.

Gage charged toward the barn. "If we can't deliver this foal, we'll lose the mare, too."

"We could cut the foal out." Ike stepped back as Gage rushed past him.

"It would kill the mare." Gage got there and saw the hard truth. His mare was flat on her side, in obvious distress and only one leg was visible.

A foal born proper had two legs come out first, followed by the baby's nose. This baby had one leg bent back. No mare could deliver a foal in such a position.

The foal needed to be moved inside the mare, and Gage couldn't help. His hands were larger than Ike's.

"Let me help, Gage. I've delivered—"

"Bailey, go to the house. I don't need a woman distracting me right now." Kneeling behind his pretty mare, there was silence as Gage assessed the situation.

"She's just too small for either of us to work on her," Ike said from behind him.

"I should've never bred her to my stallion, not for her first baby." The mare turned to look over her shoulder at him and whickered softly as if begging him to help.

"Wouldn't make a bit of difference, not in this case. Our choice here is to lose one or both. If we don't cut the foal out of her, they'll both die," Ike said.

A shove knocked Gage all the way to the barn floor. He turned to see Bailey, her hands fisted at her waist. "I can save your horse. My hands are small enough, and I did most of the doctoring of animals on Pa's farm back east."

She lifted her right hand, which had a bandage on it until a couple of days ago. One small, strong, healed-up hand. "I've done it before."

"You have?" Gage shifted his eyes from Bailey to his distressed horse to Ike.

"You think I'm lying? You think I'm hoping I can get this job, even though I have no idea how to do it?" Bailey quit stabbing him to death with her eyes, turned to the distressed mare, and started rolling up her sleeve.

Resisting the urge to stop her, Gage instead got back to his knees just as Bailey crouched beside him.

"This mare isn't a mustang. I've never seen one of them have trouble with a birthing."

"I bought her last fall after I drove my cattle to Fort Boise. One of the soldiers was willing to part with her. She's the only thoroughbred mare I've got, and this foal will be her first and bred to my stallion."

"Well, she's a pretty thing."

The mare was a dark shiny brown with white stockings and a white stripe down her face. Gage had been looking forward to seeing what she and his stallion would produce.

Dropping to her knees by the business end of a birthing mare, Bailey did something Gage had never imagined a woman to do. He really had to change his thinking about women—at least when it came to his wife.

She had to reach past that single leg and push the baby back in, using her muscle against the strength of a straining horse.

"I've found the foal's head. It's bent back," Bailey said.

The horse picked that moment to have a labor pain, and sweat broke out on Bailey's forehead as she bore the agonizing pressure on her arm until the horse relaxed.

"Her other leg is bent back, too." Long minutes passed as Bailey worked hard to line the baby up right.

And all Gage could do was watch and pray.

Bailey's wounds were healed, but this was a glaring reminder that she was still tender. The pressure from the laboring horse was crushing her arm, and the foal wanted to come forward when Bailey needed to push it back.

She did as much as she could when the mare was between contractions, and she'd silently bore it during. There was no winning if she pitted her strength against the strength of a full-grown horse.

Going only by touch, she finally caught hold of the unborn baby's jaw and dragged its whole head around. She felt every bit of that effort in her barely healed right hand. Now she had to do it one more time, with the pinned back leg. It was harder because the leg was stretched straight back and she'd almost get hold, then the horse would move or strain and the slippery baby would get away.

Her muscles screamed in protest as she pushed herself far beyond what she should. Running on pure grit and determination, she kept working, praying with every breath for strength sufficient to the task.

Finally, she got a firm hold on the little one's knee and pulled it forward, then slid her hand on down, without anything shifting out of place, to get the hoof. A solid, steady tug and she had the foal in position.

"There! It should come out the right way now. It was wiggling, even sucked my fingers when I got my hand in its mouth to turn the head. It feels pretty lively."

Bailey scooted backward on her knees and then stood. She fell over backward.

Gage caught her before she sprawled on the barn floor.

Her vision narrowed, and her ears felt hot. Her wounded shoulder burned like fire, and that wasn't the one she'd used on the mare. Her stomach twisted. Her knees wobbled.

"You haven't been well long enough for this." Gage's voice sounded like it came from far away, but his arms were wrapped around her from behind. He pulled her against the length of his body and held her upright.

"What choice did I have?" she said.

Gage grunted and held her just a bit closer. Or had she pressed more firmly against him?

Ike came over with a bucket of warm water and a bar of soap. "You done good work, Mrs. Coulter."

She studied Ike for a minute and decided he meant it. There was no way to deny how upset he'd been about the foal not birthing right. He was a man with a heart for animals, and his kindness with the warm water said that extended to women, too.

The skinny cowpoke could have let it bother him that she'd stepped in, literally shoved Gage aside, and done a man's work. Instead, he sounded pleased. He wanted this mama and baby to live just as badly as she did.

"Go ahead and wash up." Ike set the bucket down on the floor and stepped away.

"Let me loose, Gage." Bailey sounded weak to her own ears.

Gage relaxed his hold slowly.

She bent for the rag thrown over the edge of the bucket, and Gage stopped her.

"Let me help."

Because she was still dizzy enough that she might bend down and just go on headfirst into the bucket, she stopped.

He bathed her arm. She was too worn out to insist on doing it herself.

When her arm was clean and dry, he unrolled her sleeve and buttoned it.

"Your ma made me this dress. Today's the first I've worn it. She's going to be disgusted with me." She looked down at her dress. Getting the stains out was going to be a challenge.

"Your dress is probably ruined." Gage sounded so kind. Then he asked, "Isn't this from the fabric I bought you on the day we got married?"

As if she'd bought dress fabric any other time. "Yep."

Gage leaned down and kissed her gently. "I'll buy you more."

"I'll just wash it. A few stains don't matter."

"It's coming," Ike said.

Bailey had forgotten Ike was here, and she never let down her guard around men enough not to know where they were every second. She saw two little front hooves and the first peek at a white nose. She'd done it. The baby was coming as it ought.

Long, quiet minutes passed, and Bailey gathered herself while they watched the birthing.

The head delivered, and Ike said with excitement, "Look, its eyes are blinking. It's alive."

"You saved my mare and the foal." Gage bent down and kissed her again. "You can have all the dresses you want." He smiled. "And a few you don't want."

Ike stayed back from the mare, letting her finish on her own. As the foal's shoulders and middle inched out, Ike looked up and smiled at Bailey. It occurred to her that she wasn't a bit afraid of him. Was it because she'd decided he was trustworthy? Or was it because Gage was here and he made her feel safe? Or was she just too confounded tired to feel anything?

Gage turned to watch the foal come, slow but steady, into the world. He held Bailey in front of him. She shamelessly used his strength to keep herself upright. Now that things were in order, the baby came in a rush.

"It's a little stallion." Ike dropped to his knees beside the colt. The mother stood with a grunt and turned. Her ears pinned back, and she shook her head at Ike as if to scare him off.

It worked.

"Let's get out of the stall." Gage shifted his hold on Bailey and urged her away from the nervous new mama.

Ike came right behind them and swung the stall door shut. Once they were out, the mare turned to the foal and nuzzled it.

"That's a beautiful mare," Bailey said as she studied the long legs and sleek muscles of the mare for the first time—at least the first time since she and the horse were standing upright. "I see why you bought her. I'm glad we could pull her through."

"It's a big baby." Ike leaned his crossed arms on the top of the stable railing. Gage and Bailey stood beside him, watching the mother take care of her little one.

The colt lifted its head, and the mother crooned a soft sound and licked her baby.

"He's the chestnut color of his daddy but with his mother's white face and white stockings. If he grows up to look like her with the strong build of his sire, he'll be worth a fortune." Ike looked at Bailey. "And it's due to your help, ma'am. You're a fine hand with animals. Do you know a lot of doctoring tricks?"

Bailey shrugged. "I've handled a lot of horses and cows."

She was between Ike and Gage, and she was only distantly aware she'd moved as close to Gage as she could get.

Gage's strong arm wrapped around her back. "Let's leave them alone for a while. You need to get off your feet, Bailey. This was too much to ask of you."

"You have to protect your animals. God gave us dominion over them. That means they're in our care. I found the strength because it was necessary."

As they walked to the house, Bailey realized she was leaning almost completely on Gage. She wasn't sure she'd have made it if not for him.

"Oh, I just remembered. I came out here to begin with so I could talk with you without Ma listening." They were almost to the house.

Gage stopped, turned to face her. "What is it?" He leaned closer, attentive, warm. So solid.

"I w-wanted to . . ." His hand had been around her back. Now it slid to her waist on one side, right where she'd been hurt. She flinched.

He glanced down and slid his hand up, then up a bit more until it made her shiver, but she wasn't one bit cold.

"I hurt you." His concern was like a caress on her un-touched, lonely heart.

"No, it was nothing. But thank you for caring."

"Of course I care." His brow knit, and he frowned as if he couldn't imagine someone not caring.

Bailey could imagine it all too well.

His eyes seemed to look inside her, study her, wonder about her. She looked into those gray eyes and wondered back. His other hand, on her upper arm, not the injured one, slid up to her shoulder, then her neck.

"Bailey," he whispered as he pulled her closer and low-ered his head.

The back door of the cabin popped open. Ma cried out, "Bailey, you should not be out yet. You're still healing."

Gage almost jumped away from her and took a nervous look at his ma.

"I'm fine, Ma," she said.

"You've got blood on your new dress." Ma wrung her hands. She sounded genuinely concerned for Bailey, but was she? Or was she worried about the dress being ruined? Or her son being too close to his wife?

"I helped deliver a colt."

"You what?" Ma gave a squawk. "Working in the barn

is for the men. Come in at once. I'll help you get changed. Why, I just finished making that for you. I'll hurry and wash it before the stains set."

Bailey suspected it was too late for the stains.

"And you shouldn't be out and about. You aren't strong enough."

Bailey wished her husband would tell his ma that having Bailey help with the foaling had been important and he supported it. She wished he'd say she was the strongest woman he'd ever known and he was proud of that. Instead, he looked worried about her, and maybe he was worried about the dress too, after his ma's work on it.

She spared him a narrow-eyed look.

With a shrug so tiny, Ma couldn't see it, but Bailey sure did, he slid an arm around her back and urged her forward. "Yep, you need to get inside, clean up, and rest."

Gage seemed helpless to do anything other than go along with his mother. Leaning close as they neared Ma, Bailey muttered, "You obey your Ma, but you don't seem to have any trouble refusing to do things my way. Why is that?"

Gage didn't answer, just kept moving forward. Then they were too close and Bailey had to stop talking. She was sure that was exactly what he intended.

And she was too worn out to grab the man and shake him, not to mention what Ma would make of that.

Ma rushed forward, caught Bailey's arm as if to keep her from collapsing. Gage let go and stepped back. Ma hustled Bailey toward the house.

Gage said, "I'll have another look at the colt before I come in for supper." Which was two hours away. He left her in Ma's care. The coward was gone before Bailey could say a word.

Ma badgered her the whole time she helped her clean up, as she so often did. Sounding concerned but using words that left little cuts in Bailey's heart. It was so familiar to be criticized, she tried to pay it no mind. Pa had never let up. But coming from Ma Coulter and laced with concern and help, it left Bailey more wounded than Pa's shouting. Bailey knew she should say something, tell Ma to stop with the hurtful words.

But Bailey couldn't manage much herself. And Ma was the only one around, so Bailey endured Ma's veiled insults over doing such an unladylike thing as assist when a baby animal was born. For a woman from a Texas ranch, Ma seemed overly upset about the mess.

Finally, the scolding was over and Bailey was back in a clean dress. She found herself right back to sitting at the table—where she'd been slowly going mad with boredom all week.

At least Ma didn't make her stay in bed.

It was only after she rested awhile when her energy returned enough to remember she'd seen all those men leave Gage behind and she'd rushed out to talk to him. He was always surrounded by a crowd of men when he was outside.

She'd wanted to know how the investigation was going. She wanted to check over his stallion and see how he was healing, and she'd wanted to tell Gage she was ready to ride over to her homestead and check her cattle. Surely the trails were open by now. Yes, Gage could send men over there, but she wanted to go herself.

More than anything, she wanted a few hours away from Ma's sharp little claws.

Of course, she had no gumption left to do such a thing today, but she'd been up to it until she had to deliver a foal.

Ma was probably going to throw a fit over Bailey wanting to see her old homestead. She wouldn't approve that Bailey had lived there alone, and God save them all if Ma found out Bailey had worn britches.

That was Bailey's reason for wanting to talk to Gage when he was outside, but not when he was surrounded by his men.

She could whisper her questions to him at night, except she'd been falling asleep hard the moment she lay down every night.

Tonight, she promised herself, she'd stay awake and have a talk with him. It had to be better than standing by a window hoping all his men would go away and he would stay. Because she wasn't going out there to talk to him when they were around.

"Gage, I need to talk to you."

Gage's eyes shot open. His wife was awake. He'd been coming in as soon as possible at night, after giving her privacy to change, hoping to get a bit of her attention and maybe a good-night kiss.

But every night she'd already dropped down into that bed before he got here and as good as passed out. He knew she was still healing. With her wounds and her blood loss, she needed sleep to mend, so he understood. But he couldn't believe he slept next to his pretty wife night after night and never spoke to her.

Watching her be so injured, realizing how strong and heroic she was to stand over him with a rifle when she was wounded, knowing she was inside putting up with Ma while Gage could go hide by working long hours. The more he knew the true measure of this woman, the more he wanted to spend time with her and let her know his feelings were warm and growing warmer every day.

He could tell her none of this, because she fell asleep on him. It wore on a man. And now here she was, awake.

"What is it?" He rolled onto his side and propped his head up on his fist.

It was a perfect spring night, the full moon and blazing stars making the outside almost as bright as day. The glow streamed in from the window behind Gage's back. He was careful not to hover too close so that he shaded her face. He wanted to see those golden eyes turn silver in the light of the night sky. He rested a hand on her middle and enjoyed the movement as her breath rose and fell. He looked down at her, eager to hear every word.

"I've wanted to talk to you, but I've been so tired at night and I had things that couldn't be said in front of your ma. Today when I came out—"

"You ended up saving my new colt instead of getting to talk." Gage's hand flexed on her belly. She felt so alive under his hand. "I sure appreciate that, Bailey. You were there when I needed help. You knew what to do and had the skill to do it well."

And what was a man to do when thanking his wife

kindly for doing something so fine? He leaned down and kissed her. He meant to just brush her lips. A gentle kiss and then they'd go back to their talk. He wanted to talk with her, too.

Then she kissed him back and thoughts of talking fled. He deepened the kiss and moved closer until he had her nearly tucked beneath him. Her hand rested on his arm, and he got hold of himself, prepared to be wise and give her more time to heal, more time to know him better.

He lifted himself away, amazed at just how close he'd gotten.

"Come back, Gage. Don't give me time to think." Her strong, clever, lifesaving hand slid slowly up his arm, over his shoulder, and behind his head. Her fingers sank deep into his hair.

But the fear in her voice—perhaps unfortunately—brought Gage to his senses, and he reached for her hand and unwound it from his hair. Feeling like a fool to stop her, he brought her hand around and kissed it.

Her eyes glittered. She tried to get away. She was thinking and she'd asked him not to let her. But he didn't want passion to flare up between them when instead there should be honesty, and her fearful request and the grip of her hand reminded him that he'd always known there were deep secrets inside Bailey. And until she could talk them through, he didn't think she'd be able to lay them down.

In fact, she'd just proven she'd rather make their marriage real in all ways than have the talk that was long overdue.

"Why do you say that? 'Don't give me time to think.' Think about what?"

She shook her head frantically and pulled away. Caging her with both hands, he didn't let his weight settle on her. Whatever her fear—and he had an awful dread for what it might be—if he physically restrained her, it might turn her against him for good.

"Gage, let me go. If you don't want me to give you wifely attentions, that's f-fine." Her voice broke, and she fell silent. He was far enough away that he could see her eyes, as dry as a desert. She never cried.

"What is it that's kept you a near prisoner in this house since you came here? You don't like being around my men. Tell me why." He kissed her again with aching gentleness. "Please."

He fell silent and waited. She wasn't going anywhere until they got this settled. Because the other part of this night, something he now realized he wanted very badly, could not begin until he knew what haunted her.

*M*aybe if he'd shouted.

Maybe if he'd pinned her down.

Maybe if he'd goaded her or even insulted her like her pa did all the time.

Maybe then she could have kept silent.

Instead, he'd offered her warm, gentle kisses that awakened the womanly side of herself, something that confused her terribly because she'd always considered what passed between a man and woman to be an ugly thing. That was the only way she'd ever seen it, and now she was taken aback at how strongly she was drawn to him. And then he'd—

"You controlled yourself," she said.

Gage's eyes narrowed. "Bailey, I'm not going to let you rush into something you fear. I'd hate for passion to ignite between us and sweep us along, only to have you regret it afterward."

Bailey reached a hand up to touch him on the temple, beside one of his gray eyes. "Control. That's what I've always thought of when looking into your eyes. Icy control."

"Back in Texas, when I wouldn't go to war, I had to listen to some folks say terrible things to me and I didn't dare fight back. I reckon I learned to control myself."

"I considered that cold control your worst flaw, but right now I thank God for it, because . . . because you're right. I might have regretted it later." She might even regret it during, and what passed between them could become a nightmare for her . . . to go with the others she had.

"If you consider self-control something to thank God for, then I might just be the best husband you could have ever found."

"And God arranged for me to find you."

Gage grimaced. "By sending Ma for a visit?"

Bailey almost smiled. "I can't imagine much else that would have convinced you to ask me. And the bribe you offered, well, that got me to say yes. God knew He was dealing with a stubborn pair."

"Tell me, Bailey. Get your fears out where we can both see them. If that doesn't get shut of them, then at least I can share the weight of them with you."

She drew her finger down his cheek and touched the corner of his lips. "I'll try."

He bent over and kissed her, then eased back, waiting. Patient. Controlled.

It was a story that she'd vowed to never speak of, but the solitary way she lived . . . who had she ever talked with anyway? Her sisters? She would die before she'd lay her burdens on their already overburdened hearts. But Gage was strong enough to hear it.

"Kylie managed to get herself assigned as a secretary of sorts to an officer. That got her out of most of the battles. Shannon found herself in the medical corps. She still saw terrible things, but she'd go to work on the injured after the cannons quit firing."

Gage shook his head slowly. "All three of you went to war. Your pa oughta be strung up for that."

"But I never got out of the fighting." Bailey's hands clenched on the front of Gage's nightshirt as she thought of how she'd run into the middle of gunfire. Bayonets. Charging horses. Cannon fire.

"You really went to those battles?" Gage asked.

She knew he was just trying to urge her to speak of the worst of it. She didn't know how to go on. She just didn't.

"And that's why you don't like being around men? Because you were surrounded by them and saw them do such ugly things?"

A humorless laugh escaped her clamped jaw. "That ought to be enough. But I think I got through it all right. I felt like I was fighting for my country, and I saw it as a noble thing. So many of the men were terrified, too. And the company I was with, we all got tough. The terror eased, or maybe we just got used to it. I did come to see the Southern point of view, though. They were fighting for freedom. Not freedom to hold slaves, because most of them weren't slave owners. But freedom from a tyrannical government who could make laws from far away. In some ways the South was fighting for a more American thing than the North. The South saw themselves as repeating the Revolutionary War, while the North was fighting for a powerful government, a royal government like we'd just escaped."

"Did you talk like that to the other soldiers? Were they furious about it and did something to you?"

Bailey touched Gage's mouth with her fingertips. "Let me just get this all said, Gage."

He nodded behind her fingers, and she pulled her hand back and closed it. The warmth of his lips caught and held tight.

"Toward the end of the war, we were assigned to Sherman. I marched right along with him toward the sea, and we destroyed everything. We razed houses and barns, we killed and ate the livestock, we drank our fill from the wells and then we poisoned them. The whole idea was to crush the South, to leave them nothing to live on so they'd quit fighting. We did terrible things and in the midst of that madness I did them, too. I didn't kill any women or children, but many did and I felt the bloodlust of it."

She was silent, wishing she didn't have to tell the end, what left her hollow inside. But it pressed on her to come out, after all this time.

"During one raid, things went wrong and we were pushed back. The Reb troops overran our lines, and in the mayhem I got taken prisoner."

"You were in a prison camp?"

"No, I wasn't held long enough to be moved anywhere. But I got locked up in a house with about a dozen men, all Union soldiers. We were held there in different rooms for maybe two days. I got thrown in the cellar with a couple other men, both badly wounded. There was a woman living in that house. Just an ordinary woman in a nice farmhouse. It was by no means a Southern mansion on a plantation.

"She brought bandages for the injured men and helped me tend them. While we worked, she talked. I got the feeling she'd been alone a long time and hadn't talked to a living soul in ages. She asked how I could fight for tyranny. Fight against the real United States of America. She told me her husband had died in the war and her only brother and her pa. She had nothing left but this home, and we were going to burn it to the ground. Then she talked of terrible things that had happened to people she knew, especially the brutal treatment of women. I knew it was true because I'd seen it with my own eyes.

"By the time she'd said her piece, it made me sick at heart that I'd been a part of it. Then Union troops came and . . ." Bailey's throat went dry, and she wasn't sure the words could get past it. "The men came, and I knew what they'd do to her. I knew she'd endure a horror that might go on . . ." Inhaling and exhaling slowly, Bailey covered her eyes. "She had a gun, and she said, 'I can't bear what they'll do to me.'

"She turned the gun on herself, aimed straight at her heart. Moments passed, and she didn't pull the trigger. Finally she started crying and said, 'I can't do it. I can't kill myself. I'm afraid I'll go to hell.'

"She shoved the gun in my hands just as the door to the cellar slammed open. I recognized the man who was coming in, with a large group behind him. I'd heard this man boast of doing . . . doing exactly what this woman feared. They saw the woman . . ." Her voice faltered.

"Bailey, I'm so sorry," Gage whispered. He pulled her close, rolled onto his back and clutched her tight to his chest.

"We both had a hold of that gun. She held my hand right on it and said, 'Please, do it.' I looked the woman in the eye, and with the door slamming open and that man's brutal eyes on her, without a second to think, I . . ." Bailey slid her hands into her hair, wishing she could tear it from her mind. But the memory was as clear as if it had happened yesterday. "I did it. I killed her. I killed her, and her fear she'd go to hell if she did it herself was cut into my soul, because I think I'll go to hell now because I did. I did a lot of ugly things in that war, in the midst of battle, fighting for my own life. But nothing so awful as when I killed that kind woman, with her love for the Lord, her passion for freedom, her healing hands."

Bailey had never gone a day without thinking of it. "The worst of it is, maybe if I'd told those men I knew so well that I was a woman, maybe my fellow soldiers, there to save me, would have stopped. I know battle made some of them into near animals. But if I'd begged them, they might have come back to themselves. Or—"

Gage cut in, "Or maybe they'd have turned on you, too."

"A thousand times it's run through my head. Two different endings. One, the crowd of soldiers calms down and remembers they're decent men—or had been before the war. The other way, they attacked us both." Bailey looked up at Gage. "And I can't help but wonder if I killed her, not to save her from attack but to save myself from one. Which makes me a terrible coward on top of a murderer. Now every time I'm near a crowd of men, I wait for them to go mad, to turn on any woman within reach."

"Not all men are like that, Bailey."

"I think they are. I think in the right circumstances they can all turn into something more deadly than a pack of wolves."

Gage slid his hand deep into her short curls and lifted her head off his chest. "You know that's not true. I would bet my own life that your brother-in-law, Aaron, never did such a thing. What's more, I'll bet he and many other men like him would have stepped in to protect a Southern woman from his own Northern troops."

Bailey thought of how honorable Aaron was.

"The war seemed endless. God seemed so far away." Suddenly the strength and comfort Gage offered struck her as terribly wrong. She pushed away from him.

"No, Bailey, let me hold you, please."

She shoved harder, and reluctantly he let her go. She swung her legs out of bed and sat, facing away from him. "How can I accept comfort from you when she is dead?"

"She's in paradise and has been for long years. She escaped this hard life."

He sat up behind her and put both arms around her shoulders from behind, but rather than urge her to lean back, he shifted around until he was supporting her without her having to allow it. She knew what he was doing, but she couldn't resist his warmth.

"Maybe I saved her from a fate worse than death at the hands of those men, or maybe I killed her because I was a coward."

Gage leaned forward and pressed his left cheek against her right. "They called me a coward. I left my whole life behind to get away from it." He shifted again until he was beside her. Taking her face in his hands, he kissed her briefly. "It doesn't matter what the right thing was to do in that terrible moment."

"Of course it does."

"Why? What good does it do to torture yourself by wondering what you should have done? It's over. All that's left now is forgiveness. Have you asked God to forgive you?"

"Yes, a thousand times. But the weight is as bad as it ever was." She rested her face on his chest.

"That's not God refusing to forgive you, honey." His arms tightened around her. "It's you refusing to forgive yourself. God's done His part; now you have to do yours."

Bailey looked up. With the moonlight behind him, she could barely make out his features, but those eyes sparkled even in the darkness. A light in the darkness, that's what Gage was offering her. And wasn't that what God promised, too?

"How many believers did Paul kill before the road to Damascus?" Gage asked. "Have you done something worse than that?"

"N-no."

"And do you believe God forgave Paul?"

"Yes, of course He did." Bailey's eyes brimmed with

tears. She never cried, yet her eyes did burn with unshed tears sometimes. "He does forgive me, doesn't He?"

"He does, Bailey." Gage pressed his lips to her forehead. "And maybe He forgives me, too."

Bailey tilted her head back. "You really are the one and only perfect husband for me." She touched Gage's lips with her own.

"Don't say that."

Surprised, Bailey straightened in his arms. "Why not?"

"Because I think if I let you say that, I have to admit that God sent my ma here."

A laugh startled Bailey. Only moments ago she'd thought she might never laugh again.

Gage grinned down at her.

She threw her arms around him. "If God wants us to be married, then let's be married."

"You are the perfect wife, for sure." Gage rolled onto the bed and tucked her beneath him. He swooped his lips down and captured her mouth just like he'd captured her whole life.

23

It was hopeless to wait until she could escape Ma, and Gage could escape his men. Those moments were hard to come by.

And besides, she wasn't sure she needed to escape anymore. She felt as though a massive weight had been lifted off her shoulders. Maybe from talking through her darkest fears with Gage, and maybe from finding one of the sweetest joys of marriage.

Today she was a new woman, or at least almost. The new woman still wanted to check her cows. She was almost fully recovered from her injuries, but Ma was determined to run the house, so there was little Bailey could do inside. So she'd decided to go outside.

Ma had done most of the talking at the breakfast table. When the woman stood to get coffee off the stove, Bailey seized the chance. Oh, she'd had her chance last night, of course. But that ended up very differently than she'd expected. She blushed as she thought of it, and that drove her on to speak. Very carefully, because although Ma was a few steps away, and occupied, she could hear every word.

"I want to get a few things from the cabin," she said.

Gage smiled at her, the warmest smile she'd ever seen on his face. A smile that spoke of intimacies in the night that would bring on another blush if she didn't keep talking.

"And check my cattle," she went on. "If we could ride over there right now, early. I'd appreciate—"

"You just leave that sort of thing to the menfolk, Bailey dear. You're still much too fragile to go riding about the countryside. Would you risk your health in a foolish need to see an old run-down cabin?" Ma came back to the table and began pouring coffee as if the matter were settled.

"But my cabin isn't run down. It's small but built with a lot of skill." Bailey forced herself to let go of the need to defend herself. Explaining to Ma that she was a fine carpenter would only earn her a scolding for her unlady-like ways. "And I want to see for myself how things are over there—"

"Bailey," Gage said, interrupting her when she had some serious nagging to do, "I've had my men checking the trail. I told them not to go in until the snow cleared, and until yesterday they'd come back without getting through. But Manny made it in yesterday. He said the trail is muddy, but the drifts have melted finally. The herd looks good, and he fed the chickens. You've got a bunch of baby chicks. We'll bring them home as soon as we can get a wagon up the trail to your place. A group is riding that way today to take a closer look at the new calves and figure out how soon we need to move the cattle out of the canyon to new grass."

"Why didn't you tell me this last night?"

Gage's eyes smiled. "I meant to, but I got . . . distracted."

Instantly, Bailey remembered their distraction, yet she couldn't recall a single thing she intended to say. Finally she managed, "Well, good. We can go instead and save them some time." Bailey laid down her fork, eager to be on the way.

"They headed out at first light so they're already hours down the trail." In good weather Gage could get to town in an hour, and from town to Bailey's in another two. In poor weather it took much longer.

Gage reached for her hand and held it, there on the table. Right in front of his mother!

"Well, that's fine. We can go . . ." Gage's thumb moved, caressing her palm. Bailey caught her breath and had to fight to finish her sentence. "We c-can go on"—she swallowed hard—"on our own."

Gage grinned. "Today is busy. But we can ride over there real soon. When the men get back, they'll report to me. You can ask them about the herd. After we get your chickens, we can bring any of your furniture home you want. I'm not sure where we'd put it, but—"

She forced herself to say, "I trust you to take care of things. I'd just like to see my place is all."

His thumb kept caressing. Her thoughts scattered, or maybe better to say her thoughts left horse rides and cattle worries to remember their intimacy last night.

". . . bring your . . ."

Bailey saw his lips moving and remembered how tenderly they'd moved when he'd kissed her.

". . . we get what we need . . ."

Was he talking about their time together? With his mother right here? She shook her head to clear it and deny that he'd do such a thing.

". . . including all the babies."

"What babies?" Bailey's hand went to the collar of her dress. How many babies did he want? Could there be one on the way even now?

Bailey took a quick glance at Ma, who turned away with the coffeepot and busied herself at the dry sink. Gage smiled, and for a moment it was there in his eyes. He knew exactly what she was thinking of. Then his eyes followed hers to Ma, her back to the room. He shook his head as if realizing now was not the time, squeezed her hand tightly, and let go.

"Your hens and chicks and the herd is crowded with the spring calves. *Those* babies." His eyes gleamed with humor. He stood from the table. "We'll ride over there soon. In the meantime, do you want to come out and see the foal? The little guy is doing well."

"Babies at my place, babies here. There are babies everywhere." Her voice was a bit hoarse, and she cleared her throat. "I'd love to see the foal."

Gage took her hand for no reason as she rose. She wasn't about to topple over or anything, but that strong hand felt wonderful.

So wonderful, in fact, that just because she so badly did not want to give up this moment with Gage, she recognized her own selfishness. "Ma, you should come out. This foal is a beautiful critter."

Gage clutched her hand and gave her a dismayed look, which wiped off his face the instant he realized his mother was turning around.

She picked up a towel and faced them, drying her hands. "I want to get something on for a noon meal first. You two go on without me." Her gaze dropped to where Gage held on to Bailey, and Ma hesitated before she went on in a motherly voice, scolding, "But, Bailey, for heaven's sake, if a horse is giving birth again, leave it to the men!"

Ma didn't like Gage being close to her, and Bailey wasn't sure why. Gage had said his ma needed to run things. Did she resent Bailey being the woman of the house?

All Ma's cutting insults made Bailey hesitate over everything. Working inside had always just been for simple survival. Bailey could get a meal on, but she had none of the gift for doing it nicely like Ma. And though it was cloaked in kindness, Ma chided Bailey all the time.

Bailey was used to being scolded by Pa, but he was critical to everyone. Ma's criticism was much kinder, yet for some reason it cut all the deeper. And Ma didn't like it when Gage was too attentive to Bailey.

"I won't be gone long," she told Ma. "I'll come and help with dinner after I've seen the colt."

Ma nodded, glanced at their hands again, and turned back to the dishes.

Gage dragged Bailey out the door. They were halfway to the barn when Gage took a quick look back at the cabin and whispered, "Why did you invite her?"

"I invited her because I didn't want to," Bailey said and had to smile about saying such a foolish thing.

Gage stopped so suddenly he almost skidded. "What in tarnation does that mean?" Bailey laughed at his look of confusion. She hadn't done much laughing in a long time.

"What it means is . . ." Leaning close, she undeniably fluttered her lashes, just like Kylie used to. "I wanted to be alone with you so bad." Bailey stole a quick kiss. "It would've been rude not to ask her along."

Gage quirked up one corner of his mouth. "Oh, all right. In that case, I was being rude, too." He kissed her hard and fast. "But I'm still glad she didn't come."

"Gage, she's really been good to me, but . . . well, I've noticed a couple of strange things about her."

Irritation glittered in Gage's eyes. "My ma is fine."

"Yes, she's fine. She doesn't really approve of me, though, and that's with me being as ladylike as I can be. It's not who I am, and it bothers me that she would disapprove of me if she saw me wearing britches."

"Everyone would disapprove if they saw you in britches."

"Including you?" The snap in Bailey's tone drew Gage's attention.

Shrugging, Gage said, "I sort of liked you in them, but you must know it's not a proper way for a woman to dress."

She did know. She should leave off the topic of Ma Coulter; she didn't want to argue with her husband. But they got so little time alone, and after last night, Bailey suspected they weren't going to do much talking at bedtime, either. At least she hoped not.

"It makes every word we say to each other feel like a

lie. Our whole relationship is based on me putting on an act. Your ma would hate the real me."

Frowning, Gage ran his eyes up and down her form. She was wearing another dress made over from Ma's clothes. Bailey was up to four dresses now, counting the one made from the fabric Gage had bought for her. Ma really knew her way around stain removal.

"This is the real you, Bailey. Wearing the britches was the lie."

"No, it wasn't. I liked wearing britches."

"Are you saying you'd have dressed like that if your pa hadn't made you? You'd have gone off to war without him badgering you? You'd have homesteaded as a man without him pressuring you?"

That stopped her. Yes, Pa had badgered and pressured and nagged. Yes, Pa had chosen her form of dress since a young age. But there'd never been a mother in her household to put a stop to such a thing. Would she have chosen it on her own?

For some reason, she wanted to fight with Gage, and it was just possible it was because she'd so enjoyed being held close in the night that she felt too raw, too exposed. Too close to falling in love with a man who'd married her for the ridiculous reason that his mother was coming for a visit.

That chafed. That she might be setting her heart up to be crushed, just as Pa had done so many times.

She'd long ago stopped caring what Pa said and did.

Or had she? She'd let Pa hurt her the day he came to Gage's cabin. Deep inside, hadn't she gone along with

Pa's plans, not without protest, but in her heart had she always hoped Pa would someday love her as much as he'd loved Jimmy?

It horrified Bailey to think of it, because she knew it wasn't ever going to happen. She knew her pa too well.

Leaving that behind, Bailey said, "Did you notice she got riled up when you held my hand? And do you really think it was a coincidence that she came out to get me yesterday just as you kissed me? Your ma is . . . well, I think she's jealous."

Scowling, Gage said, "That don't make no sense."

"She might not describe it that way, but she doesn't like us showing any kind of closeness."

"Why wouldn't Ma want me to be close to you, Bailey? You're my wife."

"I don't understand it, except that she's been away from you for so long she might not want to share you."

"Share me?" Gage shook his head in disgust. "This is the kind of thing womenfolk waste time talking about when they should be cleaning the house. Now, do you want to stand out here yammerin' nonsense about my ma or do you want to check on the foal?"

Honestly, when he put it like that. "Let's check the foal."

He took her hand and began marching toward the barn again.

What could be done with the woman, anyway? Ma wanted to be the center of Gage's life, and if that meant shoving Bailey aside, well . . . up until now Bailey had been too tired to fight the woman for control of the house. And Gage loved his ma, but he was clearly uncomfortable with her fussing. And Bailey wished she could help the older lady get on better with her son, though she had no idea how.

"You can talk to the men and ask them anything you want about your animals and your cabin."

"You just tell me what they report." Bailey had no wish to talk to Gage's men.

They entered the barn just as Gage gave her a hard look. "I think you need to give them a chance, Bailey. After last night, I thought maybe you'd be willing to try."

Swallowing hard, Bailey almost agreed. Then, before she could promise anything, they reached the stall and the little foal sprung to its feet and wobbled.

Gage didn't look. He kept his attention on Bailey, while the active colt was her reprieve. "He's a little champion, isn't he?"

Resting a hand on her arm, he said, "I'd stay beside you at all times. But you can't make decisions based on fear."

"This colt is the future, Gage. Let's pay attention to that and let the past fade."

"Except it hasn't faded for you." Gage's hand tightened on her arm.

Bailey nodded. "Last night helped, Gage."

With a soft laugh, Gage's eyes sparked. "It helped me, too."

She backhanded him gently on the belly. "Let me get used to one thing before we start another."

"I can spend as much time getting used to one thing as you want." He slid a hand up her back and ran his fingers deep into her hair. He tipped her head back.

Ike came whistling into the barn.

They jumped away from each other. Gage let go of her hair as if it were on fire.

"Out checking the baby you saved, Mrs. Coulter?"

A heated look flashed in Gage's eyes, and for a moment Bailey thought he would throw Ike out so they could spend more time alone. Bailey wanted him to.

Rowdy came in leading the thoroughbred stallion. "He threw a shoe, Gage. I'm going to need help putting on a new one. You know this big guy doesn't handle well for anyone but you."

The mother horse whickered at the stallion, but even though she sounded friendly, she rushed to stand between her baby and the rest of the world.

Ma came in next, smiling. "I put the roast on and shaped dough into loaves for rising. I have a few minutes. I can put off the pie for a bit. I'd like to see the new foal."

Gage growled in frustration, but so quietly only Bailey could hear. He gave Bailey a frustrated look, rolled his eyes, and turned to the horse. "She's in here, Ma."

Ma came up and sidled between them. Ma didn't choose where she stood by accident. But that wasn't what stung; it was that Gage didn't protest. He was the one who needed to speak to Ma about the way she interfered and the way she treated Bailey.

True, most of it was while Bailey and Ma were alone, but Gage saw enough of it. In fact, he was seeing it right now.

The three of them faced the foal over the stall door.

Bailey stood there and tried to remember that last night she'd unloaded a lot of her old troubles on her husband, and he'd seemed not to be sickened by her.

In fact, he'd been real friendly.

She'd thought her life was going well.

Now here she stood with Ma planted firmly between them, and Gage trying to force her to talk to his men and refusing to take her to her place. Well, Bailey had been taking care of herself for a long time. She wasn't inclined to ask permission for much.

He rested his arm around Ma's shoulders and pointed at the foal and talked quietly about his dreams for it.

So Gage was no help.

Maybe it was time Bailey quit hoping for help from him and had a long talk directly with her mother-in-law.

24

Their nights together were so wonderful that it took Bailey a few days to notice that Gage was avoiding talking to her.

Night distractions she understood. But during the day he was always surrounded by men outside, and it became clear to Bailey that this was deliberate. He didn't want her embarrassing him by helping out on the ranch, or going to her own place, or investigating the attack.

"Bailey, come away from that window."

Flinching, Bailey fought for patience. How much longer could the woman stay? Bailey needed to get out of this house or she was going to say something that made Ma dislike her something fierce.

She tried to work up the courage to go out and check the foal or take a ride or something—anything to get out of this house. But there were always men. She knew Gage's men weren't dangerous, but they seemed to form a battle line between her and the outdoors.

Gage was using her most painful secret to avoid her. That made him a low-down coyote, and she wasn't about to put up with it. She had to get over this fear. Better yet, maybe she should just go home.

"Please, Bailey, pay attention."

A woman spoke to a child like that. Not her son's wife.

"We need to work on your piecrust."

"My piecrusts are just fine, Ma." They were. In fact, she took pride in them.

"You haven't quite gotten the hang of it. Yours aren't flaky like mine."

Ma insulted her. Gage avoided her. She'd thought she was improving her lot by marrying into this family, but right now she was tempted to be rid of them both. She clamped her jaw shut to keep from telling Ma just that.

"It's not the way my baby boy likes it. Now mind me."

Bailey's temper snapped. She turned from the crowd of men outside to face Ma, caught herself long enough to say a prayer. And then, as if whispered to by God, she knew what she had to say.

"Ma, can you explain something to me?"

"Of course. You know I love nothing better than to help you understand things."

"Why did you have only one child?"

"Why . . . umm . . . well," Ma said, pivoting back to the stove and taking far too long as she poured herself a cup of coffee. "Gage is . . . he's not . . . There were other children, but none survived."

"What? He's never mentioned brothers and sisters." The surprising answer had washed Bailey's temper away.

"He never knew them."

"Them? How many?"

Silence stretched.

"Gage's pa and I were married for nearly fifteen years before Gage was born. I was almost thirty when I met him. My parents died at the Alamo. I was turned over to a family who treated me like a slave. Lashes across my back, chores from morning to night."

Which had been at the root of Ma's horror of war.

"I met Jeremiah quite by chance. Women weren't plentiful. He needed a wife, and there was a spark between us. I convinced him we had to run away. I found myself expecting a child almost immediately. Jeremiah was a kind man. We were both thrilled. The baby came too early and only lived a short time after he was born."

"I'm so sorry. How terribly sad."

"Then another child came and went, and another and another. These babies didn't have a chance, as they came so early . . ." Ma's voice broke.

"And you finally had Gage." Who now lived a thousand miles from her.

"Finally we had our son, healthy and strong as any child ever born. I adored him. I was forty-five when Gage was born, and no more babies came after him. I could bear it, though, because I had him."

Ma had faced the coffeepot all this time. She pulled a kerchief out of her sleeve and mopped her eyes. Then she turned to face Bailey. To her disappointment, there was no softening in Ma's expression. "Such nonsense to talk of old, painful memories. Now, let's get to this piecrust."

"Ma . . ."

"Enough."

"But don't you see—?"

"Bailey!" Ma cut her off with a sharp tone. "If you're the sort of woman who would rather chat than work, then you're not a fit wife for my boy."

That was when Bailey remembered how angry she'd been. "He's not a boy, Ma. You have to stop talking about him like that. He's a strong, wise, adult man, one of the best ranchers around."

"He belongs in Texas."

"And that's what you really want? That's why you came, to take him home to Texas?"

"He belongs with his family."

"I'm his family now. God laid it down in the Good Book. 'A man shall leave his mother, and a woman leave her home.'" Bailey had sure done her part, while Gage was failing miserably.

Ma's face bloomed red. "Don't you try and twist the Scriptures around to keep my son from me."

Gage stepped into the room on those words. He looked between his ma, eyes red from crying, face red from anger, to Bailey. His impatience flared, and he aimed it all at Bailey. "What happened? What did you do?"

Turning to Ma, Bailey said, "Nothing happened. We were talking about—"

"Hush, child." There was fear in Ma's voice, and Bailey remembered Gage knew nothing about the lost babies. Ma didn't want her to tell him. "A decent woman wouldn't air her sharp tongue in front of her husband."

It was then Bailey noticed Gage was filthy. A trickle of blood coursed down from his lip.

"Gage, are you hurt?" Ma spoke before Bailey could. "Come in and sit down. You need doctoring."

"Gage, can I help—"

"Not now, Bailey. Just give me a minute."

Ma threw Bailey a smug look, just in case Bailey wasn't hurt by Gage's impatient tone.

Rushing to her baby boy with a damp cloth, Ma began fussing as Gage smiled up at his favorite woman in the world.

The woman he avoided in the day and seemed all too fond of in the night slipped out of the room unnoticed.

❧

Where was that woman going? Gage wondered.

And why did she have to stir Ma up? Didn't Bailey know Gage needed help dealing with his mother? Instead, she'd upset her and then left Gage to deal with her.

"What happened, son?"

He did love his mother's gentle care.

Ignoring his wife for the moment, he said, "I got kicked by one of the cows I was wrangling. She knocked me backward into a fence, and that's how I split my lip. But no real harm was done."

Ma clucked over him, quickly got him coffee and a slice of pie. And because that cow had really walloped him right in the knee, he let Ma convince him to stay inside until the noon meal.

He wondered where Bailey went, but for right now he wanted quiet more than he wanted to hunt her up.

He'd managed to keep her home for another week, trying to let her heal up, but the woman was well and that was that.

He was going to have to make the long ride over to her cabin soon, and Ma wasn't going to like it. Then Bailey didn't come in to eat with them.

Muttering, he went to their room, assuming she'd been in there pouting. He couldn't find her there, or upstairs either, which meant she'd gone outside. And Bailey never went outside, not without him.

What was that woman up to? "Ma, Bailey's outside somewhere. I'll fetch her in for dinner."

"She should know better than to show up late for a meal."

Gage didn't much like Ma's tone. It sounded a bit too much like the tone he'd heard when he came inside. What had she been saying? He'd barely noticed and had only seen that Ma was upset, while Bailey seemed her usual strong, calm self. Something about twisting the Scriptures.

It had struck Gage as wrong. But what exactly had Bailey said?

"I'll find her and be right back." He stepped from the cabin to a surprise.

"Tucker, you got down out of those mountains?" Gage had forgotten about Tucker. The man usually came down for the summer, and when he was around he often worked for Gage. He'd never brought a woman with him, though.

Shannon.

He'd gotten to thinking of his wife as alone in the world. And if she was alone, then she needed him.

But here were Tucker and Shannon.

"We can't stay, Gage. We only stopped in because we came from the south and we were passing close. Shannon is anxious to see how her sister got through the winter."

"Don't bother. Bailey and I are married." Gage grinned. He couldn't help enjoying unsettling Tucker, who didn't let much surprise him.

Shannon was on the ground after that, and she almost stumbled over her own feet as she pivoted to stare at Gage, the most confused woman who'd ever lived. "Bailey married you?"

"Yep." He waited to see how that would set with the woman. Shannon was dressed like an Indian woman. A doeskin dress. Leggings. He saw at a glance that she was increasing around the middle. And her black hair was long enough she'd managed two very stubby braided pigtails.

"Willingly?" Shannon bristled, reminding Gage of Tucker's tendency to carry hideout knives. Could his wife have taken up the habit, too?

"Of course willingly. And she grew her hair longer and wears a dress all the time now."

Shannon arched one brow as if such a thing were unthinkable. Which Gage understood, honestly.

Tucker dragged his fur hat off his head. "Never did I imagine such a thing."

He dismounted. Gage walked toward him, and the two men shook hands. Tucker flashed his animal white teeth.

"Reckon we're brothers now, Gage."

"That'll be interesting."

Shaking her head, Shannon headed for the house. "I need to talk to her."

It was going to be even harder to find any time alone with his wife. On the other hand, maybe this would keep the woman off the trail to her cabin, which would keep Ma from complaining about Bailey's strange ways. And when Ma was satisfied with Gage's life . . . she'd go home.

After that, Bailey could wear britches all she wanted, except in town. And she probably shouldn't wear them in front of the men, which meant she shouldn't wear them outside, really the only time she wanted to wear them. Yep, being married was complicated.

Gage was glad Tucker was here, if just to distract him from his woman troubles. Which reminded him he had to go hunt up his wife.

"Are Myra and Nev taking good care of Shannon's sheep?" Tucker asked under his breath.

"I have no idea. I made it over to Bailey's one day this spring and brought her out to marry me. It was a mighty hard trail. We got married, and neither of us has been to town since. A man doesn't need to be running into town all the time. And we saw Myra and Nev in town, but we didn't spend one bit of time talking about your stupid sheep."

"Aren't you keeping cattle there? Surely you notice the sheep when you're working your cattle." Tucker sounded indignant, like he'd expected Gage to go over there and inspect Shannon's sheep regularly.

"We moved the cattle off that property last fall and we haven't moved them back yet. I like to save that grass and water for later in the year. Anyway, the trails are just now clearing out. I'm surprised you could get down from the high hills."

"Shannon wouldn't let up. She was worried about Bailey. I think they got locked away from each other last winter, too. Judging by where their homesteads were, I can't imagine they could see each other. But Shannon said she always knew her sister was close and it helped her bear the loneliness. She thought Bailey had to be dying of it by now and would need some company. So we faced some mean trails to get down here."

Tucker rubbed his chin. He had no beard and he always had a beard in the spring. Being married had turned him purely civilized. He turned those sky-blue eyes to Gage. "She really married you willingly?"

Gage didn't like the sharp look. "What do you think I did? Hold a gun on her to make her say her vows?" Gage remembered his very subtle attempt to strangle her to get "I do" out of her mouth, but he didn't mention that to Tucker.

"I reckon that might've worked." Tucker nodded. "I can't imagine much else. That woman was right fond of her homestead and her privacy. But you got that canyon away from her and it didn't leave her much."

"It was my canyon, Tucker. I didn't get it away from anybody. And honestly I think she was lonely just like you said. I showed up there this spring needing a wife. She said yes a lot more easily than I thought she would. I never came close to holding a gun on her."

"And how'd you get her out of those britches?"

Gage had a sudden vision of Bailey in her britches . . . and out of them, then lost the threads of the conversation.

Tucker punched him in the arm. Hard. "What did you do to make her dress like a woman and grow her hair out and leave her homestead, Gage? If you've threatened her or forced her somehow and she doesn't like it, I'll take her side over yours."

"She was wearing a dress and her hair was that long when I came to her door." Gage wanted to punch him back, yet he respected a man who looked to the welfare of his family.

Tucker turned back to watch Shannon near the house. "No foolin'?"

"Nope. And I asked her to leave the britches behind at her cabin, and she did."

"You said you went over there needing a wife. Why is that?"

"I needed a wife because—"

The cabin door swung open. "Come in, come in." Gage's mother stood in the doorway and waved a lace hanky at Shannon. She was almost singing when she hollered, "I've got plenty of food for company."

Gage went on in a glum voice, "Because my mother was coming to visit. I thought having a wife might discourage her moving in permanent." Gage didn't mention his lies, as Tucker wasn't fond of liars.

Ma lifted her voice to reach Gage, her kerchief fluttering all the more. "Come on in, son. I've made pie for dessert. Something you've loved ever since you were a little tyke. And bring your friend."

Gage managed a weak wave back. Shannon and Ma vanished inside.

Tucker turned to Gage, his mouth pinched shut, though he couldn't quite keep the wild amusement out of his eyes. "That's your ma?"

"Yep."

"The one who wouldn't let you fight in the war for fear you'd get scratched?"

Gage didn't even bother to argue with Tucker about that description of events. "Yep."

Tucker shook his head and caught the reins of the horses. "Can I put them up somewhere? I reckon we're going to be staying awhile. If you want, I'll . . ." A laugh broke loose, but Tucker rubbed his mouth and quickly silenced it. "I'll help you plot how to get your ma to go back to Texas."

"Instead of that, why don't you help me find my wife, and after that you can help me find the man who's trying to kill me."

Tucker turned grim. "Tell me what's going on."

"I'll tell you just as soon as I find my wife."

❧

"Bailey ran away from you?" Shannon wasn't even trying to keep her voice down.

Gage dragged her farther from the house. He didn't want Ma to hear this.

"I think she might've gone home to check her cattle. She's been after me to take her, and I . . ." *I wanted to keep her safe at all costs. Wanted her to stay inside and be a lady so that my ma would go home. Wanted to pretend that she was a sweet, obedient, feminine little woman.* "I hadn't gotten around to it yet. It's a busy time at the ranch."

"Too busy to let her ride over to her place?" Shannon really had a way of cutting a man up with her tone.

Gage hoped Tucker was doing all right. "Too busy to go with her. And there's someone who's been pestering me."

"Deadly traps aren't 'pestering,' Gage. Let's ride."

Tucker came out of the barn. He still had his grulla, but he'd found a fresh horse for his extremely pregnant wife. Like the horse was the one who should stay home.

"She can't go."

"I'm going." Shannon didn't bother bickering, but instead swung up onto her horse, big belly and all.

"She's gonna have a baby any minute."

"She's going. I never leave Shannon behind. She don't like it." Tucker mounted up.

Gage looked at Shannon, trying to figure out how to get her down from there.

"Come with us or not. We're going to find your wife. We'll ask her if she's interested in coming home."

"Of course she wants to come home. She just rode over to check her cows."

"Without telling you?" Shannon asked, reining her horse and riding away.

"I didn't pay them much mind, but there were fresh tracks on the trail." Tucker headed after his wife. "She must have heard us coming and ducked into the woods without seeing who we were. Too bad. If she knew Shannon was here, she might've put off leaving you."

"Hey, there's Ma." They were nearly to the trap when Sunrise met them. Here was a woman whom Gage would like to have on hand.

Tucker dismounted and went over to her.

She swung down off her horse with agile grace for anyone, let alone an elderly, stout woman. Sunrise had raised Tucker as her own from a young age, after Tucker's ma died. Tucker thought of her as his ma, and she called him son.

"I was hoping you'd hear I was back and come calling."

"I did hear you were back, though I admit I did not smell you. Shannon must have convinced you that a bath now and then would not kill you."

Tucker laughed, and Gage couldn't help but grin.

"No fur on your face this spring. Being married has civilized you." Sunrise hugged him.

He spun her around until she slapped his shoulders. "You should come up to the high hills with us, Ma. Shannon's got a little one on the way, and I'd like you there to help her."

"Hi, Ma. I'll stay up here. Climbing on and off is a chore." Shannon's face glowed with pleasure.

"When is the baby to come?"

"Next month. We'll be down here that long."

"I'd love the company of a woman during the long winter."

Gage was tiring of the chitchat. He had a wife to corral.

"Are you leaving her alone?" Sunrise asked sharply.

"No, Ma," Tucker said with exaggerated patience. "I've only been gone overnight a handful of times and I took her when I went. She's a tough little thing. But we love you and we both miss you. Think about coming, Ma. We could build you your own cabin or add a room onto mine."

"I'll consider it."

Gage itched to get to Bailey, but Tucker insisted they stop to look at the trap.

"I didn't have much to go on in that avalanche. I had men hurt and I was in the middle of a big job. Then we were snowed away from it before we could try and find a trail. I doubt there's a trail left here you two can follow. My men couldn't find anything the next day, and I've been out here to look at things since then and found nothing. But the trap he set was unusual. Maybe if you look at it, you'll see something you recognize."

Gage led the way into the woods and narrowed his eyes. "It's gone. It was thrown off the trail right here. Some's come back recently."

"Whoever did it must have worried we could trace him through his cruel trap." Sunrise studied the ground. "He took the evidence away."

Tucker came up beside her and knelt. He ran his hand over the ground in silence, then looked sideways at Sunrise and smiled. "He took the evidence, but he left something behind."

"What?" Then Gage looked and even he could see it. "Hoofprints."

"Footprints too." Tucker pointed to one that showed as clear as day. "I've never seen them before, but if I see it again, I'll recognize it. It's a few days old, though it's clear which way he went."

"And his horse's hooves are distinct," Sunrise said, pointing to the trail. A print was visible right where the horse had left the woods for the path.

"Shod, a mustang I would say, because the prints are small but a long-legged one. The man isn't big, either. The prints are not much deeper when he is riding than when he is afoot. And look at this." She plucked at the bark of a tree and held up her hand. "He left a tuft of black fur here."

"His tracks don't show once he's on the trail." Tucker crossed his arms over the cutlass and his powder horn. He carried the same batch of knives and guns he always had. Marriage hadn't civilized him that much. "There have been riders enough to erase them, but he's headed for Aspen Ridge. We should be able to see if he leaves the path."

Gage tried to think of anyone who matched that description. His thoughts immediately went to Mo Simmons.

Shannon had stayed back. She was good on a trail, but she admitted she wasn't a patch on Tucker and Ma. Gage reached the horses and said, "So we're looking for a small man on a tall black mustang."

Gage was reaching for his reins when Shannon's hand shot out and caught his arm. "I know someone who fits that description."

Gage and Tucker both turned to her. Tucker said, "You do?"

"Who is it?" Gage asked.

Shannon gave Gage a bitter look. "It makes sense."

"What makes sense?" Gage sounded ready to explode.

"That the person with tracks like that might try to kill you."

"*Who is it*, Shannon?" Gage didn't like the sorrow he saw etched in her face, just beneath the anger.

"That sounds like Pa."

25

Cudgel looked at the two men he'd found. He'd put
word out he was hiring, and these two were the only
ones who'd turned up. That they'd found their way to his
homestead impressed him enough to make him hire them
on sight. Because getting here wasn't easy.

They were exactly what he needed. A couple of men who
knew the woods, who'd do just about anything for money.

"We need to strike hard and fast. I'll pay you and you'll
take off, leave the country."

"And you'll be the owner of a dynasty?" Ted Gacy
slouched back against the wall. He'd turned out to be a
hard worker. And Cudgel had worked these men hard
already in the few weeks since they'd shown up.

Stark was the lazy one and mean as a rattler. Cudgel
wouldn't have hired him, but he rode with Gacy, and to
fire one was to fire both of them. Much as it choked him to

admit it, they weren't going be that easy to fire. Including after he didn't need them anymore.

"I've got everything set. We need to use every skill we've got, cuz Coulter has his men on alert."

"That's because you did a poor job with that trap. You warned him, and now he's on edge. That's gonna make him harder to get."

"I'm paying you for hard work, ain't I?" Cudgel didn't like saying it plain like that. He didn't consider himself a killer. A landslide wasn't killing. And a fall from a horse wasn't, either. But Cudgel had stayed by that trap he'd set, without thinking it out in plain language, and planned to make sure Coulter died in that fall. When that hadn't worked out, Cudgel was surprised at the relief that he hadn't had to resort to cold-blooded murder.

After all, he wasn't a bad man. He was just trying to protect his family's name and build a legacy for his son. He'd expected help and loyalty from the children he had left.

Instead, each had betrayed him, one by one. He'd half expected it of Kylie, a young'un who'd never known how to behave. He'd been real disappointed in Shannon. She had the makings of a decent rancher, although those sheep would've had to go. He'd let them stay, thinking once the homestead was proved up, it would be time to hold a lamb roast. He'd been mighty upset when Shannon as good as stabbed him in the back, but he still had his toughest and most loyal child — Bailey.

But Coulter getting the canyon back, that had shown Bailey's weakness. After the bungled job of getting rid of Coulter with a rockslide, Cudgel had been snowed away and couldn't do much until spring. Then to ride to Bailey's and find Coulter there. Cudgel had gone reeling at what he'd heard when he'd listened in this spring, with Bailey right in the middle of betraying everything the Wilde family had planned to build. Betraying Jimmy.

Cudgel loved nothing more than remembering his son. Never an hour went by that he didn't think of Jimmy, sometimes even talking to him. A handsome boy, bright and strong, Jimmy had a temper, but Cudgel respected that. He had one himself. Jimmy had grown up to be the man Cudgel wanted him to be. The grief of it, the loss, the pain still cut at him and kept him awake at night and haunted his waking hours. His only goal in life was to do something big enough that Jimmy would be remembered.

And he'd needed his other children's help. It was sickening that they hadn't loved their brother enough to stick with their own pa.

Cudgel setting that trap had been a reckless attempt to put a stop to Bailey's betrayal, but he'd expected Coulter to be riding alone. There'd been three of them. When Coulter's saddle partner aimed that gun into the woods, Cudgel looked right down the barrel. Though no one could've seen into the woods the man, and just going by sound and instinct that rifle had taken a perfect bead. It'd been enough to make Cudgel drop back fast, because if Cudgel had aimed that rifle, he'd have pulled the trigger. He only figured out later that the person riding with Coulter had been Bailey.

He'd dropped back and planned his next move.

It was then he realized that if Coulter died, Bailey would

own his property free and clear, and what one Wilde owned, they all owned.

He'd ridden back to town and spread the word to a couple of men he knew who understood just what Cudgel needed.

Then he'd gone to Coulter's place and given Bailey one last chance.

"Your father? Why would he set an avalanche?" Gage knew the answer to that the second he asked the question. "To keep me out of that canyon. To help preserve his dynasty. I didn't tell you that Cudgel showed up at my ranch the day after Bailey and I got married. He was spitting mad, then tried to talk me into changing my brand to his."

Tucker laughed.

"We wondered at the time how he got out. I admit it never occurred to me that he had set the trap. One day after the accident. How could I not have even considered him? But somehow he figured out we were getting married and got ahead of us on the trail and set a trap."

"He might not have known a thing about the wedding," Tucker said. "He had to be behind the avalanche last fall, too. It stands to reason whoever did one did the other. And you sure as certain weren't sparking Bailey back then."

"If he did know, I reckon he hoped to keep Bailey from marrying me. But he must've found out because he was all set to yell at her. No surprise at all. He knew she'd be there."

"He attacked you and then went back to town and heard the news," Shannon said.

"Yep, and all that makes sense if he was close by, because he's the one who bushwhacked us."

"He could have killed Bailey along with you." Tucker scowled. "Is Cudgel that low-down?"

"Maybe." It made Gage sad to hear Shannon say that about her father. "But whether he knew about the proposal or knew only that he wanted you out of the canyon, he wouldn't have known you got married the same day you asked Bailey to marry you. He thought he still had time to stop you and hopefully get the canyon back under Bailey's control."

"If your pa did know we married," Gage said quietly, "he'd have seen it as a chance to make his daughter a rich widow. Either way, it helps him."

Gage remembered the loud thump at Bailey's house. That had been Cudgel, furious, striking out. "He came to my house and said something about there being more than one way to build a dynasty? I reckon inheriting one would work as well as building one. In fact, it's a sight less work."

Shannon whirled to look around at all the places a man could hide. "If that's right, if Pa is now thinking of inheriting, he might be gunning for you right now, Gage."

"Not gunning," Tucker said. "He's been trying to make it look like an accident."

Gage knew Bailey had a low opinion of men. When she'd spoken of her fears, she blamed it on the war. But with a pa like Cudgel, she'd expected the worst of men before she signed up to fight. He wondered if she'd ever really trust him.

His mother didn't trust him. She'd come all this way

claiming to miss him and want to see him, but by the way she fussed and fed him and tried to run everything, what it really came down to was that she didn't trust him to take care of himself. Her smothering love was why he'd ended up half a nation away from his home. Ma had followed him anyway. Now he had a wife that felt the same way, and she'd run away from him.

One untrusting woman wouldn't leave him alone. Another wouldn't stand by his side.

It was something he couldn't stand to think about.

His voice was so harsh it could have ground glass when he said, "We can hunt Cudgel up later, but right now I need to find my wife. She's not safe out there alone."

26

S he's here." Gage spied his wife, unsaddling her horse in the corral, and breathed a sigh of relief. She looked over her shoulder and glared at him, and his irritation returned.

"Looks like she's planning on staying awhile," Tucker said, sounding amused again.

Gage ignored him and rode for his wife. They were going to get a few things straight between them.

Bailey looked ready to fight as she closed the corral gate. She stormed straight toward him as he swung down. Then she looked past him and saw Shannon, and a smile broke out on her face.

He was struck hard with jealousy.

Nothing he'd ever felt before, but he couldn't deny for one heartbeat that was exactly what he felt.

He wanted that smile. He wanted her to be happy to see him.

He wanted his wife to love him, because . . . because . . .

Even standing still, Gage almost stumbled. He hadn't ever planned on it, but he wanted her smile, her happiness, her love for him. And could that mean anything but that he loved her?

It was like a squirrel banging around inside his head, trying to claw its way out. Love? Bailey Wilde?

God protect me from that woman having that kind of power over me.

As the panic settled, one thing became clear. He could never tell her. She'd just moved three hours away. She'd throw his words right back in his face. And while she was throwing things, she might add in a fist.

Wheeling away from him, she cried, "Shannon!"

Shannon's shocked eyes swept over Bailey's hair and dress. She seemed too surprised to speak, because she didn't so much as squeak, let alone yell and run for her sister. But Bailey was running enough for the both of them. Shannon dismounted, and a second later Bailey threw her arms around her sister's neck. Shannon clung to Bailey, and the two of them set up a squeal that made Gage check to see if Bailey had any hogs around the place.

He couldn't help but smile at their pleasure. Tucker hit the ground as gracefully as a cougar leaping from a tree. His gaze met Gage's. They shared a moment of mutual pleasure in their wives' happiness.

The two women started chattering. Gage only heard a word clearly once in a while. He thought he heard Bailey say "coffee," before the sisters locked arms and headed for the house.

Gage and Tucker followed their women in and watched

silently until the reunion died down. Finally, Shannon told Bailey what they'd decided about Cudgel.

"We're still at least two hours from Pa." Bailey faced Gage for the first time since she'd seen Shannon. "He lives a lot higher up than me, over a twisting trail, through some narrow passes that may still have snow in them. There's a nice mountain valley up there, but getting there is a chore. It's more rugged the farther up you go. I never did figure out how Pa got out of there so early in the season to come to your place. It's no trail to tackle in the dark."

"I think I remember him saying something about there being more than one trail," Gage said.

"He was hollering a lot, so he could've said something like that."

At the table, Shannon sat around the corner from Bailey, with Gage on Bailey's right, straight across from Shannon. Tucker sat at the end, facing Bailey. When Bailey mentioned hollering, Shannon reached over and rested her hand on Bailey's shoulder and looked grim. These girls had all gotten their share of hollering.

"Do you know of more routes up this mountain?" Gage asked.

Bailey and Shannon exchanged a bewildered look, then shook their heads.

"We've always gone up that same trail," Bailey said. "I think a body would have to do some mountain climbing to get there a different way."

"If we're going to get there tonight, we'd better head out." Gage finished his coffee with one long draw.

"We'll have light enough, I hope, to get in, but we'd

be riding back here in full dark." Bailey gave Shannon's round belly a worried look. "We should spend the night here and see Pa in the morning."

"Ma will worry," Gage said. "I never intended to be gone overnight."

Bailey liked to burn him to a cinder with her eyes. Now what was the matter with her?

"We aren't makin' it back to your place tonight, Gage, even if we push hard toward Cudgel's place right now." Tucker sounded sure of himself. "I know his homestead, and it's a rattler of a trail to get up there—nowhere you want to be come nighttime."

Bailey gave Gage such a long hard look, he braced himself. "If you head back now, you could get there before too late. You take care of your ma, and we can handle my pa."

"I'm not going to abandon you." Did she really think he'd do such a thing? It reminded him that his wife didn't trust him.

"It might be best, Gage." Shannon frowned. "It's not that you'd abandon Bailey, but you're the one Pa's tried to hurt. Seeing you might start trouble we don't want."

Cudgel needed to be locked up. If there was any trouble, Gage would be the one starting it. With Gage being the focus of his spite, would Cudgel start shooting? It didn't change Gage's mind, though it did make him feel less insulted.

"I'm going. We'll sleep here and set out in the morning." Then Gage thought of something. "I sent my men over here to work the herd. We'd have met them heading back if they were done."

"They're still in there?" Bailey didn't look happy about that.

"One of them can take a message home."

Bailey nodded. They'd stay here—at her house. She didn't think of Gage's house as hers. Honestly she didn't think of it as his, either. It was Ma Coulter's now. She ran that house. Bailey and Gage had both been reduced to visitors.

Bailey had a lot of time to cool down after she'd left the C Bar. She'd like to try to make her marriage work; she'd probably have to if she had a baby on the way. Heaven knew they'd carried on enough that it was a likely outcome. But first she had to get rid of Gage's meddling mother.

And then she'd seen her house and remembered how much love she'd poured into building a haven for herself. Of course, it wasn't hers anymore. Gage owned it. He'd made promises, but they were only as good as his word. Would he give up the canyon if she asked it of him? She suspected not. Would he toss his mother onto a stagecoach to Texas if she asked it of him? She suspected not.

Instead, he'd turn his considerable will to making her stay with him. But she'd never know if he wanted her for herself, or to placate his ma, or so that he could hang on to this prime piece of land.

"Gage, are you going in to talk to your men?" Bailey asked.

"Yep, right now."

"I'll come along." Her spirits lifted to a ridiculous degree, especially considering that men were involved. "I want to see how my cattle are doing."

"Finally we can have ourselves a little talk, wife."

Bailey felt the clash of their stubbornness and the pull of their attraction. The two were so strong it nearly ripped her in half.

"Now's your chance. But I've told you they're fine. Don't you trust me at all, Bailey?"

What in the world did trust have to do with any of this? "I'm sure your men are good cowpokes. I'm just used to taking care of things myself."

Shannon said, "I'll stay inside. It's been a long ride. There's not a crust of bread in this house. Tucker, fetch your pack off Gru. I'll get a meal started."

"I will get Tucker's pack and my own, and will help with supper," Sunrise said, then was out the front door.

After they left, Bailey wondered just how tired her sister was. She decided that Shannon should stay here tomorrow while she rode over to see Pa. Shaking her head as if to shed thoughts of just how far Pa had sunk—if they were right about who'd tried to kill Gage—she walked toward the canyon with Gage at her side.

Five of Gage's men had gathered off to one side and were busy saddling their horses. They must have finished with the cattle. There were longhorns spread all around, standing belly-deep in the grass. Dozens of calves leapt to their feet when Bailey and Gage rode in. The calves trotted toward their mothers for a reassuring nip of milk. One old cow raised her brown, speckled head, woofed at them, and waved her seven-foot spread of horns to warn them away. The rest kept munching on the lush grass.

It was a place that could challenge Eden for its beauty. Bailey had wanted it from the first moment she'd seen it. She recognized that it was pure greed. She'd known Gage owned it and had chosen her homestead carefully.

"I don't blame you for wanting this place, Bailey." She turned, and Gage was grinning at her. "I know just how you feel."

Reluctantly she smiled back. "I guess we both own it now."

"Nope, it's yours. I'd be proud to help you tend it."

Nodding silently, she turned back to study the cows, eager to see how hers were doing. Her eyes scanned and scanned as she searched for the Double W brand.

The cowhands came riding up. Gage turned his horse so that he was right beside her. Protecting her even without her showing a bit of fear. And she didn't feel much, for this was the first time she'd been near a crowd of men since she'd talked with Gage about her war experience. Now, did that mean the wounds she carried in her head had healed, or did she just feel safe so long as her husband was nearby?

A prayer for true healing came to mind.

"We didn't know you were riding over today, Gage," Manny said, who seemed to be the one in charge of the group.

"Bailey and I are going to stay here tonight and go see her pa tomorrow. Tucker's with me. Can you let my ma know I won't be home tonight?"

Manny's eyes widened in what Bailey suspected was fear.

Ma had all the hands running scared. "Sure, boss, I'll tell her." Manny tugged the brim of his hat and lifted his reins.

Before he could go, Bailey asked, "How are my cows? I haven't picked them out yet."

"Your cows, Mrs. Coulter?" Manny's brow furrowed. "Don't they all belong to the two of you?"

Bailey actually smiled. "Yes, of course they do, but I mean the ones I had before Gage and I got married. The ones with the Double W brand. All the calves were born before I left, but I just wondered if you noticed them. Did you do any branding yet?"

Manny looked sideways at the other men. "Did any of you notice a Double W brand?"

The men looked between each other nervously. They shook their heads.

Manny turned back to Bailey. "I didn't think I would have missed a cow with a different brand. There aren't any cattle in here except C Bar."

Bailey peered again at the herd. There were so many. Gage probably had over five hundred cattle here, and a good bunch of them had borne calves. That made a thousand critters to study, all spread out over miles.

"Are you telling me," Gage said, his voice cutting through the thin mountain air, "that in the times you've been over here, you've never noticed a single cow with Bailey's brand? It's two Ws, one over the other."

"You said to check the cows, boss, and we did. You never mentioned we'd be looking for that brand. There wasn't a brand with two Ws around here last fall, and there hasn't been a single one this spring."

Bailey kicked her horse to ride toward the herd.

"It's no use, Bailey." Gage's voice rang out with command, and she couldn't stop the impulse to rein in her horse and turn back to him. It annoyed her that she'd obeyed him. But he was used to running things, and right now he was in charge. "If my men said they didn't see one, then they didn't."

Bailey looked from Gage to Manny. "Where did my cows go?" Her eyes met Gage's, and she knew the answer to her own question. "Pa took them."

❦

"How long we gotta wait, Wilde?" Gacy was a restless man. Tall and skinny, with blue eyes that gleamed with impatience. The man never sat still.

"I told you Coulter would come. We're keeping watch on the gap, ready for him. When he comes, you cut him down and be on your way. I'll give you all fifty of the cows we brought over from the other homestead."

Fifty cows were worth twenty-five dollars a head. A fortune, and these two coyotes knew it. They'd never had a bigger payday in their lives.

"It's my turn to stand watch. Stark is as tired of this as I am. And he's the mean one of the two of us. Me, I'm a thinkin' man, but Stark is ready to fight at the drop of a hat, and he's been known to drop the hat himself. You oughta just let us go get Coulter, have done with it. You're makin' this harder than it needs to be, Wilde."

Shaking his head, Cudgel said, "You told me he had too many sentries and was riding careful. I gave you a chance to settle things the first week you were here."

"And I didn't take it, I know, but I'm tired of biding my time. We'll go back, and this time we'll do it right."

"No, I've baited a trap right here." Cudgel pointed to the cabin he'd built. His young'uns had helped, yet Cudgel had ramrodded the building. It had been done right. But he'd never done another thing to the house. He lived as though it were a trail camp, only with a roof over his head. He slept on a pallet made up on the floor, ate beans heated in the fireplace. He took his meal right out of the pot, the only one he owned. He didn't have time or the money for fripperies.

Paying these men off with the herd he'd brought home from Bailey's stung, but if they did their job right, Cudgel would be the proud owner of ten thousand head of cattle, or whatever Coulter's count was up to now. And giving them whatever money they could earn selling the herd made them ride off. They had to drive them somewhere to sell them.

Cudgel figured it'd clear them out. Afterward he'd go console Bailey, then move right into Coulter's house and take over.

He'd have his dynasty.

<hr>

Bailey wanted to scream and rage and maybe hit someone. But screaming never solved anything, and the one she wanted to hit wasn't here and it made no sense to hit Gage. She tried to let the words out in a rational tone.

"Why would he come in here and steal my cows?" Her voice started climbing, and she clamped her mouth shut until she could control it. Breathing in and out slowly, she went on, "Can you imagine how hard he worked to cut them out of the herd? No regular rustler would have done it. He'd have taken yours along with mine, or if he only thought to skim off a few head in the hopes of not being found out, he'd have taken whatever cows were easy to herd away. Cutting out my cows . . ." She shut up again before she started shouting.

There was silence in the canyon. Bailey wanted to storm at Gage to say something, but he was busy thinking. She'd married a smart man. A man she respected enough to sit quietly, waiting to see what he'd think up. His eyes were ice-cold. He was as mad as she was.

Finally, he dragged his Stetson off his head and muttered something under his breath. Considering the angry tone, Bailey probably didn't want to hear what he said, so she didn't ask him to repeat it.

He used the hat to swat his thigh. With a disgusted growl he said, "You men ride on home and pass the message on to my ma."

"If you're talking about trouble with Cudgel Wilde, you might want some of us to ride along with you tomorrow, Gage." Manny spoke as if he'd had a run-in before with Pa.

Gage shook his head. "I reckon Bailey and I, with Tucker along, can handle one cantankerous old cattle rustler. You men get on home."

They took their orders from Gage just like any other day, whether they thought he had the right of it or not. Bailey heard some grumbling, but they rode out nonetheless.

Gage waited until the men were out of sight before he turned to Bailey. "Now we've got another reason to go see your pa."

27

Gage was saddling horses when Bailey came striding out of the cabin wearing britches. She had a defiant expression on her face, like she expected him to protest. Instead he smiled. That woman made a pair of britches look mighty good.

Next came Shannon, who looked rounder every time Gage saw her.

Tucker frowned. "I told you to stay here, honey. You can't go for another day's long ride. It ain't good for the baby."

Shannon got that wide-eyed hurt look again. Gage took a quick glance at Bailey, hoping she wasn't watching. He didn't think he'd be able to deny her anything if she looked at him that way.

"I'll stay if you stay with me, Tucker." Shannon patted Sunrise on the arm. Sunrise looked none too pleased with the situation, either.

At least the hugely pregnant woman let Gage saddle her horse.

Tucker accepted his fate and rode into the canyon to see if he could pick up any sign of the rustlers. Gage heard him coming back at a fast clip. Too fast.

Gage spun to see what Tucker had found that upset him. Sunrise was watching him, too. It only took a few seconds for Shannon and Bailey to realize something was wrong as they watched for Tucker to emerge.

"It was after dark when you and Bailey came in and told us about Cudgel rustling her cattle." Tucker leapt off his grulla. "I didn't think of it right away, but Bailey had fifty head of cattle, and Cudgel couldn't have driven them out of the canyon without leaving enough sign your men would have noticed the first time they rode over. And we'd have seen it when we rode into the yard."

"They're not in there, Tucker." Bailey sounded mighty cranky. Gage had married himself a spitfire.

"Nope, but they didn't come out through here."

"And there's only one other way out of that canyon," Gage said.

Tucker arched his brows. "He used the trail you blasted open."

"He knew all about that trail because he set off the avalanche," Bailey said. "And while he was making his plans last fall, he found another way into his place from over there. I only knew one way to get to his homestead— through a gap that fills deep with snow and melts mighty slow. I've been trying to figure out how he got out of there early enough to know Gage proposed to me."

Shannon said, "I just thought if Pa got through it, we'd be able to."

"Let's ride, Tucker. We're burning daylight." Gage swung up on his horse. He almost smiled as he watched Tucker help Shannon onto her mustang. The little woman was probably just fine climbing on.

"Tucker, you think she needs help climbing on her horse, but you're lettin' her ride into the middle of a fight. That don't make no sense."

"Lettin' her?" Tucker snorted like a grumpy horse.

Gage had taken his turn trying to convince all the women to stay behind, but he wasn't going to bother anymore. He reined his horse toward the canyon. If Cudgel used this route and drove fifty head of cattle over it, then they'd have no trouble following him.

They rode up and over the canyon rim, and Gage had to admit there was little evidence of a herd coming this way. Cudgel had worked to cover the signs. But once over the saddleback Gage had blasted, the stolen herd was easy to track.

Tucker rode up beside him after only a few yards. "Three men, Gage. Cudgel has hired some help."

Gage hadn't even checked. He looked at Tucker, then glanced back and saw that Bailey and Shannon had moved up close behind him, riding side by side. They were listening to every word. Well, he'd accepted by now that Bailey didn't trust him.

And wasn't that just exactly what he'd decided was the biggest problem keeping his wife from being happily married? Not trusting men? He decided then and there that no matter how bad the news, Bailey was going to hear every word of it. And why not? His wife was as tough as a bootheel.

"Three men, not one old man alone." He met Bailey's eyes with his. "Thanks, Tucker. I'm mad enough to chew up nails and spit bullets. I need to calm down and be more careful. You think they'll be watching this trail?"

Tucker jerked one shoulder in a shrug. "Depends if he drove them straight to market, planning to take the money and start up somewhere else, or he took them to lure you to another trap."

Gage considered that for about three seconds. "It's a trap."

From a few paces behind, Bailey said, "Bushwhacking seems to be his style."

"Ma, come up here." Tucker pulled his grulla to a halt for Sunrise to catch up with him, and everyone stopped. "We're all leaving the trail. I don't want to ride straight for Shannon's dear old daddy."

"Don't blame me for the way he turned out. I didn't raise him." Shannon rested her hand on her stomach, and to Gage it looked like she took a minute to pray for her little one. Or maybe to pray for herself that she'd be a better parent to this child than what she'd had. That shouldn't be too hard.

"Gage, we're easy pickings here. We need to slip up on him by surprise, and I don't think we can do that in a group of five. There are three ways to Cudgel's cabin from here—an uphill trail to the north, and two to the south. We have to cover all of them, because they all have good spots for a lookout and we can't know where Cudgel might have posted them."

"You mean *if* he posted them," Bailey said. "Pa's not usually that careful."

"He's not usually a cattle rustler, either," Gage said.

Bailey nodded. "Good point."

"The high trails are rugged, but they don't fill in with snow like the gap Shannon and Bailey know."

"I'll go on the northern uphill side of the trail," Sunrise said.

"Bailey and I'll take this one, and you and Shannon can take the one to the south."

"Be on the lookout, Ma, in case he's got it set to spring another trap."

"And don't forget," Gage said, "he's got two extra men. Cudgel's a yellow-bellied coyote, so he might not come right at you, but we don't know a thing about the men he hired. They're working the cattle well, so maybe they're just regular cowpokes. Still, I wouldn't trust them. So be looking for when the trail stretches below a likely spot for dry-gulching."

"Bailey, if we're trying to sneak in, it's all the more reason to have only a few of us," Gage said. He had to try one more time. "You should go back to the cabin and help Shannon. Let us handle this."

"No," Bailey broke in before Tucker could add his voice to Gage's. "I'm coming with you. This is my pa and we're after my cattle."

"Bailey, I don't—"

"She stays with you, Coulter," Tucker cut him off. "We're done wasting time arguing."

"Thank you," Bailey said, more sarcastically than was needed.

Tucker shook his head helplessly before turning back to Gage. "I know this land, and the first likely places for a lookout are still a ways ahead. But there's a decent trail to the higher ground right here, and I want to get up there where I can see. Gage, there's another one on ahead where a stream flows out of pure red rock."

"I know the spot. I always remember water holes." Gage wasn't as good in these mountains as Tucker, but he'd ridden far and wide searching for good pastureland. That spring flowed year-round, but there was no grass, nothing but aspen growing out of rock for miles. "I'll take it. Now let's go, we're burning daylight."

Tucker smiled. "We'll meet up at Cudgel's cabin and ask dear old pa for a cup of coffee."

"Nope, we'll drag that polecat out of there and his men too if they fight us."

Tucker looked at Shannon. "Are you sure you're up to this? We'll ride a ways, then be on foot. It's rugged land."

"I've . . . I've decided maybe I should go back," she said.

"You have?" Gage wheeled his horse to face her.

Tucker said, "What's wrong?"

"Are you all right, Shannon?" Bailey asked.

All three of them spoke at once and stared in shock at Shannon.

It wasn't in these Wilde women to stay safe at home when there was trouble. Which meant . . .

"Tucker . . ." Shannon's voice was deep and dark and sharp. The tone of it cut Gage to the bone.

292

Tucker reined his horse so close to Shannon they bumped knees.

"The baby's coming." Shannon hadn't been praying for the baby; she'd been feeling a labor pain.

Which meant there was trouble, sure enough.

Tucker's mouth opened and closed, then opened again. "I need to catch Ma."

Shannon's hand shot out to catch Gru's reins. The feisty mare tolerated it, which was only right. Two females . . . no doubt they were in cahoots. "I need to get back to Bailey's house. Now."

"Let me get Ma. You'll need her to help deliver the baby. Then we'll—"

"Now! And we can't take Ma, because Gage and Bailey will need her."

Gage couldn't believe he'd brought a pregnant woman to a gunfight. Surely that was such a big sin that it was written right down in the Bible somewhere. Probably in big letters. He wanted to ride off right now and tackle this whole mess alone. Him against three men, two probably hired guns. That sounded a lot better than staying here with a woman birthing a child.

Bailey grabbed his stallion's reins.

"What?" He jumped, nervous as a cat. He glared at his wife, wondering what the Wilde women had against horses—always grabbing reins.

"You were getting ready to run," she said.

He'd have denied it, but he'd sworn off lying . . . unless his ma really had him cornered.

Shannon said, "Tucker can handle this by himself."

"This? Handle this? What exactly are you saying I can handle, Shannon?" Tucker sounded for all the world like a man who couldn't handle anything.

"I want him with me," Shannon said. "You go arrest Pa and stop by your cabin and introduce him to his grandchild on his way to jail."

Tucker's eyes got real wide. Gage had seen scared horses that looked a lot like Tucker did at the moment. He also might be in some pain, judging by the gritted teeth. Gage was pretty sure Shannon's grip had gone straight through his buckskin coat to sink into his flesh.

In fact, Tucker looked as scared as Gage had ever seen him, which didn't prove much because he'd never seen Tucker scared before. Even so, the man was scared out of his wits.

"We'll do whatever you want, honey." Tucker the Wild Man had turned into an obedient puppy dog.

Gage hadn't seen that coming.

"Shannon," Bailey said, sounding uncertain, "I don't think it's at all proper for a husband to attend to his wife while she's giving birth."

Tucker perked up at that, as if the man had one single shred of concern about being proper.

Bailey swallowed visibly. "I should come, too."

"Go with Gage." Deep and dark and sharp.

Bailey sat still as Shannon and Tucker rode off.

Then they looked at each other.

"I did pretty good with that foal." Bailey sounded just the tiniest bit hurt.

"You might want to go," Gage said. "Sunrise might want

to go. I reckon whether he wants to or not, Tucker's got to go. But I'd rather go on to this gunfight alone than help Shannon deliver that baby. In fact, I'd rather go fight the Civil War single-handedly than deliver that baby."

Bailey nodded. "I said I should go, not that I wanted to."

Gage found a moment of accord with his wife.

Then she said, "Tucker was going up. I'll take that trail."

"No, we're staying together," Gage said.

"You heard Tucker. These trails all lead to high spots, and any of them could have a sentry posted. We have to cover all the trails."

"You're not striking out into the wilderness alone with at least three gunmen out there."

Bailey sat silently, staring at him.

Finally Gage asked, "What? I'm safer with you, too."

"We're going to do this right, Gage. We're going to cover this land like we are supposed to, and get to my pa's house alive and well."

Gage looked at the narrow path Bailey planned on taking, disgusted that she wouldn't let him protect her better. "You don't trust me at all, do you?"

A furrow appeared between her brows. "I trust you more than any man alive, Gage."

That sounded good, but since she trusted no man at all, she might only trust him the tiniest bit and he'd still be ahead of everyone else.

"I never thought for a minute anyone was behind my cattle disappearing but Pa."

"I don't mean you think I'm a rustler; I mean you don't trust me to protect you. You're taking your own path, fighting this fight on your own, instead of staying with me to let me protect you. It wears on a man to have a woman wearing the pants in the family."

Bailey looked down at her clothes.

With a snort of disgust, Gage said, "I'm not talking about your clothes. I'm talking about your attitude. I miss those britches, and I wouldn't mind you wearing them anytime you wanted."

"Except your ma wouldn't like it." Bailey sounded mighty unruly when she said that.

Gage wondered why. "Nope, she surely wouldn't."

Bailey closed her eyes. "I wonder just how long Ma is planning to stay."

Gage wondered that many times a day. "Let's ride."

❦

Gage rode straight for the spring Tucker mentioned and guided his horse up a steep, cracked spot in a high rock wall. This was the way they'd gotten the herd in. There were plenty of tracks left by the cattle, with the ground turning into a narrow passageway between two bluffs. Gage peered up at the top of the bluffs, expecting a shot to ring out any second.

His horse took a step onto sheer red rock, onto a ledge hardly wider than the horse's hoof. Gage could see the cattle had passed this way. Bailey had kept mainly longhorns, good climbers and a fearless breed. So Gage didn't hesitate to give his stallion his head. Besides, Gage had lived in these rugged mountains long enough to know a horse wouldn't willingly continue on a path that went nowhere. If his stallion thought the trail was passable, it most likely was indeed.

He climbed in silence, save for the buffeting wind and the clopping of shod hooves on rock. His horse took a hairpin turn in the trail, and they walked along with rocks higher than his ears on both sides.

He had an itch between his shoulder blades and kept looking forward, back, and overhead.

The trail rose sharply and widened to reveal a small patch of grass. The cattle kept going from here, but it looked like the edge of the mountain was right ahead, where Gage would be able to see down into Cudgel's valley. It was time to get mighty sneaky. Gage picketed his horse there and proceeded on foot.

He walked silently until he nearly reached the top. In fact, his head would have cleared the surrounding rock walls with one more step. Gage dragged his Stetson off his head and picked a spot where a few straggly junipers sheltered the top of the draw.

He inched his head up behind the pines until he spotted a man standing guard. Or rather sitting guard, with his gun leaned at his side.

Gage crouched low and silently drew his gun. He had to get the drop on this sentry, and the man looked to be loafing. He'd tie him up and go on toward Cudgel's.

Gage hoped the man didn't panic and start firing because Gage had never killed anyone and he didn't want to start now.

28

*B*ailey left her mustang behind. She was in thick woods, walking a trail so faint it might've been her imagination.

The aspen had sheltered her as she climbed, but they'd given way to juniper and oak as the ground leveled out to a high mesa. She wound through the forest and the landscape took a downward slope.

That wasn't right. She expected to get to a high spot where she could study the land for sentries. Instead, it looked to be leading her straight to Pa's cabin. The trees started thinning, and in another few yards she'd be in a clearing at the top of a slope that would lead them into the valley Pa had homesteaded.

She moved to the last big tree before the woods mixed with thinner, younger growth and then aspens again. From where she stood, she could see Pa's cabin, and though he didn't have the best grass, his homestead could support a few head. Of course, he had the five or six cows he'd managed to gather since they'd moved in, and he had fifty head from Bailey. The spring grass was grazed thin.

He couldn't keep her cattle. He planned to drive them to market. She took another step, almost out in the open, which wouldn't matter up here, then stopped dead in her tracks.

A man stood watch off to her right, a good two hundred yards away, with a deep gully between them. He was facing the trail they'd have been on if they hadn't split up.

Gage should be on that side of the hill, but then her trail had taken her in unexpected ways. Maybe Gage's had, too. But there should be two of them. And Pa could be out here standing watch, too.

A movement wrangled a smile out of her. Behind the guard about thirty feet away.

Gage.

She had an angle on the man that showed Gage crawling forward behind a wall of rock.

Her husband was going to take care of the guard. She wanted to see it, but the trees blocked part of her view. She needed a better angle. Then one step farther and she sheered away and dropped to the ground, silent as a ghost.

She'd found the second watchman. All she could see was the muzzle of a rifle and nothing else.

And just as she had a good angle on Gage, so did he. His gun was rising, aiming straight at her husband. With no time to slip around, she moved toward that stretch of fire iron.

Seconds ticked loud in her head as she crawled forward, trying to be silent but with not a second to spare.

Any noise from her might warn him. She had her gun out and ready. Though she wanted a sneak attack, if she didn't have time, she prayed the man would hear her and turn away from Gage, even if it meant drawing his gun on her.

Gage surged to his feet.

"Get your hands in the air." Gage's ice-cold voice sliced through the mountain air.

The man jerked to his feet, his gun falling sideways. His hands slowly rose as if he was afraid of doing anything suddenly and maybe making a nervous gunman flinch.

Gage leapt out of the cut he'd climbed in and rushed the man. There was no time to do anything else, even though he'd never found the second man and now he was completely exposed.

Bailey rounded the tree, coming at the lookout from behind, and brought her gun down with all her strength on the man's head. She reached around him and snatched the gun out of his slack fingers before a twitch could trigger it. The man fell forward, facedown.

The noise drew Gage's attention for one brief second, yet that was all the man needed to dive behind the boulder he'd been using as a chair. He brought his gun up and fired without exposing his head.

Bailey had no way to cross that gully.

"Stay down!" Gage was already moving, running to the side to get out of the path of gunfire. When the lead started flying, Gage dove flat on his belly.

The man shifted his gun, following the sound of Gage's running feet. Which brought the bullets in Bailey's direction, because her foolish, heroic husband was trying to get between her and that gun.

She'd only get in his way if she came out from cover, so Bailey ducked just as bullets struck the rock right overhead.

She took a long, hard breath, peeked out to see Gage crawling around the rock out of the line of fire. She aimed, knowing this was a shot she had to get right. Her gun blasted, and the men ducked. That gave Gage some cover from the flying bullets.

The man quit shooting at Gage and turned his gun on her. She jumped behind a tree and heard the bark explode only inches away. Seconds later, the shooting stopped. The silence was so profound, it echoed in Bailey's ears. Hesitating to come out, she listened, hoping and praying Gage was all right.

"You can come out now, Bailey. I've got him." Gage's voice. "Thanks."

He was alive. She let out a breath of relief and said, "I've got one over here, too."

Gage turned and waved at her. "You saved me, Mrs. Coulter." He smiled so wide she could see it all the way across the gully.

"And you saved me, Mr. Coulter." She really had married a mighty good man . . . with a troublesome mother.

"The gully's too deep to cross," Bailey called out. "I'll meet you at the bottom of the mesa."

"Let's tie 'em up tight, then head for your pa's place." He looked back at the man he'd caught, and his expression went from satisfaction to fury. "I know who this is. Do you recognize yours?"

Looking at the man she'd knocked cold, she shook her head. "I don't, but then I've been mostly hiding from people since I moved out here."

"Well, mine is Gus Fowler. He's Rance Boyle's ranch foreman."

"So Boyle is in this with Pa?" Pa didn't cooperate with anyone all that well.

"I thought we only had one cantankerous old man to deal with, and his two hired men. But if Boyle's involved too, we might keep meeting men ready to shoot us all day long."

Shaking his head in disgust, Gage said, "It's time to find out what part Cudgel even has in this thing. Maybe we've been wrong about him right from the start. He's an old hermit. Maybe he doesn't know who it is he hired."

Bailey shook her head. "Pa's tracks were in my canyon, and he drove the herd here. He's in it deep enough to have stolen my cattle."

"Whatever part he's played in it, your pa is the least of our worries."

She studied the gully between them. Even on closer inspection, Bailey saw no way across it.

"Don't forget, there might be more than these two men keeping watch."

"I won't forget. See you at the bottom, Gage." She headed for the trail that led down to Pa's valley.

29

They reached the bottom, and Gage itched to ride over to Cudgel's cabin and give the man a thrashing, just for the hurt he'd seen on Bailey's face.

He met up with Bailey after a long, treacherous ride.

But if Boyle was involved, there might be more trouble ahead. "I'd hoped there'd be a couple of horses here. We've got some open space to cover to get to your pa's place. We'll be exposed the whole time."

"I wonder how Shannon is doing with the baby," Bailey said.

"And I'm wondering where Sunrise got to. She'd be a mighty big help, I reckon." Gage pulled his gun and checked it. "Let's move. If Cudgel or anyone else standing guard heard that gunfire, they're expecting us. The longer we wait, the more time they'll have to dig in."

"Let's go arrest Pa." Bailey reached her hand for his.

Walking hand in hand to a fight. Gage sighed. His life had gotten really strange.

They reached the bottom of the trail and stopped, peering out of the woods.

"From the minute we step out in the open, we're in range. We've got about a hundred yards to cross. I don't see how even someone as foolish as your pa could not be waiting for us." He turned and looked at Bailey.

With some uncertainty, she said, "I don't think Pa is a murderer, Gage. He's never been a man to look another in the eye and fight. I'm talking about our neighbors back home. He could complain and insult folks and be nasty, but he never even swung a fist, let alone drew a gun. The sneaky way he attacked you, with the avalanche and the spiked trap—that sounds like Pa. I don't think he'll shoot us."

"It's a long chance, Bailey. I doubt he'd gun down his own child. That might be why he hired help, to do the dirty work for him. He might hold back, hoping his sentries come to help him. But we're risking our lives on that." Gage shook his head.

"I think I'll walk in there, and Pa will tell me my cows are his. He'll think he has a right to keep them at his place. A judge might even take his word, until you tell them they're your cows now. So I expect bluster from him, though he'll be too sure he's in the right to shoot."

They looked at each other for a long minute. Gage knew she wasn't that sure, and it was a terrible thing for a child to wonder about. "Let's go."

They'd walked to within twenty feet of the house when

a gun blasted, and dirt kicked up a couple of yards in front of Gage's boots.

It reminded Gage of the way Bailey used to treat him.

He kept walking regardless. Bailey moved closer to him, and he knew she was trying to protect him. He fought the instinct to shove her behind his back. He'd married a tough woman and he knew she wouldn't put up with hiding.

Another bullet blasted. "This is how we started out, Bailey. It reminds me of our courtship."

Bailey shook her head and kept walking.

"I think you're right. Your pa isn't going to shoot us."

"He's not as good a shot as me," Bailey said. They closed on the house, and another bullet fired, this one off to Gage's left and behind him. With Bailey on his right, maybe Cudgel was aiming wide to spare her.

They finally arrived to the house, close enough that Cudgel probably wouldn't risk firing again.

"We're coming in, Pa." Bailey jerked on the door, a heavy, clumsily made thing that rested its weight on the ground.

"Git out. You're not my child, not anymore. You've betrayed me." Cudgel Wilde, bleating like an injured sheep.

Bailey pulled her gun. "Step back, Pa. I'm gonna shoot my way through this door, and we're gonna talk."

Gage thought it was wise Bailey didn't mention they planned to arrest him.

"Don't you bust up my door."

"Then open it. Right now. You've got no call to shoot at me and Gage like that." Bailey waited, her gun aimed at the door. If Cudgel had a heavy plank barring the door, they'd have trouble getting through it, but they would do it all the same.

At last, there was a heavy thump behind the door, and Cudgel dragged it open. Gage knew that Bailey, Shannon, and Kylie had helped get Cudgel's cabin started, and he could see it was squarely framed and the walls solid. It was obvious when his daughters quit and Cudgel went on alone. He'd done a poor job of chinking cracks between the logs. The windows and doors were sagging, and the floor was nothing but dirt. Cudgel didn't have the skill his daughters possessed, and they hadn't come and finished the cabin for him.

Bailey holstered her gun and marched inside. Gage had to hurry to keep up. How was he supposed to protect her if she wouldn't wait for him?

"Pa, you stole my cattle." Bailey plunked her hands on her hips. "We're taking them back."

Cudgel glanced past Gage almost like he was expecting help. It made Gage step far enough into the room that he could keep the door covered. It was the only one in the ten-by-sixteen-foot shack. Gage had heard this was the required minimum size of a homestead cabin, and Cudgel hadn't made his one inch bigger than that.

There was no one at the door. Gage wondered if Cudgel hoped his guards were coming. Gage looked back and saw that Cudgel still had his gun in hand, though he was pointing it toward the ground.

"We got your sentries tied up in the hills, Wilde. They won't be coming to help you out." Gage strode straight for Cudgel and ripped the gun out of his hand before the man could bring it up. Then he took Bailey's arm and shifted farther into the room so that Cudgel was between him and the door. That was where Gage wanted him, in case he had men beyond the two they'd taken out of the fight.

"I wasn't gonna shoot you. You got no call to barge in here and talk about cow thieving." Cudgel's eyes were yellow and sunken. The man had always been thin, but now he seemed almost skeletal. His sickly look struck Gage as more than the man not eating right. He had a strong feeling that Cudgel was a dying man. Maybe they didn't have to arrest him. If his days were numbered, there didn't seem to be much point.

"Pa, I built my herd by shagging unbranded strays out of the hills, feeding my cows right, and helping with a birthing when I needed to. I rounded up mustangs and broke them and sold them to raise money to buy more cows. You didn't help me, not for one day. Those cows are mine, and now that I'm married they're my husband's, too. If you agree to let me ride out of here with them, this will be the end of it. But if you don't, we're taking you to the sheriff and having you arrested for rustling."

No mention was made of the attempts on Gage's life, and he didn't aim to overlook that. But maybe they could put off talking of them for a while.

Cudgel's head jerked back. "My own child would say such a thing to me? Threaten to have me arrested?"

"My own father would steal my cattle?" Bailey's tone was a mocking echo of Cudgel's.

"You married a man with thousands of cows, then complain because I want a mere fifty? It was my idea to come out here, my hard work driving a wagon all this way. After all I did, you betray me and end my hope of building something in Jimmy's name. You owe me, and you're lucky I was willing to settle for only a few head of cattle."

"We're not here to talk, Wilde," Gage cut in. "We don't have the time. Because one of your daughters is right now having a baby back at Bailey's house." Gage had a bright idea then. "What if Shannon had a son, Cudgel? A grandson of yours would be something to build on, wouldn't it?"

"Shannon's here? Having a baby, you say?" Cudgel's eyes softened some, but whether because of his concern for his daughter or a new chance for a male in the family, Gage wasn't sure. Yet for once he did appear as though he cared about someone in his family. Gage figured that would last about until he met the little one, and then Cudgel would no doubt find something else to complain about.

"She went into labor while we were riding out here," Bailey said. "Tucker took her to my place. We need to get back in case they need help." She gave the door a nervous glance, as if she wished she could see through the mountains to her cabin.

Cudgel looked in the direction Bailey had. "It might be a son, mightn't it?"

As if Tucker would let Cudgel within a mile of his child. Gage smiled. "It surely might be."

With a blustery show of anger, Cudgel said, "Fine, take the cows back."

"Nobody move." A metallic click brought everyone's

eyes to the open door. Rance Boyle stood there, his gun cocked and aimed, a huge man who had to duck to step inside.

Bailey whirled to face the door, her gun drawn. Boyle froze.

"You won't win this gunfight, Mrs. Coulter."

"One step more and I fire. I might die, but so will you."

Gage saw two men behind Boyle. Neither of them were the men tied up in the hills. Gage couldn't shoot, as Cudgel was between him and the door. But that didn't stop him from bringing his gun up. Wilde might not be a stone-cold killer, but Boyle and the men with him had murder in their eyes.

Bailey held her fire, but she'd been to war. Gage had no doubt she had the courage to fight. And because of the way Gage had them standing, she'd die and he just might live.

Rance knew that and hesitated. He needed Bailey and Gage both dead, but he didn't see how he'd kill them and not die himself.

If he managed to kill them both, Royce would move in on the C Bar. His men would make a fight of it, but how many of them would be willing to die for a boss who couldn't pay them?

Ma was at his house. And Ma and Pa were Gage's natural heirs, save for Bailey. Boyle would likely kill her, too. Gage stood to lose everything. His ranch and even his life were the least of it. He braced himself to shoot and keep shooting, even if a bullet struck him. He had to stop all three men before they killed Bailey.

"Boyle, what are you doing here?" Cudgel stood sideways, glancing up at Boyle, then at Bailey, then back at Boyle.

***

"You really didn't know, did you, Pa?" Bailey saw death in Boyle's eyes. She'd never seen the man before, but she'd fought shy of people and didn't know hardly anyone.

"Know what?" Cudgel kept looking between her and Rance.

"That the men you hired worked for Rance Boyle."

Without taking her eyes off of Boyle, Bailey could feel Pa looking hard at her, then turning to Rance. "You planned this from the minute you heard I was looking for men?"

Boyle's eyes shifted between Cudgel, standing in the line of fire between him and Gage and Bailey. Though she probably should have fired, she'd hesitated, and Boyle was watching her again.

He didn't give his men the order to come in, and he was so big he blocked the door so they couldn't get their guns into the fight. It was in his eyes that he knew to step forward was to start the war. Bailey would fire. But he had his gun aimed right at her heart.

"Yep, you wanted help with your little scheme for Coulter to die so it looked like an accident, but you wanted your daughter alive to inherit. Then you'd try and move in on her and run the C Bar, even name it after your worthless son. You'd have your dynasty for the small price of Coulter's life."

Pa's face took on a ruddy look as his ugly plan was laid

bare before Gage and Bailey. It was enough to cause Pa shame. She'd thought he had none of that.

"The avalanche was just to scare him off, to discourage him from breeching that canyon wall."

"A real dangerous way to scare a man, Cudgel," Gage said.

Bailey didn't take her eyes off Rance. Somehow she knew she was going to die. She saw no way out of it. She prayed harder than she ever had in her life, that God would forgive her for going down fighting because she wanted nothing more than to save Gage's life.

God, please don't condemn me if taking another life is my final act.

She tightened her hand on the gun and hoped and prayed God would answer such a prayer.

"Cudgel, you can walk out of here alive if you stay out of it," Boyle said. The man didn't look at him; he only watched Bailey.

Bailey remembered the war, remembered being in the heat of battle. The roaring of cannons and gunfire, so loud it was like being deaf. Men running, shooting, bleeding. Cannons exploding all around. Everything slowed down. She would see things, make decisions where to aim, where to run, when to duck down. Time stretched out, even though only fractions of seconds had passed.

This was a moment like that. Her hearing was only for Boyle. Everything else faded. She heard each breath, saw a trickle of sweat run down the side of his face. He was nervous, although it didn't show in his rock-steady hand.

"And leave Bailey here?"

"That's the only way you live, Wilde."

Moments stretched long and slow, yet they passed in a twinkling. Pa didn't move, didn't try to save himself.

"Leave you to kill my . . . my . . ." Out of the edge of her vision, still locked on Boyle, she saw Pa turn to her and really look at her for the first time in years, maybe the first time in his life. He said firmly, "Leave you to kill my daughter?"

He'd never said that word, not in her memory. He'd never admitted she was a girl. Not because he didn't know, but because he'd always considered it such a terrible disappointment.

Bailey saw the shift in Boyle's eyes, the twitch of the muscles in his hand. He pulled the trigger just as Pa threw himself at Boyle, right into the blasting gun. Boyle fired again and again. He shouted in what sounded like pain. Pa's slight weight shouldn't have been enough, but Boyle staggered back and went down.

She aimed, expecting the other two men to charge into the room firing, yet with Boyle down, what she saw was . . . Sunrise.

Sunrise jerked Boyle's gun out of his hand, then dragged Pa outside, leaving a trail of blood.

Gage was on Boyle in a flash and slammed a fist into his face. One blow was enough to make the man go limp. Then Gage jerked a piggin' string off his belt and trussed Boyle up like a maverick calf. Sunrise pulled a knife out of Boyle's gun arm.

Her knife. Bailey recognized it.

That had been what caused the shout of pain.

Bailey holstered her gun and had to wait precious seconds for Gage to finish and stand. She then climbed over Boyle, who lay unconscious in the doorway, and rushed to Pa's side. The other two men lay unconscious on the ground. One was bleeding from his head, a bloodstained rock lying on the ground beside him. How had Sunrise gotten them both?

Bailey made a note to never underestimate the tough mountain woman.

Pa's shirtfront was covered with blood. His eyes blinked open and locked on Bailey.

She knelt at his side and tore his shirt open. Three gunshots, high on his chest, and a fourth in the gut. Mortal wounds. Bailey knew it and didn't even try to staunch the blood. In his few seconds remaining, Bailey wanted to look into his hazel eyes, so much like her own.

Gage was kneeling across from Bailey.

Pa coughed and whispered, "If Shannon has a boy, ask her to name him Jimmy."

Bailey smiled as generously as she could. He'd acknowledged her as his daughter and had given his life to save her. She wouldn't begrudge him his love for his son as his dying wish. She also wouldn't make a promise about the name.

"I'll ask her. I'll tell her it is your wish. That grandchild means your family goes on, Pa. Whether boy or girl, the child is your blood and maybe the baby will build a dynasty."

More likely the child would grow up in the mountains and maybe someday build a cabin. Not much chance of a dynasty there.

Pa looked at Gage. "The avalanche was to scare you off. I knew I could hurt you, but I was too mad to care. Then that trap I set. I overheard the proposal and rushed for town to waylay you. I never thought Bailey would marry you on the spot. I can't swear to you I didn't want you dead, but I've never killed a man, not in cold blood."

Bailey thought that was an odd thing to say. Had Pa killed a man in his life in the sneaky way he'd tried with Gage? Bailey decided not to think about it.

"I'm mighty sorry, Coulter. I'm an old fool. You're the son I wish I'd had." His gaze shifted back to his daughter. "You're a good rancher."

He coughed again, and flecks of blood tinted his lips. Dragging in air, he forced the words out, "A better rancher than I was." His eyes fluttered closed then, as if he couldn't bear to look her in the eye when he said, "And a better rancher than Jimmy would have been."

He exhaled until his lungs held no more air. With the last breath that passed his lips, he said, "I'm proud of you, girl."

30

*B*ailey looked up at Sunrise's solemn, wrinkled face. "You took care of both men."

"All three, honestly." Sunrise wasn't bragging. It was just fact. "They were paying attention to what went on in the cabin. Too busy to look behind them. Now I need to get to your cabin and see if there is time to help deliver the baby." She turned and walked away.

Sunrise had to do everything.

Hot tears burned in Bailey's eyes . . . again. Pa's unexpected last words had healed a wound deep inside her. Even knowing if he'd lived, he almost certainly would have been his same cruel self, for one moment when it really mattered, he'd saved her and shown her respect.

Then she realized Sunrise and Gage and Pa had saved her. She'd stood ready to kill and die to save them, but in the end she'd done nothing. Pa had thrown himself onto a firing gun. Sunrise had taken the men out of the fight. Gage had leapt in and knocked Boyle cold.

The tears burned, yet they didn't fall. She never cried and she didn't see any reason to start now.

"Pa said he was proud of me." The sentiment toward her pa then faded somewhat because of a lifetime of unkindness. "About time."

"He saved you, Bailey." Gage wrapped his arms around her. "He took those bullets for you."

Nodding, she turned back to her father. "In the end he cared more about me than he did himself. I hope he had a moment to ask God for forgiveness before his last breath."

Gage patted her shoulder. "Let's bury your pa, Bailey. Say a few words over the grave. Then Shannon can rest up at your place while we take these five men to town."

Bailey nodded.

"I'll find a shovel. You stand guard over the prisoners."

"They're unconscious."

"I'm in no mood to be careless, so watch them."

The job was about the easiest thing she'd ever done.

They draped the other men over their saddles, including the sentries, and rode to her cabin. As they arrived, Tucker came out of the house and waved them in, a smile on his face that liked to dim the sun by comparison. They went inside to see Shannon cradling a bundle. A tiny arm waving as if the baby were greeting them.

Sunrise went to Shannon and spoke softly, then lifted the baby and brought it to Bailey. "Hold your nephew."

She placed the baby in Bailey's arms and adjusted her hands. Bailey had never held an infant before. Her throat clogged, but she didn't waste time with tears. Instead, she looked down at the tiny thing. His eyes were puffy and closed tight, but he waved at her and wriggled as he lay wrapped in a piece of soft leather. Bailey glanced at Shannon and saw she had only one of her leggings on. The other was now a baby blanket.

"Shannon, I have never in my life seen anything as precious as this little one." Bailey looked at her sister and found a love so deep for her and her child that it shook her and spread to every one of these people.

Looking from Gage to Tucker to Sunrise, she said, "Shannon was having her baby. I was in the center of a gunfight, and in the end you three took care of us. It's like nothing I've ever known before."

Shannon said, "No one much took care of us growing up, did they?"

"Nope, but we have a fine family now." The baby squeaked and drew Bailey's attention. She could even now be expecting a baby of her own. If not, the way Gage carried on, she no doubt would soon. Something powerful and wild came to life in her heart, a longing for her own child. She kissed the baby's forehead and was in awe of how soft the little guy was.

Bailey looked up at Gage, and he might well have read her mind because he gave her a very private smile that seemed to share that longing.

He said, "Yep, a fine, growing family."

"Pa's dying request was that you name your son Jimmy." Bailey watched Shannon roll her eyes. "I'm just telling you what he said. I never told him you'd do it."

"We're naming him Matthew Tucker Junior." Shannon glowed.

"Foolish name." Tucker shook his head. "I wanted to name him Wilde Eagle Tucker."

Sunrise nodded. "That is a fine name."

"A mighty fine name, but Shannon won. We'll call him Matt, since I don't really use that name anyway."

Bailey wondered if there was a Gage Coulter Junior in her future. She certainly hoped so.

⁓

They didn't linger, because the men they'd taken prisoner were going to be easier to transport when they were knocked cold.

They left Shannon, Tucker, and Sunrise behind until Shannon felt ready to ride. Gage and Bailey were well on their way to town before any of the unconscious men stirred.

Boyle raged about being tied up and draped over the back of a horse.

"Should I gag him, Bailey?" Gage led the way, while Bailey brought up the rear. "He's wearing on my ears."

The rest of the men were silent, though Bailey saw they were now awake. "Nope, I like that we've made him mad." Bailey added, "Just so you varmints know, the only one of you here who killed a man is Rance Boyle when he shot Cudgel. The more you help us figure out all he's been up to, the better your chances are of not swinging from a noose."

While Boyle raged on, a couple of the men looked sideways and caught Bailey's eye. They looked eager to get out of trouble in any way possible.

They reached Aspen Ridge just as the sun was setting. The jailhouse was unlocked but empty. Gage got the prisoners off their horses and in a cell while Bailey knocked on doors until she found the sheriff.

Bailey had advised the sheriff that she thought several of the men had stories to tell, but they'd need to be separated from Boyle for their own safety.

When they got back to the jail, Gage had all five men lying side by side in the cell, still tied up. Gage shook the sheriff's hand. "I didn't want to untie them while I was here alone."

Bailey and Gage were a long time telling their story, with Boyle shouting at them every minute or so about what an important man he was. By the time the sheriff finished asking his questions, it was so late that Bailey felt unsteady on her feet with exhaustion.

"Is there anywhere to sleep in town, Sheriff?" Gage put his arm around his wife to keep her upright on her feet.

If she were a crying woman, she'd have wept with relief not to have to face the long ride home.

"The parson headed for the mountains, so the building he used for his church and home is empty. Folks passing through town sleep there, but no one's there tonight."

When they stepped inside the church and Bailey was finally able to lie down, she was afraid the day would run through her head and keep her awake. But she blinked her eyes and it was morning. She turned her head to see Gage asleep beside her. How had her life changed so much in such a short time?

She studied him. So peaceful. None of the icy control, none of the ghosts were there as he slept. She rested her eyes on his handsome face, and in the quiet of early morning she realized she was in love with her husband.

Not just romantic love, but love so deep, so full of respect, so full of gratitude for saving her from loneliness. He'd protected her when no man ever had before. She didn't even fear it or regret how vulnerable it made her to love Gage. It was too powerful, too wonderful.

A smile spread across her face as she lay there, ignoring all they had to do today so she could spend another minute or ten or an hour studying him, loving him.

"Good morning, wife."

She'd been lost in pleasure and hadn't noticed Gage's eyes were open. He was watching her, and she had to wonder what he'd seen in her expression. She almost spoke, almost told him she loved him, but she didn't have the courage. "Good morning, husband."

He leaned over and kissed her, a lovely way to start the day. "Let's get moving. It's time to go home."

Before heading home, though, they had to return to the jail and answer more questions. Ma had to be worried sick.

Ma would fuss over Gage, then wait until he'd left before turning her small, cutting criticisms on Bailey. Somehow now, knowing how much she loved Gage, she thought she could bear whatever nonsense Ma got up to.

At least Bailey had left the britches behind. She hated doing it, but even in the middle of transporting five prisoners, Bailey could hear Ma finding fault. Yes, she'd bear it, but she still wanted to get that woman out of her house.

They were done at the sheriff's office before long. He'd found Wanted posters on two of the men, each offering reward money. The sheriff told them the money was theirs.

Bailey noticed the two wanted men weren't the same ones who'd looked at her yesterday as if they'd be willing to betray their boss.

The sheriff had already wired for a judge to come for the trial and found a couple of deputies to ride with him to wherever the men ended up spending the next few years.

It was almost certain that Boyle would hang.

"Let's ride for home, Bailey."

"Gage, about home, uh . . . your ma . . ." Bailey wasn't sure how to say what was on her mind. It was a sure thing that Gage would defend his ma, and the fact that he would defend her at the cost of Bailey's happiness hurt worse than Pa's cruelty, because she'd expected it from Pa. But Gage was usually so good to her.

Except he had this one blind spot. And Ma was careful not to show the unpleasant side of herself to Gage. Although the way she fawned over him was plainly unpleasant.

"I'm worried about her, too." Gage strode for the livery, clearly eager to saddle up and run home to his mama.

"When do you think she's going home?" Bailey had to hustle to keep up. She wasn't going to drop this. Her father had been much worse than Gage's mother, but in her own way, Ma was coming between them and something had to be done.

"I don't know." Gage didn't seem interested in the topic.

Bailey caught him by the arm. "Gage, we need to talk."

"Sure, Bailey. About what?" He looked as innocent as Shannon's newborn baby, the big idiot.

Before she could explain, a clatter of wheels turned them toward the south edge of town where the main trail came in.

The stage came rushing into town. There hadn't even been a stage last year, and this year it'd brought Ma Coulter mighty early in the spring, and now here it was again. Aspen Ridge was getting purely civilized.

Bailey and Gage had been standing in almost this exact spot when Ma had arrived. Bailey couldn't help the rush of dread she felt.

The stage was heading straight for them, so they had to leave off their talk and move to the side of the street. It pulled to a stop and was nearly swallowed by dust. Bailey waved her hand in her face. Before the dust settled, the stage door opened, and a tall man with dark hair streaked with gray jumped down without using the steps.

Bailey stared at him, and his eyes met hers, looking straight out under the brim of his Stetson. Then he turned his warm, brown eyes to Gage.

Gage blinked. "Pa? What are you doing here?"

"I've come to fetch your ma home, son."

Bailey decided right there on the spot that she loved Pa Coulter with all her heart.

31

"I'm sorry to see them go," Gage said. He stood beside Bailey in Aspen Ridge as his parents' stagecoach headed out of town.

This was the happiest day of her marriage so far.

Bailey had never been so glad to see the back of two people in her life. Pa was all right, but Ma was a fright. But Gage loved his ma, and thankfully Bailey hadn't needed to say a single discouraging word to get rid of the woman. For all that, she had no trouble smiling and agreeing with Gage.

"Let's ride for home, Bailey. Shannon and Tucker should be coming in a couple of days."

Yesterday, two weeks after the baby was born, Sunrise had come over to tell them that Shannon was feeling fine and ready to come to Gage's for a long stay.

Tucker was ready to go to work. Myra and Nev didn't want to give up Shannon's cabin, and Sunrise was living in Kylie's. The one Aaron had built was now owned by the new doctor in Aspen Ridge. Shannon and Tucker would be living with Gage and Bailey for the summer, and Bailey couldn't believe how much better it was to be surrounded by family than to always be so alone.

She didn't count Ma Coulter.

Loving Gage and talking with him about all her old burdens had helped her to heal from the war. After all this time, she felt safe enough to trust people, even Gage's hired men.

As they rode out of town, Gage said, "We'll be lucky to have one day to ourselves before your sister shows up."

He reached across the space between them and took her hand as if he wanted to cherish that single day to the fullest.

Bailey smiled. "It's an unusual thing to hold hands whilst riding a horse."

Gage laughed. "It is indeed, Mrs. Coulter."

The trail got narrow ahead, but for now they rode along, talking of what needed to be done to get ready for a baby in the house. They also talked of the letter that had come from Kylie full of news of her new baby, Aaron Masterson Junior. Another missed opportunity to call a baby Jimmy. Bailey wasn't going to be any help when her turn came. There weren't going to be any baby Cudgels, either.

Kylie said there was a much more peaceful spirit in the Shenandoah Valley than right after the war and life was good. They were building a house on the site of Aaron's old home, and she'd even had some neighbor ladies in to tea and she described in detail the new bonnet she'd worn.

It was the perfect moment for Bailey to share her news.

"Gage, we'll be having a little one of our own long about February." They'd be married ten months when the little one was born. Bailey was so thrilled by it that she thought maybe she'd finally found something she liked well enough to keep her from wanting to run her own ranch.

He whipped his head around so fast his Stetson fell off. He had to let go of her hand to catch it. She hoped that wasn't some kind of bad omen.

"Really, a baby?" He pulled his horse to a stop and swung down. He lifted her right out of her saddle and kissed her long and hard. "You're sure?"

Bailey shrugged. "I talked with Sunrise about it yesterday." Bailey wasn't about to go into the personal details with Gage. Even Sunrise had to drag the embarrassing information out of her. But in the end, there'd been no doubt. "She says I'm definitely expecting."

"February, in the depths of the winter. This one shouldn't catch us out on the trail like Tucker's baby did."

Nope, she planned to stay home from about November to May whether she wanted to or not, so it should be okay.

"You should have said something to my folks before they left. It would have made Ma real happy to hear the news right straight from your mouth."

Yep, that would have been the polite thing to do.

"I wanted to have a moment when we were alone to talk about it, and the chance never came until now." Because Ma had stayed up with them so late last night that finally Bailey had given up and gone to bed. The woman wanted every moment with Gage.

Then he'd been gone when Bailey woke in the morning. In the kitchen and listening to his tearful mother's long goodbye.

She could have told them all at once, but she'd been afraid his parents might delay their departure. The stage was coming through every two weeks now, and another two weeks of Ma made Bailey's throat threaten to swell shut. That couldn't be good for the baby.

"Pa said there's room for me in Texas if we want to pull up stakes and go back there."

A shiver of fear that made Bailey remember a lonely Christmas Eve spent in a stable stormed through her whole body. She tried to keep it from showing, and only years in the war made that possible.

"And what did you say?" She was amazed at how calm she sounded.

"I told them that life here suited me fine. I like the change of seasons. The heat of Texas wore on me worse than the cold of the northern Rockies. I like having something I built myself." He nodded. "I probably should have talked with you about it. Would you rather head south and get out of this rugged land?"

Bailey found the most genuine smile of her life. "I like it here, Gage. It suits me, too."

"You're an easier woman than my ma. Much as I love her, I have to admit I'm glad to see her head home." Gage added, "Pa says the trip is too hard and it's doubtful if they'll be back, but I suspect Ma might come up to see the baby."

With gritted teeth behind her smile, Bailey decided she'd worry about that when the time came. Then she perked up. No letters went out of Aspen Ridge in February. They couldn't let Ma know until the spring. At least Ma wouldn't show up the minute the baby was born.

For now, as they stood there in the sheltering pines, in the cool mountain breeze with plenty of warm summer days ahead, Bailey knew it was time she told Gage one more little thing.

"I'm never going to claim my homestead and that canyon from you, Gage. I am so glad you came and dragged me out of my cabin and bribed me into marrying you."

With a flashing smile and eyes so kind that Bailey couldn't imagine them ever being cold, Gage said, "It's worked out better than I ever dreamed. I knew you'd make me a good rancher's wife." His hand came up to run through her hair, still too short to tie back. She didn't mind, for Gage seemed to like the way it felt on his fingers. "But I never expected to be so in love with you, Bailey."

A gasp escaped her lips just before Gage's mouth came down and kept the words she wanted to say inside. When he lifted his head, his eyes blazed with more than warmth, but with heat, with desire for her. With love.

"I love you too, Gage." Her arms had somehow gotten around his neck, so she held him tighter. "I was so lonely in that cabin." She snuck in a kiss. "I'm pretty sure I'd have said yes even without the bribe. I'd have done most anything not to be alone again."

Gage's brows lowered to a straight line. "You would? Then why'd you make all those demands?"

"I was just afraid. I was so sure I couldn't be happy at your ranch, not with all the cowpokes you had around the place. For a woman who's faced terrible things and who prides herself on being strong, I've been afraid all my life."

"God tells us to depend on Him, Bailey. You should never be afraid."

Bailey laughed. "That's fine to know. So I'm not only afraid, I'm also a sinner. That makes me feel a lot better."

Gage didn't laugh. "I will protect you with every ounce of my strength all our lives, Bailey. But I don't like the idea of you burying so much fear inside. I've always thought you were a woman who didn't need anyone."

"In a way, that's right. I don't need anyone."

Hurt flared in Gage's eyes.

"I mean I don't need anyone to run my ranch. I don't need help feeding myself or clothing myself. But I need someone to love me, Gage, and I need someone to love. I've found that with you. I consider being married to you a blessing straight from God."

The hurt faded from Gage's expression, replaced with happiness and love. She realized how much she could see of his feelings now. He'd left the usual cold of his eyes far behind.

"Let's go have the house to ourselves, woman. It's high time." He kissed her thoroughly.

And they rode for home. His ice had thawed. Her fire had calmed. They'd thrived alone, but there'd been no happiness.

Together they were better, stronger, wiser, more faithful.

Together they'd forged their fire and ice into the warmth of true love.

Mary Connealy writes romantic comedies about cowboys. She's the author of the acclaimed TROUBLE IN TEXAS and THE KINCAID BRIDES series, as well as several other series. Mary has been nominated for a Christy Award, was a finalist for a RITA Award, and is a two-time winner of the Carol Award. She lives on a ranch in eastern Nebraska with her very own romantic cowboy hero. They have four grown daughters—Joslyn, married to Matt; Wendy; Shelly, married to Aaron; and Katy, married to Max—and a little bevy of spectacular grandchildren. Learn more about Mary and her books at:

maryconnealy.com
mconnealy.blogspot.com
seekerville.blogspot.com
petticoatsandpistols.com

More From Mary Connealy!

To learn more about Mary and her books, visit www.maryconnealy.com.

Living in disguise, Kylie Wilde is homesteading for profit so she will be able to live comfortably when she moves back East. But her plans—and her claim to the land—are jeopardized when Aaron Masterson discovers her secret. Will he choose to protect her or uphold the law?

Tried and True
WILD AT HEART #1

When Matthew Tucker accidentally angers a grizzly, he sprints straight into feisty homesteader Shannon Wilde, and they're both forced to jump into a raging river to escape. After they return from their adventure in the wilderness, can these two learn to live together—for better or worse?

Now and Forever
WILD AT HEART #2

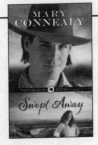

The Civil War may be over, but the adventure has just begun for this ragtag group of soldiers who became friends while held captive in Andersonville Prison. When they cross paths with three one-of-a-kind women, there's going to be trouble in Texas!

TROUBLE IN TEXAS: *Swept Away, Fired Up, Stuck Together*

You May Also Enjoy...

While doing volunteer work for the Weather Bureau, Sophie van Riijn uses an abandoned mansion as a resource and a refuge—until the long-lost heir catches her trespassing. Quentin Vandermark has returned, with his young son, to put an end to the rumors about Dierenpark. But as secrets come to light, will tragedy triumph or can hope and love prevail?

Until the Dawn by Elizabeth Camden
www.elizabethcamden.com

At Irish Meadows horse farm, two sisters struggle to reconcile their dreams with their father's demanding marriage expectations. Brianna longs to attend college, while Colleen is happy to marry, as long as the man meets *her* standards. Will they find the courage to follow their hearts?

Irish Meadows by Susan Anne Mason
COURAGE TO DREAM #1
www.susanannemason.com

When Miranda Wimplegate mistakenly sells a prized portrait, her grandfather purchases an entire auction house to get it back. However, after traveling to the Ozarks, they're dismayed to learn their new business deals in livestock—not antiques! While Miranda tries to find the portrait, the handsome manager attempts to salvage the failing business. Will either succeed?

At Love's Bidding by Regina Jennings
www.reginajennings.com

⬧BETHANYHOUSE